Critics Cheer John Dunning and His Extraordinary National Bestseller
THE BOOKMAN'S WAKE

"*The Bookman's Wake* not only kept me up far too late one night, but got me up two hours early the next morning."
—Geoffrey Stokes, *The Boston Globe Sunday Magazine*

"Mad, fantastical, and darkly original. Bookbinding has never been so spellbinding."
—*Kirkus Reviews*

"Dunning is a hugely talented writer. . . . *The Bookman's Wake* is the book we've all been hoping it would be. . . . Even more memorable than the plot are Dunning's characters and the harsh secrets they keep."
—Tom and Enid Schantz, *Denver Post*

"The author . . . immerses the reader in this intriguing, little-known milieu without losing sight of the page-turning yarn he's spinning. In the end you may be disappointed that the last plot twist has finally played itself out."
—Pam Lambert, *People*

"John Dunning writes stunningly good mysteries. The characters, settings, complex plots and rare book lore that he imparts are like Grayson's editions—inspired, and without a flaw."
—*The Times-Picayune* (New Orleans)

Books by John Dunning

For orders other than by individual consumers, Pocket Books grants a discount on the purchase of **10 or more** copies of single titles for special markets or premium use. For further details, please write to the Vice-President of Special Markets, Pocket Books, 1633 Broadway, New York, NY 10019-6785, 8th Floor.

For information on how individual consumers can place orders, please write to Mail Order Department, Simon & Schuster Inc., 200 Old Tappan Road, Old Tappan, NJ 07675.

THE HOLLAND SUGGESTIONS

JOHN DUNNING

POCKET **STAR** BOOKS

New York   London   Toronto   Sydney   Tokyo   Singapore

A Pocket Star Book published by
POCKET BOOKS, a division of Simon & Schuster Inc.
1230 Avenue of the Americas, New York, NY 10020

Copyright © 1975 by John Dunning
Introduction copyright © 1997 by John Dunning

ISBN: 0-671-00353-4

First Pocket Books printing December 1997

10 9 8 7 6 5 4 3 2 1

POCKET STAR BOOKS and colophon are registered trademarks of Simon & Schuster Inc.

Cover art by Danilo Ducak

Printed in the U.S.A.

For Helen

Introduction

IRVING STONE, THE OLD LION, WAS HOLDING COURT, and I was one of the young lions sitting on the floor across from him. It was October 1980.

Stone had been with Doubleday about two million years and had become one of the colossal bestsellers of his time. He had arrived at this party in the Colorado mountains in a sour mood. He was haggling with his publisher over $250,000 in expenses he had incurred while living in England researching his fictional biography of Charles Darwin. At any rate, this was the story that was bandied about that night.

But Stone was an advocate of a strong author-publisher relationship. He was of the old school that had flowered in the twenties and reached its peak in the thirties and forties. He believed staunchly that a writer was best served by getting with a strong house and staying there throughout his career. Look at Hemingway and Scribner, Michener and Random House—the list could be long if we wanted to compile one. He looked at me and asked, "Who's your publisher?"

"Well," I said uneasily: "I've had Bobbs-Merrill and

"Prentice Hall. And Gold Medal is doing two of my books in paper. And the one I've just published is with Times Books . . ."

Stone shook his head. "This is not the way to build a career. You should get with one house and stay there. This is the best advice I can give you."

That's fine, I thought, if you happened to write *Lust for Life* right out of the gate and were in the driver's seat from the beginning. *Get with one publisher and stay there?* I would have killed for such a setup.

Stone was a kind man and I liked him, but I still think he was pretty far removed from the agony and the ecstasy (mostly agony) of the working writer trying to get a foothold on the slippery slope of the book world. Authors who become bestsellers early in life have a warped view of the process. In this sense, Scott Fitzgerald nailed it dead center: the rich *are* different. I'd be the last to suggest that Irving Stone had never paid his dues, but I think he was speaking that night from a pinnacle of success that had begun in 1934. That's a long time removed from whatever lean-and-mean days he might have had.

Here's how it really was, for this working writer.

The first struggle you have is with yourself. Getting up the gumption to put 80,000 reasonably cohesive words on paper can only be understood by those who have done it, or, perhaps on a darker and deeper level, by those who have repeatedly failed in the attempt. Raymond Chandler had a term for the latter: the "not-quite writers," he called them. They are "tragic people," he said in a letter to his agent; "and the more intelligent they are, the more tragic, because the step they can't take seems to them such a small step, which in fact it is." Chandler then added a line so haunting that I will never forget it. "And every successful or fairly successful writer knows, or should know, by what a narrow margin he himself was able to take that step."

This writer knows.

It would be great fun, and certainly more colorful, to say that my first novel, *The Holland Suggestions,* is a lost masterpiece of adventure fiction, grossly overlooked in its day by knuckleheaded editors and critics everywhere. But since I never reread my old books (a constitutional barrier against pain), I'm not quite sure what it is. I get a hint occasionally, when some reader tells me he found it "still a damn good mystery," or when another says that "that book sounds *nothing* like the author of *Booked to Die.*" I thank the first reader and assure the second: both books indeed came out of the same haphazard woodpile. If the cells of the body replace themselves every seven years, I'm a new man three times over since *The Holland Suggestions* banged its way noisily out of this manual typewriter's venerable first cousin, sometime in 1973. But the brain cells do not reproduce: what you have at twenty is pretty much your allotment for life, and what you do with it over the next sixty years depends on your vision, passion, experience, tenacity and luck.

I look at the writer's journey as a three-part trip: the struggle to write, the struggle to be heard, the struggle to survive. Each is a mighty battle, unless the writer's luck is on constant overdrive. The writer can be hamstrung at the start, never getting past the struggle to write. I have known some gloriously talented wordsmiths who could not write a novel, though they tried, literally for decades. Until I was thirty-two, I shared that aching inability. I had great ideas, I thought, and time after time I headed boldly into fiction's choppy headwaters, hoping the heat of the idea would carry me to the end. But the ideas all failed, usually about seventy-five pages in. The heat cooled down, leaving me with no power source for that trek across the novel's vast, dreaded interior.

I simply couldn't write a book. I could turn a phrase with the best of them—so I thought—but I couldn't take that brilliant glimmer and sustain it for three or four hundred pages. It always went bad somewhere south of page one hundred, and when your prose goes bad, the stench can rival a rendering plant, a stockyard or a paper mill.

What do you do? The writer and the not-quite writer are afflicted with the same bottomless self-doubt, and there's no way to know whether you're a real writer or not quite. The constant lure is that this very piece you're working on may be the one that breaks you through. So you push ahead, with absolutely no assurance that there's going to be a payoff anywhere this side of the grave. But you've got to keep going—what else is there? Occasionally you resort to silliness in the desperate attempt to find that missing piece. This sense of desperation led me, when I was very young, to dabble in self-hypnosis. I had been seduced by a rumor, never confirmed, that Swedish boxing champ Ingemar Johansson had been in a state of autohypnosis when he took the heavyweight crown away from Floyd Patterson in 1959. This was downright thrilling. If a fighter could do that and win the title, why not a writer? Maybe with hypnosis I could at least find the strength to wade through that awful prose and get to the end of something.

For a full year I dabbled in the subconscious. I was captivated by *The Search for Bridey Murphy* and all that it implied. I read all the self-hypnotism books then in vogue, notably the works of psycho-hypnotist Leslie LeCron. But even with LeCron in my corner I could never "go under": was never able to get any deeper than a pleasantly hazy state of full awareness. This only heightened my sense of failure. Then there was a second fight, Johansson fought like a man in a real trance, and Patterson quickly reclaimed his title. Meanwhile, I was hardly encouraged by the news that only the intelligent can be effectively hypnotized. This was not the stuff of chumps.

Between novel attempts I wrote short pieces for magazines. My success at this was spotty in the best of times, enough to keep me in typewriter ribbons and that was all. I did have one major advocate, a working wife whose faith (blindness? . . . insanity?) never wavered, and in 1972 I acquired another—an agent from the time-honored firm of Harold Ober Associates in New York. This would prove to be a major turning point in my leap from the ranks of the not-quite writers into the mystical kingdom of 40-carat, nickel-plated, USDA-government-inspected, approved-by-*Good-Housekeeping*, scratch-me-and-I-come-up-writing writers.

I had had a small success in magazines and, bolstered by it, had written a short query to the Ober agency. Ober was one of the great names of the golden era: agent to Scott Fitzgerald and William Faulkner, his agency also handled J.D. Salinger, Ross Macdonald and many others in the top tiers of literature. I had always believed in shooting first at the top, and the letter went off though I had yet to complete a book-length manuscript. It was promptly answered by Phyllis Westberg, one of four agents in the Ober office (Ober himself had died in 1959), but Miss Westberg was only mildly encouraging. The magazine market had become so depressed that it was hopeless trying to make a living at it. Ober never took on new clients solely on the basis of their magazine sales, and I shudder to this day thinking how close Miss Westberg was to becoming my not-quite agent. But she added a final line to this effect: "If you have anything that looks like a book, no matter how rough you think it is, I'd be happy to look at it."

There's a saying I love—when life says you're on, you'd better be ready. I was far from ready, but here was this lady in New York asking me to send her something. She wasn't asking me for $300, like all those so-called agents who advertise in *Writer's Digest;* she wasn't operating out of Sarasota, Florida, with a briefcase full of manuscripts and an office in the bus station. Her zip code, 10017, was literarily correct, and, unless I failed yet again, she was going to be my agent. I had to write something, fast.

At a time like that, you look to what you know best. I had been studying radio history, having come of age just in time to remember when our national entertainers were Jack Benny and Jack Armstrong. I thought an encyclopedia of radio was needed, and in two or three weeks I wrote out the entries for the letter A. Now it can be told: I did absolutely no research for this, there simply wasn't time. I made up the parts I didn't know, and this fiction had a flowing kind of logic when I wrapped it between the facts that I did know. My thinking was strangely sound: I wasn't writing this for publication; there would be time later to do the actual research, but if I didn't impress Miss Phyllis Westberg right now, today, with the wonder of my prose, there wasn't going to be any tomorrow.

Again she responded quickly. Finish this and I will try to sell it. Build it and they will come. Get your hands moving, get down in the trench and start shoveling. She probably phrased this more delicately, but you get the point.

The point is, *I* got the point. There is something magical, galvanizing, about getting a letter like that from a real agent who has nothing to gain unless she can sell your work. On that day, my life as a not-quite writer was over. I had not yet completed a book, but suddenly I had the work ethic of an old pro. I would finish this book, there wasn't a doubt in this world. I eased down into the trench.

Suddenly I was working eleven-hour days. I worked like I never believed I could work on a piece, and when it was almost finished I began thinking about my next book.

My next book.

I had survived the struggle to write. I was a writer.

My next book was *The Holland Suggestions,* the mystery-adventure that has had the audacity to fall into your lap. The leap from journalism to fiction is sometimes a long one, but by then my writing schedule was so well fixed that I had little or no downtime. My year had been one of rapid and exciting growth: I had learned that bad writing is not an automatic death sentence, that you get another shot at it, tomorrow and the next day and the day after that. If your characters sometimes seem like temperamental actors, that's okay because you are still the director. There's always the cutting room floor, so why not let them do it their way for a scene or two? I gathered some fictional people and gave them a situation to confront.

I knew it would be the story of a treasure hunt. I had been in Colorado almost ten years, arriving here from South Carolina in 1964 with a tenderfoot's instant fascination for the mining towns of the Old West. I had spent some time wandering in the high country, where the remnants of real ghost towns still dotted the hills. I walked up the rutted street of Apex, peering into what had once been a saloon and dance hall. The roof had caved in years ago, covering the stage with dusty rubble, yet the place seemed alive with color, voices, stories. Picture yourself snowed in here, I thought. I saw my people, a man and a woman, climbing a path above the town. In my mind the day was windy and cold, coppery and ominous.

Colorado is full of treasure stories. One local scribe has collected them in a book that has become a local evergreen. The same writer had given us a descriptive guide to the state's ghost towns, and as I followed its directions from one sad ruin to another I felt a growing sense of what Michener has so aptly termed "emotional freight." The land was alive with it.

For story I would use what I had learned about hypnotism and the subconscious. Henry James was right: nothing is ever lost. I can tell you something about the composition only because I am a great saver, and I saved it all. I have before me the first halting steps into character—the name Jim Ryan written on a small sheet of notepaper. Other character names would follow. Some would stick and become the book's cornerstones; others were mere names, falling away as they failed to come to life. I have the outline: it seems strange and remote today, since my method (if you can call it that) now excludes all such abstract plotting. Today I would grope my way into it: I would follow the most painful sequence of trials and errors. If a character now wants to turn off and follow his heart, I let him do it; then, if his heart errs, I rein him in and grope back through the hopeless-looking morass to see where we went wrong. This is not an easy way to write a novel: impossible, some would say, and if I had saddled myself with such madness in 1973, I have grave doubts that this novel or my subsequent career would have amounted to anything, even with Phyllis Westberg encouraging me on from New York.

I wrote the outline, then I wrote the book I had outlined: it was almost that simple. The outline consisted of twenty chapters sketched out in the briefest prose imaginable—eight lines to half a page for each would-be chapter. Somewhere along the way I discovered the virtues of rewrite, for the outline is heavily corrected, as if at various later times, in different pencils and inks, and the first draft is likewise marked almost into obliteration. A veritable book is written between the lines, and in the margins and on the backs of pages. Dialogue is scoped, often in pencil, and working notes are sometimes added on the sidelines.

I discovered new things about the subconscious. It feeds you material out of order: it gives you stuff you may never use, or may bring to life in another novel years from now. I remember one chapter that wouldn't work until I removed it from the first third of the book, cut it in half, and plugged it as it then stood into the last third. The process is difficult, painful, and endlessly interesting. For this novel, the process took about six months. Phyllis balked at the last two chapters, I rewrote them yet again, and the book went off to market.

And I settled into my next book. Rejections began accumulating in New York on both *The Holland Suggestions* and on the radio book. It would be more than a year before either book sold. Then both sold, and I had finished my third and was into a fourth.

This is the writer's life. You've got to keep moving, keep your hands busy, keep growing and, hopefully, keep getting better. You do the best you can and you move on.

I wish I could say that lightning struck, as it had for Irving Stone when he was that age. Well, it probably isn't *Lust for Life*. I should be happy, and am, that people still find it viable. Fiction tends to have a short half-life. Much of it is biodegradable, and books far more noble than this have perished in the same brief time span. The writer has no way of knowing: all he can do is shore up the trench and write another one. In the eighteen years between *The Holland Suggestions* and *Booked to Die*, I probably wrote millions of words. There were many disappointments, a few heartaches and lots of bloody footprints left in the snow. But Phyllis Westberg is still my agent and my working wife is finally out of the gravel quarry. The good things keep getting better. And that may be the most obvious virtue of not finding too much success too soon.

JOHN DUNNING
Denver, Colorado
March 1996

THE
HOLLAND
SUGGESTIONS

1

TWO SEPARATE FORCES, LONG SINCE BANISHED FROM my life and buried, returned that fall to put the nightmare in motion. Naturally, at first I tried to push it away, but once it started, there was no stopping it. Judy brought her pressures to the conscious element; my subconscious did the rest. Before I could begin to understand it I was drawn in and found no way to go but straight ahead to the end of it.

Judy's part, limited as it was, provided the initial impetus. It was Judy who first began to ease my mind—then jolted it—into that early critical examination of my past. Though she never asked specifically about the Holland experiments, her interest in her mother was tied directly to the time when Robert Holland and I were taking those long dips into my id. Either I was too blind to see it in its early stages, or my subconscious had screened it out the way psychologists say it sometimes does for self-protection. Later it became too obvious to ignore. The beginning was probably sometime after Judy's fourteenth birthday, and I began to notice it the following year. Suddenly

I saw that she was experimenting, and learning many things about her mother from my reactions to her experiments. She's quite a kid, Judy. She looks so much like her mother that I am still startled when she enters a room without warning. Judy has always looked more like Vivian than me; I guess that's her blessing, but it leaves me a strange feeling of sadness and discontent to carry into my middle life. Dull pain, bone deep, that you can never find and snuff out completely. Judy helped bring part of that to the surface.

Teenage girls are a joy. They seem to develop overnight: Now they're kids, and soon there are breasts and curves, and they're testing the old man's reaction to all the artificial lures of womanhood. Judy tried them all, and I let her do it, with one exception, until it had run its course. The exception was orange lipstick. I just hated that, and I told her so. But Judy has always been a sane kid, and I know she would have abandoned it in a week or so anyway. She settled on a subdued makeup that was almost a replica of Vivian's. How she arrived at it I couldn't then guess, but she was developing an amazing instinct for her mother's taste. I thought it had to be instinct, because I knew—wrongly—that she never got any clue to Vivian's character from me. We never talked of Vivian beyond the fact that she had lived and had once been my wife and was Judy's mother. I didn't know where Vivian was and I had no interest in knowing.

I should pause a minute. I've just caught myself in a lie, and if this is to have any value, I guess it should be done without all the little ego-saving games that people always play. In fact, Vivian has always been the most fascinating woman in my life. I would have suppressed my interest in her then, but deep inside me it has never waned. Vivian has affected my relationships with other women through the years, the most recent being my secretary, Sharon Welles.

Sharon blames Judy for that, perhaps with good reason, but Judy was merely the manifestation of Vivian. Vivian has always been my millstone. I still do not feel at ease talking about her or even thinking about her beyond those flashes that have passed through my mind several times a day for fifteen years. So when I first noticed Judy's strong resemblance to her mother, when it became so strong that I could not ignore it any more, I began to watch her growth with a morbid brand of depressed fascination. I was eager to write it off as simple mother-to-daughter physical heredity. Now I find my lack of insight into the needs of my growing daughter terrifying. Early in her life, Judy sensed my inhibitions about Vivian and constructed inhibitions of her own. My hangup fed her fantasies, and, in a different way, Vivian became the most fascinating woman in Judy's life too. With her only weapon, her looks, she fought my reluctance to discuss it. With an utter lack of material to go on, Judy reconstructed her mother's image for me. It was a slow process of trial and error. But when I first saw her in one of those 1950s sweaters with her lips touched a pale pink and the hair that she always wore in a bun flowing out behind her, my reaction must have gratified her. I dropped my drink down the front of my shirt.

She refined the image slowly, adding and subtracting touches here and there, but never again did she catch me so unprepared as she had that first time. Gradually I learned to live with the fact that Vivian, in the person of our daughter, whom I also loved very much, had come back to me.

When she wasn't being Vivian, Judy was going through all the perils of adolescence. Boys flocked around, and she was in and out of love more times than I thought possible in a school year. We had some very frank talks that year, the kind that most girls have with their mothers, but I think I handled them well. I strived for an open, honest relationship built on mutual respect, and it seemed complete in every aspect except where Vivian was concerned. Judy's spirit is strong, but her mind is reasonable. I could always guide her, but never boss her, and I think she knew that, though she never put it to a test. My strongest influence over her will always be the value she places on my respect. I hope I can keep that forever, though I have to admit I have occasionally abused it. The Vivian problem seemed to be our only serious hangup. I saw to it that Judy understood about sex at an early age, yet I never failed to marvel at how much solid information she picked up on her own. Street-level sex education in action. When she turned sixteen I suspected that she was going deeper into sexual experimentation than I wanted her to be, and the object of my suspicion—a pimply right guard on the football team—was hardly the man you always hope your daughter will someday bring home. I suspected he was into pot, a rumor I picked up third-hand through the parental grapevine. But I found out how reliable the grapevine was when half the varsity football team was arrested for marijuana possession and Judy's pizza-faced hero was *not* among them. When the cops came crashing through the door, he and Judy were at the movies.

Naturally, she dropped him just as my doubts were beginning to subside.

The second element in the Holland story began on the same day that the first came to a head.

I awoke that morning two hours before the alarm went off. Beyond my bedroom window there was not even a hint of light, yet instantly I was awake and peering through the darkness for some explanation of what had awakened me. I lay there for several minutes, then turned back my blanket and sat on the edge of the bed. Some noise had done it; I was certain of that, because normally, when the house is quiet, I am a sound sleeper. I did hear a noise; sharp, clicking, like the closing of a door in the lower part of the house. I got up and moved to the door, then peeped out into the hall. At the end of the hallway Judy's door stood open, and the small nightlamp at the head of her bed was on. I moved quietly to the head of the stairs, looked into her room and, satisfied that she was not there, went downstairs. A light was on in the kitchen, and there was a half-finished glass of milk on the table. The back door stood open a crack; it does that unless you slam it hard. I stood just inside the doorway and looked outside. Judy was sitting alone in my backyard workshop. The inside of the workshop was dark, but I could clearly see the round whiteness of her face as she sat at my work table and looked out through the window. I stepped outside and felt the cold night air penetrate my pajamas. The walk across the back lawn was short, less than twenty yards, and I knew that she would see me approach and would already be deciding whether to tell me what was troubling her.

But she didn't see me at all. She was so engrossed in thought that I came right up to the toolshed door without revealing my presence. I was about to speak to her when something held me back: some instinct perhaps, a feeling that my voice would be a gross violation of her privacy. I stopped then and took a step backward. My mind filled with conflicting thoughts. Later I could ask her about it, if that was the proper thing to do. Then I heard her say the word *mother*. My heart beat faster. She said her mother's name, Vivian, and, in a whisper, words that sounded like "somehow he's got to realize . . ." I took two more involuntary steps backward, turned, and walked quickly back to the house.

It was disturbing as hell. I waited for her in the kitchen, watching her intermittently from the window. For more than an hour she did not move. When at last she did come out of the shed I hurried upstairs to avoid embarrassment for both of us. I fell into my bed and lay there until the alarm went off, then got up to shower and shave. As always, she had breakfast ready when I came down, but she did not eat with me.

"I've got to run," she said. "I've got an early test and I need the library time for studying."

She kissed my cheek as she brushed past, and the door slammed as she went out. I walked to the front door and watched her walk away, briskly, as though she were racing the first bell. I went back to the kitchen and thought it through over a second cup of coffee. The conclusion was inescapable: Judy was going through an identity crisis, Vivian was at the root of it, and I had promoted it by making Vivian our household Mata Hari.

The question was, what should be done about it now? Without doubt it would all have to come out, but how and when? *Soon.* Movement and action always helped relieve emotional logjams; I had seen it work many times. I went upstairs. She had closed the door to her room, as always, but I turned the knob and pushed it open. The bed was unmade, and several copies of teen magazines were scattered across the floor. Just as I had seen it three hours ago. I stepped into the room, feeling immediately guilty for violating her sanctuary. But never mind that; I justified it under the righteous cloak of parental concern. I did not touch anything; I did not pry, unless just being there was prying, as I suspect it was. I just walked through the room, stepping carefully around the magazines, and had myself a good look. It was the first time I had ever gone into her room without an invitation, and rightfully, I felt like a prowler.

Since I was a prowler, then, I let my eyes prowl across the top of her bureau. There were lipsticks and a cologne bottle and a few snapshots of Judy and her boyfriends, and one of me. At the end of her bureau lay her lock-up diary, apparently locked, but if she had left without putting it away, perhaps she had neglected to lock it as well. All the answers to my sudden questions would be there, just the turn of a hairpin away; but under no circumstances could I do that. I did not touch it, did not even go near it. In fact, I had just decided that I had already overstepped the rights of parental concern and was turning to leave when I saw, in a corner, the small stack of canvas paintings she had done for art class. Something about that first one caught my eye; it was not one I had seen before, though I had assumed that she always showed me her work. I moved up for a closer look. Yes, it was a new one: a faceless woman standing in a fog, with a deeper blue that might have been a river running behind her. The painting had a ghostly, morbid quality that I hated at once. Her signature was in the lower right corner, with the date below it. The painting was two years old, and I had never seen it.

I flipped back the canvas to look at the painting behind it. This one I knew well; it was the seascape that had won first prize in the freshman competition two years ago. Behind that was another new one, a full-face portrait of Vivian. It was so real and so good that I was truly shocked. It was called *Self Portrait by J. Ryan.* That was a relief, but when I looked at it again, the relief dissolved. She had painted a small mole over the right cheekbone, where Vivian had always had a mole but where she, Judy, never had. I stood there looking at it for a long time, remembering small things about Vivian that I had put out of my mind years before. In almost every respect the portrait more closely resembled Vivian, just twenty-one years old the last time I had seen her, than it did her sixteen-year-old daughter. I studied it for so long that I had to rush to work; only as I was backing my car out of the garage did I remember my morning schedule of the vital meeting with the boss and an important new contract.

Harper Brothers Construction Company is located in the valley, on the far side of town. The company actually is owned by Al Harper, who bought out his brothers Joe and Vic more than twenty years ago, when all were struggling young builders. Nobody is struggling anymore. Al has grown fat and prosperous, and he pays his employees well. At least, I've got no kick. For a contractor located in a medium-sized semi-Southern town, Al Harper has done all right. He's still a hustler, and he gets plenty of jobs away from the big outfits in Richmond and even in Washington, D.C. But I'll write Al's success story some other time. After my initial reaction to the lateness of the hour, my thoughts came back to personal matters. Before I was halfway across town I had made a decision: The time had come, was long overdue, to get everything about Vivian out in the open. By now I had no doubt that what I was observing was an early symptom of something unhealthy, and it bothered me more the longer I thought about it. *Tonight;* I would start it tonight: throw out the subject myself and see where it led us. Perhaps that was all that was needed; maybe it would resolve itself. Judy's reaction would tell me everything. If she accepted it, we were still on solid ground. If she withdrew, we might be in trouble. That might mean that what I was observing was not an early symptom, but some advanced indication of her identity involvement with her mother. It was not a thought to start a big day with.

I pulled into the Harper parking lot just behind Sharon Welles. Sharon had parked near the door and was walking briskly into the office before my car had even stopped. Her aloofness was almost part of my life; after all, our little cold war had been going on for almost a year, and there was no reason for her to change tactics now. I shrugged it off, got out, and went through the main office. The working offices at Harper are along a narrow corridor that leads from the showroom to the shop; mine was at the end of the corridor, a two-room job that allowed me to keep a door between Sharon and me. These days, that had to be a plus. I walked through without speaking. She was turned away from me, as always, this time ostensibly looking through the filing cabinet for some document, so there was no need for any morning greeting between us. She would fake it like that until we got through the unpleasant business of beginning the day; then the momentum of the job would carry us through to the end. Sharon played an excellent woman scorned.

With the door closed between us I loosened my tie, hung up my coat, and sat down at my desk. The phone rang immediately.

"Jim? Al Harper."

"Al. You been trying to reach me?"

"Just once; no sweat. Look, we'll have to postpone our meeting this morning. I've got to fly to Richmond."

"If you want to, but I can handle it."

"I'd like to be there. I've already called them and moved it back to next week, okay? So just hang tough till I get back."

That was that. I had blocked out the whole morning for the meeting, and now I had nothing on my agenda until one. I sat at my desk, doodling on my notepad, for about half an hour. Then Sharon came in with the morning mail and the coffee. As usual, we had nothing to say. She poured my coffee, then put a stack of mail on my desk and left, with a malignant glare at the portrait of Judy in my bookcase. That annoyed me; it always had, but there was no way I could thin the bad blood between Judy and Sharon now. So I would have to live with it or find myself a new secretary. Often I thought that that might be the best answer for both of us.

There followed more doodling and a superficial examination of the mail. Sharon had opened and thinned it for me, handling by herself the kiss-off letters and passing on the rest, in order of importance as she judged it. I sifted through it quickly. There wasn't much; there never was on Monday: the usual engineering crap, sales pitches from field agents. Nothing even mildly interesting until, at the bottom of the stack, I found a thick, padded manila envelope. I turned the package over and examined it. The postmark was New York, two days ago, and on both sides someone had stamped the word PERSONAL. Naturally, Sharon had not opened it. I tore it open and pulled out a large photograph, wrapped twice around with a long rubber band and protected on both sides by corrugated cardboard panels. I slipped off the rubber band, pushed away the cardboard, and turned the picture face up. I expected it to be some technical shot of one of Harper's big jobs, but instead I saw a primitive mountain trail that dead-ended at the base of a wall of rock. The trail seemed to drop away into a canyon. The drop was sheer and I knew it was deep. There was a cave among the rocks at the end of the trail, and as I looked at it a strange sensation passed over me; the feeling that everyone has at some time in his life of knowing a place where he's never been. In this case it was nonsense. I have a slight problem with heights, and I knew I would never go out on a ledge like that.

I looked inside the envelope for some explanatory

10

note, but there was nothing. There was no writing, other than my name and HARPER BROTHERS CONSTRUCTION COMPANY and the address. I examined the cardboard and the back of the print. Nothing. The picture was intriguing in a vague sort of way. I looked at it again, carefully this time. It was not a particularly good shot. The sun had probably been behind the mountain; at any rate, there was too much darkness. But it was clear enough. The trail looked treacherous. Scattered along its length were many loose rocks; any of them might send a careless climber plunging into the canyon. The thought gave me the shivers. It was difficult to get a perspective from the print, especially since there were no people in it, but I guessed that the trail was no more than three feet wide. Again I felt a wave of distinct familiarity. Absurd.

The buzzer. "It's your daughter," Sharon said coldly.

"Put her on, please."

I had time for just a brief reaction: mixed surprise and apprehension. There was a click and a loud background noise; a shuffling of feet and the hollow sounds of hallway talk.

"Judy?"

"Hi."

"Something wrong?"

"No, everything's fine."

"Well, then, what's the occasion?"

"I just wanted to apologize for running out like that."

"I didn't even notice."

"Look, I know you're busy and all."

"As a matter of fact, my whole morning's suddenly free. What's on your mind?"

"Nothing really. Just what I said."

There was a long pause while I gathered my thoughts. Obviously she was fishing, groping for an opening to discuss whatever was bothering her. Just as obviously, she wasn't finding it.

"Listen, I'll be late for class," she said.

I pondered it. It would have to be done, but not now and certainly not by phone. "Okay, you run on then. But don't cook anything tonight. I just might be in the mood for a night out. How about dinner at the Roadhouse?"

"Really?"

"Sure. Just the two of us, okay?"

"Great."

That little gesture, I told myself as I hung up, was a stroke of genius. I felt confident again, and I decided to work the Vivian thing out in my mind now, as long as I had a free morning. But then Sharon came in, dropped some drawings on my desk, and went out without a word. I made a mental note to get her replaced, absolutely and irrevocably; to have her shifted into someone else's office, even if I had to answer the goddamn phones myself. With that decided, my mind wandered and settled, strangely, on Robert Holland.

Actually, some of the things I had learned long ago from Robert might be of help in my little family crisis. Hypnosis had always scared the hell out of me, and now, considering it half seriously, I felt like a kid about to make a wild dash through a cemetery at night. I had not done it in fifteen years, yet there was not the slightest doubt in my mind that it would be as easy now as it had been then. I fought with it for another minute, then got up and turned off the lights. My fingers tingled with the excitement of it, and I sank back in the comfort of my chair, still too nervous to try anything. Gradually I relaxed, staring at the opaque window, and I went into a light trance immediately the first time I tried. I went deeper. The room darkened around me, and the window became a point of light in the darkness. I deepened the trance again, and Vivian's face came into focus. Or Judy's. At first I couldn't be sure. Then I saw the tiny black mole and knew it was Vivian. I heard her voice, though I could not yet make out the words. I had almost forgotten the soft quality of her voice. Such effective camouflage for deadly poison. One level deeper and I would have her. I would see her and hear her, and if I wanted to I could reach out and touch her. Robert Holland had said that *you can relive any experience in all five senses under hypnosis,* and I knew the truth of it. I'd done it.

In the outer office I heard a filing cabinet drawer slam shut and Sharon swore, but the image of Vivian did not fade. My mind wrestled with both worlds at once and handled them with ease. I went deeper and the image sharpened; now I could see the little red lines above her green eyes, and the holes in her earlobes where the earrings went through. Behind her, the apartment where we had lived then, with the battered red sofa and the picture on the wall never hanging quite straight. She said *Hello, Jim;* it was letter perfect, precise, like a video-tape replay fifteen years later. I wanted to go closer, to step into the apartment with her, but instead I backed away from it. That cold, unreasonable fear forced me back, the apartment faded to an obscure black and white, and Vivian melted and became part of the blur. I came out of it very fast. The window focused in my eyes, and I saw that in the few minutes I had been under, it had started to rain. I sat there for a long time, just listening to the rain falling on the pavement outside. My mind was all a mixture of Robert and Judy and Vivian. Sharon pushed her way in by slamming another filing cabinet and saying "goddamnit" just loud enough for me to hear.

All right. Enough.

I barked into the intercom: "Sharon."

"Yes."

"Get the hell in here."

I was surprised at the toughguy sound of my own voice, but the scene itself was carried through without emotion, as I knew it would be. We had come to a point where we could no longer communicate, and I wanted another secretary as soon as possible. She could handle it any way she liked: with a request to Al Harper for a transfer or with a resignation. I didn't care what she did. She took it without a word and left me alone. Finished, and it felt like scratching a sore that had itched for a long time. Done. After simmering for a year, the matter of Sharon Welles was settled and disposed of in thirty seconds. Vivian might be as easy, once the preliminaries were out of the way. My eyes fell on the mountain photograph, and in a quick flush of impatience I swept it lightly, wrappings and all, off the desk and into the wastebasket. Then I picked up my coat and walked out, asking Sharon to *please* cancel my afternoon appointments.

I did a lot of driving and thinking that day. When I got home Judy was already dressed for the Roadhouse. She waited for me in the living room, reading her new *Seventeen* while I showered and changed. Then we were off. The restaurant was an old favorite, located ten miles out of town on a hill overlooking the valley. We sat at a window table with a view of the patio. I was calm and confident right up to the moment when I had to face it. A bad case of nerves set in, and I ordered a strong Scotch to help get me started. I was halfway through my second drink before I decided to bite the bullet and do it.

"I know you've been wondering about your . . . mother . . . for a long time." My voice cracked and the words seemed to stick. I looked at her, but she was staring down at her water glass and would not meet my eyes. "Look at me, Judy," I said.

"I can't."

14

"Sure you can."

With that she did look up, and I saw that her eyes were filling with tears.

"Isn't this what you want?" I said.

"Yes."

"Then we'll do it together. I'll tell you about Vivian, anything you want to know."

"When?"

"Soon. I want to go through some papers first. I've got some stuff filed away that might help. Sometime in the next few days we'll get it all out and go through it together, okay?"

She nodded. Both of us were relieved to have that initial thrust behind us, and we looked for a new topic of conversation. We unwound slowly through the night and got home sometime before midnight. It was after two when I went up to bed; I fell asleep immediately.

I awoke in a panic. I jumped up and ran to the bedroom door, stumbling over a chair that blocked my way. The hallway was dark. Judy's door was closed, and there were no sounds or lights from the lower part of the house. I went back and sat down on the bed. *Now what the hell?* I looked at my bedside clock; the luminous dials said three-thirty. I had not slept two hours. *The dream.* I had been dreaming, not about Judy or Vivian, but about Robert Holland and that mountain trail in the photograph. A strange, screwy dream, but coming with it was one of the strongest impulses of my life, an overpowering need to save that picture from the janitor's fire. Morning would be too late; the janitor would have come and gone by the time I got there. I dressed, crept quietly downstairs, opened the garage, started the car, and drove to the office. I let myself in with my side-door key and went straight to my desk. The picture and all its wrappings were still in my basket, just as I had left them. I gathered up everything, cardboard, envelope, even the rubber band. By the time I got home it was almost five o'clock. I went into my den, unlocked the filing cabinet, and filed the photograph in the drawer marked ROBERT HOLLAND. Then I pulled the drawer handle to be sure it was locked and retired to my room for what little remained of the sleepless night.

2

THE HOLLAND FILE WAS MY PERSONAL PANDORA'S box. I had avoided it for fifteen years; now I devoured the contents in one sitting. Thanksgiving came and went, and Judy left with a girlfriend for two days in the mountains. I had the house to myself all day Friday and Saturday, and I intended to use the whole time reading the Holland file. Only after a careful screening would I throw it open to Judy's inspection. Call that censorship if you want to; under the circumstances, I still believe I did the right thing. As it turned out, I censored nothing. The screening process was not nearly so painful as I had feared, and I found nothing that anyone could possibly object to showing his teenage daughter. The deeper I read into the Holland material, the more aware I became that the basic problem was mine.

First, there was Robert's unfinished manuscript on hypnosis. Even in its incomplete state it was thick and cumbersome. Reading it took half the morning, but it refreshed my memory on many of the small technical details that had gone into the Holland theories. Then there were three handwritten journals of our experiments, all very subjective, containing Robert's impressions of the Jake Walters project as well as his straight descriptions of each session. Supplementing the journals were ten lengthy tapes, verbatim transcripts of each session. The tapes took all day and most of the night to hear; I played them while I read through the journals. When I was finished I noticed that the last journal contained reference to a *fourth* book, though the journals and the tapes finished at precisely the same point. I searched through the file but found no other books anywhere, and I assumed that Robert had died before beginning the fourth journal.

There were some old photographs showing Robert and an incredibly young me, and another set of pictures showing Robert and his old pals from college. I found a small package of newspaper clippings; I knew at once what they contained and tried to push them away until later. I realized then that there was no later, that I had been doing just that for fifteen years, and I forced myself to go through them now. There was a series on the experiments and a small story telling of Robert's dismissal from the university. I read them through quickly but thoroughly. Done at last. I was through the worst of it. A few more papers; a letter; some photocopied articles on hypnotic trance. The life story of Robert Holland, tied together in five fat manila folders and ten reels of recorded tape.

Only one more folder—the Vivian folder—remained in the file. This one was dismally thin; indeed, there were only a couple of documents filed there. I removed the folder and opened it, feeling a little sadness as the dust spread into the air. It was almost appalling how little material was there. Stupid of me to feel that way, when all along I had known I would not find much. Vivian didn't write letters, never allowed her picture to be taken, and had an inherent distrust of tape machines. I remembered the time she'd gone into a rage when I recorded a conversation on the sly. She had sought out the tape while I was at work and burned it, then smashed Robert Holland's tape recorder and called it an accident. As far as I knew there was only one picture of her—the one I was holding in my hand—and it was a poor one. Judy had never seen it, but now I would show it to her. In the picture Vivian was sitting alone in the living room of our apartment, just as I had seen her this week in my little regression experiment. A vase of flowers was on the mantel behind her; another was on the table. Her love of flowers was another facet of her character that I had forgotten. She was not looking at the camera, because she never knew I had taken the picture. Had she known, she would have found it and destroyed it, just like the tape. Even after all these years Vivian would have been uneasy if she had suspected that I had her photograph. Beyond this, I was willing to risk good money that there was no record anywhere of her voice, no fingerprint on file, no evidence in public or private folders that she had lived. Marriage license—yes, I found that—and possibly a social-security card under some phony name. I have never met anyone so private as Vivian. She should have married Howard Hughes; undoubtedly their offspring would have been born invisible.

The Vivian folder took less than ten minutes, most of which was spent staring at her picture and thinking about it. At midnight I put it all away, locked the filing cabinet, and went to bed. Again I spent a restless night and was up before dawn. I was having a hell of a time sleeping these days, but that probably wouldn't be remedied until I got the whole mess over with. I decided to talk with Judy Sunday night, and that left me all day Saturday to think it through.

Impulsively I drove over to Wyllis, the little Blue

Ridge town where I had first seen Vivian. It was only a three-hour drive, but I hadn't been back since I had taken her away from all that in 1955. I packed a lunch and took my Vivian file with me, though there wasn't anything in it. At the last minute I also threw in the photograph of the mountain trail, and I didn't know why I was doing that either. The drive was dull until I got within twenty miles of Wyllis and began looking for old signs. I remembered absolutely nothing of the town. The drugstore where Vivian had worked was gone; that whole block had been ripped out and a shopping center was going up. I made a halfhearted attempt to locate the druggist who might have remembered her, but that was a lost cause from the beginning. Probably he was dead. I left Wyllis with mixed feelings of sadness and relief.

To my surprise I didn't go straight home but drove along the Blue Ridge Trail, then turned west into West Virginia. In the late afternoon I parked the car and climbed high into the mountains, but nothing here even remotely resembled the mountain in the picture. For a long time after that I sat in my car and studied the picture and its wrappings. The only new factor I found was that the address on the envelope seemed fresh, while the envelope itself looked old and faded. The word PERSONAL apparently had been stamped there a long time ago, and there was a dark dust line at the top, as though it had lain under other parcels— perhaps for years—before being mailed. The rubber band that held the picture and the cardboard panels together was old too; its outer surface had dried and hardened, and it broke easily before it was stretched out to its old limit.

None of this helped me, except to reinforce my growing conviction that the picture had a tie to Robert, or at least to the era when I had known Robert, and that something new was happening in the matter.

It was disturbing, but too much for my tired mind to cope with. I drove through the night and got home in the early morning. Again, I could not sleep more than a few hours. After tossing restlessly for a time, I got up and made a big breakfast. Then I went into the den, opened the Holland file, and sat at my desk with the mountain photograph before me.

I was doodling, thinking about it in that shallow trancelike state that is familiar to anyone who has ever been hypnotized. I don't know how long I sat there, pencil in hand; it might have been half an hour or just a few minutes. I was in that twilight state that comes just before a deep trance when the sound of an ambulance passing a block away brought me out of it. I looked down at the pad and was surprised to see that my doodles formed symbols and numbers. I had drawn a Maltese cross and had written beneath it the numbers 50, 96, 12.

Automatic writing?

I hadn't done anything like that since the days of the Holland experiments.

But it was automatic writing beyond any doubt. I had drawn the Maltese cross without looking at the pad—in fact, without any awareness of my finger movements—and the numbers were strongly written and perfect. The cross was about the size of a marble. I rummaged in my desk for a magnifying glass and studied the cross for a minute. The cross was encased in a perfect circle, and the only imperfection I found anywhere in the drawing was a spot in the lower arm where perhaps a quarter of that arm was missing. It was as though a faulty ballpoint pen had run out of ink at precisely that spot, but I had been using a pencil with a finely sharpened point, and the point was not broken.

I began to examine the photograph under the magnifying glass. I looked closely at each rock on that treacherous trail, letting my glass meander along to the base of the cave. For a long time I examined the gloom of the cave, as though the glass would help me penetrate that darkness and would thus reveal the who and why of this picture's sudden intrusion into my life. As I moved the glass along the rocks lining the cave, I felt a cold sensation creep along my spine. Clearly imprinted in the rock was the Maltese cross.

Holy Christ! I sat back and rubbed my eyes, which by now were watering badly. When I could see clearly I looked at the picture again. The cross was still there, an exact replica of the one I had just drawn. Obviously it was very old; part of the lower arm had worn away with time; but the circle and the upper arms were complete and in good condition. Had I subconsciously "seen" and stored it with my earlier examinations of the picture? Was that possible? Without the glass, the cross appeared as nothing more than a blur. Even with the glass it might seem just a peculiar rock characteristic, had I not drawn that precise image less than five minutes before. The matter of the cross bothered me more than anything I had yet encountered, and I had to fight down an urge to destroy the picture and the rest of the Holland file as well. Instead, I filed everything away, pulled the drawer handle to be sure it was locked, and went out along the lake for a long walk.

When I got back Judy was home. I saw her coat on the cedar chest and I heard vaguely the sounds of the shower water running upstairs. I went into the den and unlocked the filing cabinet, then went to the kitchen and poured myself a stiff drink. I looked at the clock; it wasn't yet one o'clock, a bit early to start boozing, but today, I told myself, I had an excuse. A sense of urgency had come over me and I knew that our little talk would not wait until tonight. Judy came down in about fifteen minutes; she smiled and said hi and kissed my cheek; I said how was your weekend and she said fine how about yours. Small talk, but I guessed that she had been through the same indecision that was now my constant companion. There was no time for any more guessing games in handling the problem; I had a strong need to get it all out at once, to have it behind me before I could find another excuse to put it off for one more day.

"Let's go in the den and talk," I said. She followed me through the French doors and took a seat in the chair facing my desk. I sat at the desk, stared out of the window in a last desperate grasp for an excuse to delay, then got up and took the folders out of the filing cabinet. When I turned and looked at her I saw that she was tense; her jaw had tightened and her hands gripped the leather arms of the chair. She had been looking at the top drawer of the filing cabinet, the one she had never seen open, and now she was staring at the files I held in my hands.

"Relax," I said, trying to put us both at ease. "There's nothing in here to be nervous about." I placed the folders on the edge of the desk and sat in the chair beside them. "There are some tapes in here too; we can play them sometime if you want to hear them. Right now I'm not sure the tapes will add anything to the questions you have about your mother. We'll see, okay?"

She nodded nervously.

First things first. I opened the Vivian file and took out the photograph. "Your mother."

She looked at it for a long time. "She's pretty," she said at last.

"You look just like her."

"I'm not nearly . . ."

"Not yet, but you will be soon. Yeah, Vivian was a damn fine-looking woman. How did you know you two looked so much alike?"

"I didn't know. Your expressions, I guess, more than anything."

"How'd you know about the mole on her cheek?" I asked, realizing that I wasn't supposed to know that she knew that.

She didn't bat an eye. "You told me once, remember? When I was just a kid you told me. It's the only time you've ever said anything about her."

I didn't remember, but I passed over it. "Except for that, you could be her double."

She looked again at the snapshot. "I'm not nearly . . ."

"Modesty's always been one of your finest traits, but you look just like her and you know it, okay? Let's get on with it; we've got a lot to cover."

My words excited her. They excited me too, in a different way. "Any questions?"

"A few."

"Yes?"

"Why is she looking away like that? It's really a pretty bad picture. Do you have anything showing her full face?"

"She didn't like pictures; I had to shoot this one with Robert's camera on the sly. It might have come out better if I'd been able to use flash. But as far as I know there are no other pictures of her anywhere."

"Was that a superstition or what?"

"I don't know what it was. Probably a superstition. Yes, I guess that must have been it; a superstition."

"Where were you living then?"

"In a little town not far from Richmond. I was a student at William Schuster U; that's a small college for kids who can't make it at William and Mary for one reason or another. In fact, I think it's closed now. I used to get propositioned all the time for money, but I haven't had anything from them now in five or six years. Anyway, your mother and I, we took this place because it was cheap and we were broke. My parents were trying to help me through school, but they didn't have much money either. That year I had to drop out. Vivian was working in a department store and it was near Christmas, like now—yes, it was this same time of year. I dropped out at midterm because we just couldn't make it. She was making forty dollars a week."

I stopped there, lost in some irrelevancy, and it might have been several minutes later when I looked up and saw Judy waiting expectantly. "You want to hear all of this?"

"As much of it as you want to tell me."

"A lot of it's just junk. It doesn't matter to anyone now."

"Why not . . . get it all out? . . . see what matters?"

I swallowed some Scotch, said, "Good idea," and forced my mind back to that Christmas. "She was making forty dollars a week. I remember she was very bitter about that. Let me tell you, your mother had a fine mind, like yours; she really resented making forty dollars a week. She hated her work, thought it was demeaning; but jobs were tight then and we had to take what we could get. I took a job in a gas station. That's almost a cliché today—everyone who's poor goes to work in a gas station—but I really did. So we were making eighty dollars between us."

"But you were just starting out."

"Yes, I was, but there wasn't any room in Vivian's mind for that kind of thinking. She wasn't interested in potential, only results. She was impatient with change; everything moved too slowly for her. I don't think she ever worried about next year or last year, only now. In a lot of ways I guess she was really practical."

I went into the kitchen and refilled my glass. "Besides," I called through the hallway, "we were horribly mismatched." I came back to the den and deposited the Scotch bottle and the ice bucket on the desk. "I guess that comes out a criticism of her from my view-point, but she isn't here to defend herself, and I guess you'll have to take all this with a grain of salt. I mean, I keep wanting to say things like bitch and whore, and that's not credible at all, is it?"

"I don't know."

"I really learned to hate her. After she left me, when she was gone for five or six months and I knew she wasn't ever coming back, I began to methodically destroy her in my mind. I must have cursed her name a thousand times, maybe more. It seems silly to me now, but I believed then that it was the only way I could make it. I do know that it was the worst period of my life, no question about it, and it lasted two years. By then I had distorted her image so that I didn't have any real grasp of her anymore. Then I forgot about her, or thought I did. I guess my subconscious never did let me forget, though, did it?"

She married me to get away, you know. She had been in some kind of trouble in Wyllis when she was just eighteen. I never did know what that was about; only that she was under a court order of some kind. She refused to talk about it, just as she refused to talk about losing her department store job later, after some employee had poured red paint over the carpets one night after closing. I was an easy out for her, so we got married and moved up near Richmond. She hated that almost as much as she had hated Wyllis. Vivian hated everything. From the beginning, I knew, with the bleak certainty that some men know those things, that it wasn't working. Knowing it didn't help. When she wanted to leave, she just left. And when I got in her way she tried to cut my throat with a broken milk bottle.

I was filling my glass again and Judy was staring out at the gray day. Maybe I could stop here and finish another time; but no, it was coming up like a rotten meal and I could not stop until it was all out. Telling Judy about the milk bottle wouldn't help her, but at least I had faced it and passed it. Now I could move on to something else. I noticed that Judy was staring at the bumpy scar on my neck, where I was feeling it with my fingers, and I took my hand down and busied my fingers with my glass.

The Scotch was having a dulling effect on my brain. That was what I wanted, but not too much or too soon. I sipped it and pushed the glass away from me.

"Where did she go?" Judy asked.

"I haven't got the slightest idea. I haven't seen her to this day."

There was a long pause while we both reorganized our thoughts. Nothing came of that, so after a while I asked her if she had more questions.

"I don't know," she said. "Is there any more?"

"A little." I sat up and opened the first of the Holland folders. "The next part of the story involves an old friend of mine. You know the name Robert Holland?"

"I've seen it on your filing cabinet. I always thought he was someone else you didn't want to talk about."

"I guess that's true; I don't know. Robert and Vivian were having a . . . thing . . . together. When I found out about it I wanted to hurt Robert, and I did. I did a really lousy thing; it cost him his job and probably would have ruined his life, but he died soon after it happened anyway. Here's his picture." I passed her the faded snapshot. "He's the one in the middle, a lot younger here than when I knew him. They were on an outing in Colorado, I think, when this was made— probably sometime in the middle forties."

I leaned over and looked at the picture, upside down in my vision as she held it. Robert, young and beardless, was wearing an assortment of hiking gear.

"Who are the other two with him?" she asked.

"The man on the left is Kenneth Barcotti. The guy on the right is Leland Smith. Robert told me they were inseparable, great pals in college. I've never met either of them." I sipped my drink. "Let's see—Kenneth Barcotti—did I say he was the one on the left? Yes, your left—Kenneth was the explorer, member of National Spelunkers, world traveler; he disappeared on a trip in the Colorado mountains just before Robert died, and I don't think he was ever found. Leland Smith became a psychologist, like Robert, and moved to the Midwest to teach, or maybe to practice—I don't know. Like I said, I never knew them, and I haven't even thought about them for fifteen years. So Leland Smith—well, I don't know where he is or what he's doing now."

I shuffled through Robert's papers, found his manuscript on hypnosis, and the small package of newspaper clippings fell from between the pages. It fell face up on the table, and I knew that Judy wanted to pick it up and look through it. Her fingers were twitching.

"We'll get to these soon," I said. "Just contain your natural female curiosity and let's take it one step at a time."

I was really getting tight now, so I pushed my drink away to the far corner of the desk. Then, in an unsteady voice that seemed to belong to someone else, I told her the story of Robert Holland.

"The first time I saw Robert was in the fall of 1955. He was my psychology prof, you know. He'd been on the skids in the early fifties—Robert had a bad drinking problem all his life—and it had been up and down for him ever since his graduation. Mostly down, from what he'd told me. His friends tried to help him; they did what they could, but there wasn't really anything that anybody could do. Robert Holland was a drunk, plain and simple.

"By 1952 he had pulled himself together and had taken a job as an account executive with a little advertising agency in suburban Washington. The following year he got back into teaching, when the chancellor at Schuster gave him an associate prof's job. The chancellor was a real bastard; he kept two or three guys like Robert around all the time, just to help feed his ego. Warren Rice, his name was; Warren Rice. Yeah, well, this Rice never let Robert forget that he could be sent back to the skids with one little stroke of the pen. Robert worried all the time about his job; Rice terrified him. He had reason to worry, because he was into hypnosis again and Rice had ordered him to drop it. That was about the time of the Bridey Murphy thing, you know; the publicity on that was still going strong. And some of it wasn't very good publicity. There had been a move to discredit Bridey, and Rice never liked the hocus-pocus that seemed to go with hypnosis anyway. So he ordered Robert to cease and desist; to stop all experimentation and all classroom discussion on hypnosis at once. But Robert couldn't stop. By fall, when I arrived, Robert was conducting secret experiments with a few select students—those who had checked out in class as good subjects and could be counted on to keep their mouths shut. I became his best subject. I could go into a trance immediately, three and four levels deep. Most people, even good subjects, never accomplish that.

"We began doing some strange things. I would go to his house, at first alone, then later with Vivian, and we fooled around with age regression. Robert believed that a good hypnotic subject could relive any experience from his past, in all five senses. When the Bridey book broke— Do you remember the story about the girl who was sent back under hypnosis to a previous life?"

"I read it last year," Judy said.

"Good. Well, Robert always believed in Bridey—not necessarily in *that* experiment, but in the concept. At first we used fairly simple techniques, like automatic writing. . . ."

She shook her head. "I don't understand."

"It's just another way the conscious mind can communicate with the subconscious. You go into a light trance and soon you begin to write. What you write is a direct message from the subconscious." I saw her doubt and tried to emphasize my point. "Listen, it's really a valid force. Psychologists use it all the time now. Look it up yourself if you don't believe me."

"Okay," she said, still not convinced.

"Let me tell you what I did once with automatic writing. My dad once gave me a gold watch. It was one of those heirlooms that had passed from father to son for I don't know how many generations. One day it suddenly disappeared; I couldn't find it anywhere. It had a strong sentimental value and I felt lousy about it for weeks. For a while I even suspected that Vivian had sold it without telling me, but that was one time she wasn't guilty. I found it through an automatic-writing experiment. It was in the watchpocket of a pair of plaid slacks that Vivian had bought me that fall. I hated them, but wore them once, just to please her. Wearing my dad's gold watch seemed to make the slacks more bearable, so just that once I took it out of its case and carried it with me. By noon I'd completely forgotten that I had it. Later I hung up those terrible pants and never wore them again, and I forgot that the watch was still in the pocket."

"What did you write?"

"Just two words—*plaid pockets*—but they were enough to jar my conscious, and then I remembered."

"That's fantastic. Can you still do it?"

"Probably. But listen, Robert and I were into things

like that all the time. The watch thing was just my first experiment with the practical use of hypnosis. There were others, more than I can remember. It's all there—in his journals. Vivian began going with me, and she developed a kind of morbid fascination with both the hypnosis and the hypnotist. I didn't know anything about that then. . . ."

Surprisingly, Judy shifted the talk away from her mother. "What else did he do?" she asked.

"I can see now we're going to have to play the tapes. But not today, okay?"

"Just tell me the highlights."

"Robert conducted a long series of age-regression experiments. He sent me back to specific days in my past, which I described in great detail. I mean, I remembered what was on the radio, what the weather was like, damn near everything about any specific day. We checked it in the newspaper morgue and it was all accurate. I never missed once. My voice changed as we went back into my childhood—it *became* a child's voice. But you'll hear that on the tape."

"Go on," she said; "there must be more."

"We went back further and further, until I was speaking baby gibberish. Then Robert decided that we were ready for that big experiment, back beyond birth, you know, just like Bridey. What we got was a man named Jake Walters in the 1870s. The name didn't mean anything to me; still doesn't. We researched my family tree but never found any record in my parents' or grandparents' lives of a man named Jake Walters."

"Who was he then?"

"I still don't know. I only know this: He was a vicious killer. He spoke in a gravel voice and used a dialect that was almost middle English. The first time I heard his voice on tape, I wanted out. I told Robert I didn't want any more of that. He insisted that we go on, find out more about Walters, see if we could uncover some tangible proof that he had lived. That scared the hell out of me. I learned to hate that voice. If I had been Walters in the 1870s, I didn't want to know about it."

"So you quit the experiments?"

"Yes." My head was clearing again so I reached across the table and picked up my glass. "Robert was crushed, but I didn't have any choice. My grades had dropped; Christ, I was a physical and mental wreck. I almost flunked out that year, and I blamed Robert for that. I started blaming him for a lot of things. Then, when I found out he was seeing Vivian, I wanted to hurt him and I did."

I opened the package of newspaper clippings and unfolded the first yellowed sheet. Under the headline ANOTHER BRIDEY MURPHY? was my picture and the words *First of a Series.*

"An acquaintance wrote that, a young reporter I knew. I gave him the whole thing, even let him listen to the Jake Walters tapes. You can imagine what happened. Robert was fired on the spot. Vivian and I fought over that and I got caught up in a defensive position. I know now that it was a rotten thing to do, but things done are never undone. Robert was fired and left town and that was that."

"And that's all of it?"

"Just about."

"There's more?"

"Not much. You were born four months later, and six months after that Vivian left us. Then, a few months after she had gone, there was a knock at my door late at night. I thought it might be your mother come home, but it was Robert. He looked like death warmed over, and at first I thought he was on the skids again. I remember we just stood there looking at each other for a minute; I remember that part so well. Neither of us knew what to say. Then he came in and we sat and talked for a time. We both apologized. He asked about Vivian, but I got the feeling that he really wasn't interested anymore. He had come back to . . . to do . . . one final experiment.

"I told him he was out of his mind, but before I could ask him to leave he told me he was dying; some liver problem. The doctors had given him less than a month, and he wanted one more try on the Jake Walters thing. He was almost in tears; he was begging me; in another minute he would have been crawling to me, and I don't think I could have stood that. So I did it. How the hell can you refuse something like that? I was scared, I've got to tell you that; I was so goddamn scared I almost couldn't bring it off. It was the hardest one we ever did. There were so many things bothering both of us, and it was the first time I had ever seen his hands shake. But we finally did it; I don't know how long it took, but when it was over he told me that it had failed and he wouldn't be bothering me again. Then he picked up the reel of tape and walked out. I never saw him again. Two weeks later I got a letter from his friend Leland Smith, from somewhere in the Midwest, saying that Robert had come to see him and had died there."

At last I had come to the end of it. Judy came to me and hugged my head against her breast, and when she had gone my head was wet where her face had been. But she had handled it fine; we had both done fine. There were a few odds and ends, but maybe she would never need to know those things. Some things were better left unsaid. Like Vivian's obsession that her child would be a demon from hell, a throwback to Jake Walters. Like the day I found Vivian standing over Judy's crib with a plastic bag in her hand.

Yes. Those things were better left unsaid.

3

But it was only beginning. I dreamed about it that night, and in the morning I remembered parts of the dream: a collage of faces; Robert's, Vivian's, Judy's, and the face of an ugly man I had never seen. I dreamed of the mountain ledge and Robert was there, smiling and pointing to that cave. Again I was up at exactly three-thirty with a headache and throbbing eyes. I was in for a bad day.

I had some important appointments, so I showered in cold water and slowly consumed an evil potion that had been billed in a magazine as a sure cure for a hangover. It was a horrid mixture of V-8 juice, raw egg, and Worcestershire sauce that didn't help me worth a damn. I was in bad shape all day. I barked at Sharon and she sulked for hours—par for the course, except now she had cause. I was even short with Al Harper, and later I had to apologize. Somehow I got through the morning, and in the afternoon, when I had to drive over to Richmond for a project inspection, the fresh air pouring in through the open window helped clear my head.

Something about the Holland matter would not let me rest. At first I thought that it was the natural remorse that comes with reopening old wounds. But fresh air should work a healing trick, and this was lingering like a cancerous sore. It preyed on my mind with increasing intensity; even Sharon's reassignment in the second week of December did not bring me any relief. What particularly bothered me was that I could not get near the cause. Often I would wake out of a deep sleep always at that ungodly hour of three-thirty, and would be awake until dawn. On those nights I reread parts of the Holland file, but if there was any help for me there I was missing it. By the third week in December I had read everything in the file three times and was starting on a fourth reading of Robert's hypnosis manuscript.

Christmas. A drab affair. Judy seems to have come out of the Vivian thing in fine shape. Today she has her hair in a bun; she hasn't worn it that way in more than a year. I think the Vivian thing is over for her. The process has begun to reverse and her interests are turning to other things. I wish I could say the same for myself.

In the late afternoon we sat watching the bubble lights of our Christmas tree. She had spent most of the day preparing a big turkey for just the two of us. But I had not been able to enjoy it and she was hurt. At seven o'clock the new boy in her life came by and they went out for a couple of hours. With Judy gone and the house dark, a wave of depression stronger than anything I had known in years came over me. It came with such crushing swiftness that I actually felt like crying out from the pain of it. I forced myself out of the house and felt some relief in the stinging cold of the night air. Driving downtown offered a temporary respite, but the end of the drive brought an end to the relief. Depression, cold and clammy, set in again. For a long time I sat in my car at the edge of the town square, staring at the big Christmas tree and watching the people as they went out in twos to early movies. I went to a movie too, alone of course. At first I thought a blue movie might help, but they are hard to find in my town; so I settled for an old Steve McQueen adventure, sat in a back row, and left before it was half over. A private topless club was my next stop, but some drunk there was picking fights, and I was in no mood for that. I left almost immediately, just as bare tits and a lot of skin flopped past me toward the stage.

I had stayed out longer than I'd planned. But the house was dark when I turned into my driveway; either Judy was also out too late or she had gone to bed as soon as she had come in. In fact, she had done neither; I found her sitting in the dark living room, watching the lonely street through the big picture window. I saw her outline as I came in, and she made no effort to move as I turned on the little nightlight at the end of the coffee table.

"What's this?" I said.

"Just thought I'd wait up for you."

"In the dark?"

"Why not? I've seen you sitting in the dark sometimes. I guess I just didn't feel like having any light on."

"Something on your mind?"

"You've been on my mind. Something's been bothering you; I can tell."

"I've just been tired. Maybe I need a vacation."

"Why don't you take it, then? You've got it coming. It might do you good to get away for a couple of weeks by yourself."

"What about you?"

"I could stay with Peggy. Her mother always says she'd be glad to have me. I'm no problem, Daddy."

I smiled. "Yeah, well, let's sleep on it, okay?"

"I've got some hot chocolate on the stove."

We sat up for another half hour and I forced myself to be gay and promote Christmas cheer. It all fell apart when she went up to bed at midnight. I felt more desolate and alone than ever. Sometime in the early morning I put aside the hot chocolate for Scotch, a bad habit I was getting into lately. My liquor bill had tripled this month; natural, probably, at this time of year, but we had had few guests, and yet the cabinet was empty. Christmas cheer for a party of one.

Judy was probably right to worry; I was worried myself. The worst of it was, I had no idea what was causing it. Yes, there was a twinge of sadness and a spurt of regret whenever I thought of Vivian and Robert, but that was all there was to it. They were ghosts now, part of an unchangeable but fading past. Hadn't I faced that one and come through it with healthy acceptance? *Que será será;* it was done. Why, then, this lingering uneasiness? Why the restlessness and depression?

That was when I first thought of seeing a doctor. One thing was clear to me: something would have to be done soon, before the strain cost me my job and left me a blubbering alcoholic. Maybe a psychologist, if I could find one with good understanding of hypnotic technique, could help me sort out the meanings of these old and new forces in my life. I took that thought to bed, awoke at three-thirty after only an hour's rest, and went through another terrible morning.

That was how the week went, a monotonous string of ups and downs. But by Saturday I had rejected the idea of seeking professional help. Like most men, I was rebelling against the suggestion, even the gentle self-suggestion, that there was anything wrong with me. Besides, there was occasional basis for optimism. After a horrid New Year and a so-so January, February was a good month. I did not go into the Holland file at all during the first three weeks of February; at the end of the fourth week, when the depression had returned, I took Judy away for two days in the mountains. That was a mistake. The mountain scenery only reminded me of the photograph, and I stayed in the lodge all weekend, drinking and brooding, while Judy hiked in the hills.

Monday morning: 3:30 A.M. Things are as bad today as they ever have been. Christ, I don't know how I'll get through the day.

I got through it somehow. But now, for the first time, came an ominous warning.

Darlene: "Mr. Ryan, Mr. Harper on one."

And the heavy voice of Al Harper: "Jim, come over here for a few minutes, will you?"

Al's secretary wasn't yet in, so I walked past her desk and knocked on the hardwood door. Al called me in and motioned me to a chair while he finished a phone conversation. That done, he shuffled through some blueprints on his desk and pushed them toward me.

"Did you okay these?"

I leafed through them. "Sure I did." Looking closer now: "Is something wrong with them?"

"Look for yourself."

I didn't need a magnifying glass. The problems were right before me, circled in red.

Al swung around in his swivel chair and gazed out of the window. "Normally I don't double-check you. I guess it's a good thing I did this time."

"A damn good thing," I said. I felt the blood in my

cheeks, and I knew there wasn't anything I could say in self-defense. For these kinds of college-boy errors there wasn't any defense.

Al swung around to face me. "What the hell's wrong with you these days?"

"I don't know, Al. What can I say? It's just a stupid mistake."

"It's not just a mistake."

"You mean there've been others?"

"I mean you're off in a goddamn dream world half the time; your eyes are bloodshot and you've lost ten pounds. You drove Sharon to the verge of a nervous breakdown and then made her move to another department. . . ."

"The thing with Sharon was personal. It didn't have anything to do with this."

"Didn't it? I'm not so sure. All I know is you've got a problem. Is it booze or what?"

That was Al Harper for you: straight to the point with no diplomatic waltzing around the touchy areas. For a moment I didn't know how to answer him. Telling him that I had my drinking under control wouldn't sound believable under the circumstances, so I said, "Look, you're right; I have had a problem and it's been a real bitch. I'm still having trouble handling it. It's just a personal thing, Al, and it isn't booze, if that's what you're thinking. My word on that. I'm just sorry as hell that it's starting to affect my work."

"Judy's okay?"

"Sure, she's fine."

"Anything I can do to help?"

"It's just something I've got to work out myself."

"Well, I hope you get it worked out soon, old buddy. A mistake like this one"—he shuffled the prints—"could cost me plenty."

"I know it. What the hell can I say?"

"It sounds to me like you're going through something I used to call occupational menopause. It happens to a lot of guys your age; hell, I went through it myself twenty years ago. A man gets tied to a desk, a steady routine, he starts wondering if maybe life isn't passing him by, if maybe he ought to get out where the action is."

I tried to laugh in protest but managed only a smile.

"I'm serious, Jim," Al said. "And if that's what it is there's just one cure for it. Take a few weeks off; get the hell out of town and see how other people live. Look, have I got to order you to take a god-damn vacation?"

"I'll put in for it."

"You don't have to put in for anything; just go."

"How about the first three weeks in May?"

"What's wrong with right now?"

"Christ, Al, if you're going to make me take this vacation, at least let me go when the fish are biting."

He frowned, then smiled, then frowned again. "Go ahead, put in for it," he said at last; "now get out of here so I can get some work done."

Later, in the privacy of my own office, I tremble at what might have happened. But I know that Al is right: I do need to get away, and soon. But not too soon. Something inside me says May, and that is how I will have to play it.

Morning business. Darlene buzzed; phone call from a project boss in Front Royal. Coffee. The morning mail. Even before I began leafing through it I noticed the familiar manila envelope at the bottom of the stack.

In all aspects it was a duplicate of the other. It had the same yellowed appearance, similar dust lines, and the faded word PERSONAL stamped on both sides. The postmark said New York, two days ago; again, there was no return address. I turned it over and saw that it was sealed with Scotch tape. The tape was old and beginning to crack, but still it held tight. I slit the top of the envelope and took out the picture with trembling hands. It was the same mountain trail, but a better photograph, taken closer to the cave and in better light. Now I could easily see the Maltese cross without a glass; I could even see into the cave for a short distance. There were objects on the floor: a coil of rope; a backpack; a digging tool of some kind. I turned the picture over. Taped to the back was a gold coin.

It was Spanish, very old, with tiny, intricate engravings. I examined the coin under the magnifying glass. Among the engravings was a tiny Maltese cross near its upper face-edge. It was about the size of an American quarter and, I guessed, very valuable. I knew at once that I would never sell it, and under those circumstances I did not even want to know its value. I placed the picture and its wrappings in my desk drawer and locked it. At the end of the day I retrieved it, took it home, and filed it with the Holland papers. Then I locked the cabinet and joined Judy at dinner.

Today I tried another automatic-writing experiment, with strange results. I wrote three words—"blood of Christ"—and again the numbers 50, 96, and 12. It all means something, but what? I wonder if I will ever know.

By the first of April there was no longer any question in my mind: I was going to New York. I put in for three weeks beginning in May; Al rubber-stamped it, and for all practical purposes I was on my way. Then a curious thing happened. From the moment my decision was made, my depression vanished. April was a good month. Only twice did I wake at three-thirty, and then I was able to get back to sleep in about half an hour. Still, my newfound peace of mind did not create any false sense of security. I was painfully aware that it might be temporary; that its existence was tenuous and easily explainable. My subconscious had accepted my plan and had made an uneasy truce with me. That's what Robert Holland would say, and even though I had no idea what would happen in New York or how I would function there, I believed it. For my own peace of mind I had to go and at least make an effort. The game plan was so simple on paper: In three weeks I would try to find the person on the other end of these mailings, in a city of eight million anonymous people. How? I had no idea. The thought of hiring a detective crossed my mind, but I would deal with that possibility later, on the scene. I looked into my savings account and prepared to spend some money.

Away from work, my thinking zeroed in on a single purpose. I wrote a possible newspaper ad: "Will the party who sent Jim Ryan the mountain scenery please contact Mr. Ryan at the Hotel . . ." Not very specific, but *he* would know what it meant. I would try it anyway. I would try anything that occurred to me, no matter what the odds. But until I knew who he was and what it all meant, I was playing by his rules.

There were the usual last-minute problems, things that should be expected whenever a divorced man with a teenage daughter and a devotion to his job suddenly uproots for three weeks. Al Harper had half a dozen minor crises and Peggy Harris suddenly reneged on her offer to have Judy as a houseguest because her three cousins were coming in unexpectedly from Illinois. I worked around everything. We found Judy a place to stay just before I was to leave. Linda Coughlin was delighted to have her. The parents seemed okay, Judy was comfortable, and that set my mind at ease.

Finally there was the matter of the camping gear. Ostensibly, I was going fishing, and I didn't want anyone to know I was in New York. So I took some camping gear with me. I bought things I had always intended to buy and use but never before had had the time: tough hiking clothes that I could use later in the Shenandoahs; a pair of boots; a large backpack. I took only casual clothes. Four heavy flannel shirts, a knitted skullcap, tough work pants, and a thermal overcoat. I packed thermal longjohns too, and never once stopped to wonder if maybe I was overdoing it. I would stand out in New York like the Midnight Cowboy.

In my backpack I took some warm blankets, an ax, and, at the last moment, a full bottle of bourbon. I debated the last, then decided to take it, I laughingly told myself, in case of snakebite.

I was so anxious to be on the road that I knew I wouldn't sleep at all. In fact, I slept more soundly than I had in months. A feeling of strength came over me as I pulled the blanket up over my shoulders. Yes, I was awake at precisely three-thirty, but it was not an awakening of distress or terror. I got up calmly as though I had set an alarm clock, filled with anticipation and enthusiasm; I *could not wait to get on the road!* In the three hours before Judy got up I loaded my car, checked the gear, read last night's paper, and rechecked the gear. I put one envelope containing the mountain pictures in a suitcase and dropped the suitcase into the back seat of the car. I was ready to go; more than that: I was aching to go.

Then, the parting. We locked the house and I drove Judy to school. We ate breakfast in some noisy little cafe about two blocks from the school building, and there we went through the final checks. I double-checked the Coughlins' home telephone number, and we passed small talk back and forth for half an hour over our empty plates. "I'm going to miss you," she said. I assured her that I would miss her too, and I would. Sometime in the next day or two I would call her and let her know exactly where I was and how I was doing. She wanted to walk, but I drove her the last two blocks and watched, with a growing reluctance to let her go, as she disappeared into the building.

Now I found that some of my initial enthusiasm had burned out. For a long time I sat outside the school. I called it thought organization, but there was nothing to organize. There was nothing left to do but go.

I know the way to New York by heart. There was no need for a road map and in fact I did not have one. From my home it is a straight shot down to Richmond on Interstate 64; then north to Washington on I-95. Actually, 95 goes all the way to New York and beyond, so there is nothing to remember. *Nothing left to do but go.* But I resisted going the straight, easy way that I knew so well; I passed the I-64 overpass and continued on out of town. The road came to a dead end at a narrow state highway that cut through a long section of woods and, I thought, joined Route 29 somewhere up the line. Rationale: *Just now I don't feel like facing the hustle of the interstate; I'd rather drift through the country and think about it some more.* Logic: *Goddamnit. I've had weeks to think about it; why not get on with it?* Decision: *The hell with it; it's my vacation and I'll go any damned way I choose.* So I turned north on the state highway and found that it did indeed join U.S. 29, which cut diagonally across the state in almost a straight line to Washington. It was probably as fast as the interstate, if not faster.

I don't remember much about that morning's drive. There were many towns, I know, and once I hit a bad spot where they had the road ripped up and cars were just crawling through. Somewhere I lost 29 and slipped over onto Route 17. It must have been early afternoon when I stopped for a hamburger at a roadside ice cream freeze. The morning had slipped by so easily I could hardly believe the time had gone. And when I started out again I saw that I had left 17 and was now on Route 50, heading west. My first reaction was strong disgust, but that was replaced at once by curiosity. The road *felt* right, even though the sun was in my eyes and the highway marker said Route 50 West. I resisted the urge to stop, check my direction, and correct it before I lost the entire day meandering. But that was too much trouble. It was too easy to go on and too much trouble to stop; as in a hypnotic trance, I knew exactly where I was and what was happening to me. I knew I could bring myself out of it any time I wanted to. But proving it just wasn't worth the effort.

When I crossed the West Virginia state line I forced myself back to reality. Damn it, I *was* going the wrong way. I stopped for gas in a town called Capon Bridge. While the attendant was filling the tank I went inside and got a road map. But I stuffed the map into my back pocket and forgot it was there. I did notice the time; a large wall clock said five to one, and here I was some goddamn place in West Virginia, probably as far from New York as ever. Possibly, by pushing it, I could still make it late tonight, but I didn't want to drive like that, especially when it wasn't necessary. The worst of it was this strong new sensation I felt, almost an ambivalent attitude toward the whole New York project. My eagerness of the morning had vanished; doubt had taken its place. I paid the man and forced my attention backward, edging into the eastbound lane and accelerating quickly. Almost in tempo with my rising speedometer needle came my strongest attack of depression since mid-March. It grew, consumed me, and became a physical monster, clutching at my gut and ringing in my ears as though some little man inside me had set off the burglar alarm of my nervous system. Faster, harder, and louder it came: I had to stop; I was surely having a heart attack.

I stopped at roadside and waited, breathing hard. Nothing happened. Immediately my distress eased and disappeared. Indigestion? Maybe, but I thought it was something else. Gingerly, remembering the numbers 50, 96, and 12, I eased around to turn back into the westbound lane. Only one car was coming up behind me, a large black Oldsmobile. I waited for it to pass, then turned back toward Capon Bridge.

My decision took less than ten seconds. New York was out, at least for the moment, and something else was in. I watched the speedometer needle climb with mounting excitement.

At dusk I crossed into Ohio.

4

THE FLASHING LIGHT OF A SMALL MOTEL CAUGHT MY eye sometime after seven. Though the lure of the road was difficult to resist, I was simply too tired to go on. I turned in and registered, getting the last available room, if I could believe the old woman who rented it to me. The room was unnecessarily large, with a double bed, a single, and a rollaway. The fifteen dollars I paid for it was, I thought, a bit steep; since I never argue over bills I paid it, took the key, and made myself at home. I didn't unload the car; took only my overnight bag and the Holland folder, locked all the doors, and headed nonstop for the shower. The water had a kind of yellow tint, like rust, but that cleared up in about five minutes, just as the temperature began to vary from freezing to boiling. But I felt better after the shower; I dressed, went outside, and walked down Main Street looking for a restaurant.

It was one of those towns where everything closes at seven o'clock. I passed two dismal cafes, both happily closed, and reached the end of the main drag in about ten minutes. Here the highway turned, zigzagged through a small residential district and continued across country. Just around the bend was a walk-in-drive-in combination, where I ate a greasy hamburger and resolved, for sure, to eat something good tomorrow.

On the way back to the motel I saw an ice machine and thought of the bourbon in my backpack. I passed it by, feeling no need for alcohol of any kind. I would sleep well enough. For the first time in months I felt completely at peace with myself. I paused at the motel entrance and observed the car parked directly across the street. You don't see many big black Oldsmobiles any more, and somewhere, today, I was sure I had seen this one. That might not be anything more than an unlikely coincidence, two travelers crossing paths twice in one day; but, curious, I crossed the street for a closer look. The first thing I saw was that it bore Florida license plates with the numbers 38–3414. I walked around the car and peeped in through the window. The inside was nicely done, with thick carpeting and new seat covers and a tape deck. There was a telephone too, rather an unusual piece of equipment for a car. The ashtray was full. And that was all I noticed about the big black car before I began to feel conspicuous. I hurried back to my motel room.

In the darkness I undressed; then I slipped between the sheets of the double bed. It was hard and good and I was asleep almost at once. I awoke at three-thirty, after seven hours' sleep, my mind clear and ready for the long drive ahead. When I came outside I saw that the black Oldsmobile was still parked innocently across the street. I shrugged it off, still not completely satisfied that it was a coincidence, and eased my own car out into the westbound lane of Route 50. In a moment the town's business section slipped into the gloom behind me.

I turned the bend at the end of town, passed the grease pot where I had taken my last meal, and stopped. My nagging hunch about the black Oldsmobile would not pass, so I parked under a tree at the side of the road and got out. The walk back to the bend was short, but even before I reached it I saw the headlights of an oncoming car. I jumped behind a tree just as the car turned the bend; it was well past me before I tried a look. It was not an Oldsmobile, at least not *the* Oldsmobile, because the first thing I saw was a large silver star painted on the door around the word POLICE. Local cops always scare me anyway, but this police car coming at this time was especially sobering. I had no doubt that I could be jailed and held for at least a day on nothing stronger than the fact that I was ducking around a dark street in a small Ohio town at four o'clock in the morning. That and my being a stranger might actually get me a jail term in some police courts. So I stood in the shadows until the car was out of sight, and since the bend was just a few steps away, I quickly walked to it and looked far down the street. It was at least six blocks back, but there were sporadic streetlights, and I could just make out the Oldsmobile still parked across from the motel, where I had last seen it.

A light rain had begun to fall by the time I left the town, and when I got to the next town the rainfall was heavy. I found an all-night restaurant, stopped, and got some black coffee for my thermos. The rain was even heavier when I got on the road again; it pounded my windshield with a monotonous patter. I drove slowly, keeping both hands on the wheel and my eyes on the slick pavement. A Route 50 West marker flashed by; then a sign that said Athens and something that looked like 25 miles, but might have been 35 or 55. It didn't matter; Athens was nothing to me. It was just something I noticed the way a traveler notices signs on the road and ignores them at home. My fascination with the road, if it had ever existed, was worn thin. I wanted badly to get on with it, to get where I was going, and, most of all at the moment, to get out of this goddamn rain. There was a long straight stretch, and as I made the bend I saw a light bobbing at the side of the road. It was a flashlight. The person who carried it began to swing it in a wide arc, as though trying to flag me down. Nice try, but I had no intention of stopping. As I drove past I heard a cry for help. There was no question about it; the voice was female. For an instant my foot hovered between the gas and brake; then I touched the brake and brought the car to a stop.

I was fully a hundred yards past her, and in the rear-view mirror I could see her light bobbing as she ran to catch up. I backed the car toward her; in a moment we met and she was peering in through my steamy window. She pulled open the door.

"You going to Athens?"

She was young. Even in the dim light I could see that clearly. Her face was smooth and the features delicate. A small curl of black hair dropped from under the hood she wore and a stream of water dripped off her hair and ran down her cheek.

Thunder rolled and I shouted over it: "I don't know; is that on this road?"

"Yes, it's straight ahead."

"Then I'll pass through it."

"Can you take me there?"

"Get in."

She almost fell into the seat beside me. The hood dropped away, revealing a thick growth of black hair, which now fell down over her shoulders. She was breathing hard, and for a minute neither of us said anything. I got the car going, and when her breath came easier she said, "Sorry about all the water. God, I was afraid you weren't going to stop."

"I usually don't pick up hitchhikers at four o'clock

in the morning. Come to think of it, I don't know if I've ever seen one. You seemed to be in trouble."

"No trouble; not now. I just had to get away from here."

"What's the rush?"

She glanced at me out of the corner of her eye. "I guess you've got to know that."

"Only if you've just robbed a gas station. Look, as long as it's legal, what you do is your own business."

"Okay. Can I get these wet things off first?"

"Sure. Put your coat under the heater; that'll help dry it out."

I didn't push her. For a time she arranged her coat, hood, scarf, and sweater under the heater, then sat back and stared blankly at the dark road. She seemed to have lost any inclination she might have had to tell me about herself, so I figured what the hell, she would soon be gone anyway. She spread out the sweater more evenly, shivered, then hugged herself for warmth, even though the heater was up full and the blouse she wore seemed fairly dry. When I had given up hope of getting conversation of any kind from her, she half turned on the seat and said, "Thanks for stopping."

I nodded. "You're going to . . . Athens, did you say?"

"That'll do. At least till I get a job and make some money to get me back to California."

"That your home?"

"I can get by there. I've got friends."

A long time passed before either of us spoke again. She was not going to tell me her life story and that was just as well. We were getting close to Athens now; there were some houses and lights and a gas station, a grocery and more houses. I looked over at her, but she was staring out at the rain-spattered darkness.

"Anywhere in particular?" I said.

"No." She sighed. "One place is as good as another, I guess." She turned and smiled a sad, strained smile. "Are you going on?"

"Yes."

"Far?"

"I'm not sure. I'm on vacation; just driving to see the country. But yes, I'll be on Route Fifty for a while yet."

"Any chance you'd take me to Cincinnati?—if you're going that far, I mean."

I hesitated. "I don't know."

"Well, I'm not a fugitive, if that's still bothering you. I just want to get away from here, from this whole part of the country, you know? I'm afraid Athens might not be far enough—or big enough."

"It still sounds sinister. Look, miss, it's just my vacation; I'm not James Bond or anyone like that. I just don't want to get mixed up in something I don't understand."

"I'm leaving my husband. It's as simple as that."

"And that's why you have to leave at four o'clock in the middle of a storm?"

"Yes, now, while he's still sleeping it off from last night. I just reached the end of my rope with him, you know?"

I didn't know, but she was into it now and I figured she would tell me the rest.

"He's just a mean, rotten bastard and I finally had enough. Haven't you ever known anybody who's just twisted and ugly inside?"

I started to say no, I never had, but then I remembered Vivian and I didn't say anything. That seemed to do it for her; I would have to take her or leave her on that basis. I drove through Athens without stopping, and when we were once more on the open road she relaxed and began to breathe easier. Again, a long time passed between words. I watched her occasionally out of the corner of my eye, but if she noticed the surveillance she did not seem to mind it. Soon her eyes closed and her breathing became deep and regular. I thought she was asleep but she said, "What's your name?"

I told her.

"I'm Amy. Thanks for not putting me out."

"Sure. I'll take you to Cincinnati if that'll be any help."

"How old are you?"

I found the question surprising, but I answered it: "Thirty-seven."

"You don't look thirty-seven. I'm twenty-two."

I looked at her. "Come to think of it, you don't look twenty-two."

"I guess that makes us even."

I found this new line of talk disturbing, and I decided to pursue it. "Not quite even. Listen, do you have some ID with you?"

"What for? You're not a cop, are you?"

"No, but I'm getting bad vibrations. There are laws about transporting minors."

"Oh Christ; look, I'm not a minor."

"Do you have a driver's license?"

"No." She looked at me for a long time, waiting for my reaction. "Goddamn, you're a worrier," she said at last. "Do you want me to get out?"

"I might; we'll see. I will take you to the next big town, anyway."

"I appreciate that. You don't mind if I rest now, do you?"

Her voice was cold. She leaned back and closed her eyes; her breathing became very heavy again and I wondered if she was asleep. I adjusted my rear-view mirror downward and to the right, bringing her face into sharp focus with my line of vision. She was nice-looking. There was no telling if she was really of age, so somewhere along the line I would have to make that judgment for myself. In this position she looked all of twenty-two, but then she shifted and the soft dashboard light offered a profile that looked almost babyish. Until she shifted again she might have been no older than my Judy. That illusion, the rain, and the wind vanished almost simultaneously. I turned on the radio, softly, so I wouldn't wake my passenger, but all I could find was some morning gospel hour and a really crappy country-music show. I turned it off and drove in silence until the sun came up.

We were well past Chillicothe when the girl stretched and yawned. I gave her one last long look, then straightened the rear-view and adjusted it until I could see the road behind me. In that stark morning light I decided with finality that she was at least twenty-two. Like so many of her liberated generation, she wore no bra; her breasts were fully developed and, while you can't really go by that, she presented an early-morning image of mature womanhood. So she was no kid, and I could forget about that. But I didn't want to forget it, not completely; it was a nice excuse, a nice option to have if I wanted to dump her along the way for any reason. I still felt uneasy about her sudden appearance, and nothing she had said had made me more comfortable with her. She stretched and opened her eyes.

"God—what time is it?" Her voice cracked.

I looked at my watch. "Almost seven. Good nap?"

"Yeah, great." She rubbed her eyes. "Where're we at?"

"Somewhere past some town that begins with a C. I can't pronounce it."

"Chillicothe. I thought you'd be farther along than that."

"Yeah, we passed it quite a while back. I haven't been pushing it."

"You still taking me to Cincinnati?"

"I said I would. Cincinnati's a big town; you ought to be able to find work and get lost there—if that's what you want. But that's the end of it for me, okay? You can get yourself over the state line."

"God, I really don't believe this," she said a little sarcastically. "Can you really look at me and think I'm under eighteen?"

"Look, do you want to go to Cincinnati or not? I said I'd take you there."

"Fine, fine." She held up her hands, suggesting that we drop it. "In fact, Cincinnati's just great."

"Good. Right now, how about breakfast?"

I found a truck stop soon, and we went inside and took a booth in a corner. Amy excused herself and went to the ladies' room, which was located down a dark corridor on the other side of the room. The waitress came and I ordered coffee for both of us. Amy returned in less than a minute—hardly long enough to have made the trip worthwhile—and slipped into her side of the booth.

"That was quick," I said.

"Just wanted to splash some water in my face."

"Have anything you want; I'm buying."

"I've got some money."

"Save it; you'll probably need it before you get to California, or wherever it is you're going."

She looked at me with strange eyes. The waitress came for our orders, and Amy had a full stack of pancakes and an order of bacon and eggs. Either was enough for me; I took the hotcakes. While we were eating she surveyed me with her eyes, much as I had watched her on the road between Athens and Chillicothe. I did not know if she was being intentionally obvious, but I pretended not to notice. Breakfast finished, she settled back with her coffee. "Any idea how much farther you're going?"

I shook my head no.

"I was just wondering. With my money as low as it is, well, the closer I can get to California the better off I'll be."

I shrugged. "Nothing personal. In fact, I've enjoyed having you along. It's just that right now I don't need any grief, and I might be letting myself in for a lot of it."

"You aren't. I can promise you that."

"Besides," I said, "what's the big deal? Rides are easy to get, especially for a girl."

"That's just it. Girls never know what kind of creep might stop for them."

"How do you know I'm not *that* kind of creep?"

She smiled, and there was just the hint of a flirt behind her eyes. "I just know it." She shrugged. "So look at it this way—you might be keeping me out of the hands of some mad rapist, right?"

I thought about it. "No, I can't do it," I said finally.

Again she lapsed into a sullen silence. I thought the matter was closed, but just as I was finishing my coffee she took out a small billfold and produced a plastic-covered driver's license. She pushed it across the table toward me.

"I thought you didn't have one."

"There it is. It's a horrible picture of me, and that's why I don't show it around."

In fact, it was a very good picture. The name on the license was Melinda Lewis, and the date of birth was January 6, 1950. The license had been issued just last month in Denver, Colorado.

"Melinda?"

"That's my real name. Please call me Amy."

"And you live in—Denver?"

"That's my home; my husband—he's from here." She reached across the table and plucked the license from my fingers. "At least you know now that I'm not lying about my age, right?"

"Okay, Amy; let's play it by ear. How does that sound?"

She smiled. "Fine."

Again she excused herself and bowed out to the ladies' room. I got up to pay the check. At the register I could just see into the restroom corridor. At the end, almost engulfed in darkness, was a telephone booth, and my friend Amy was talking on the phone.

5

It was a long day. At ten o'clock I got very sleepy and Amy offered to drive. I was reluctant, resistant to relinquish control and make that final concession to her right to be here. But when my head bobbed a second time I gave up the fight. We exchanged places, I told her to stay with Route 50, then I settled back in the seat and closed my eyes. She had to move the seat up, cramping my legs against the glove compartment and making sleep difficult. Periodically I opened my eyes, studying her driving restlessly; she was a good driver, careful and slow. When we had gone sixty miles that way she said, "Look, why don't you relax? I'm not gonna wreck your damn car."

Her words came almost like a commandment; I did close my eyes, and when I opened them we were halfway through Indiana. It was after noon. We stopped at a hamburger stand near a town called Bedford and pushed into Illinois at midafternoon. Not much passed between us, and at three o'clock I took the wheel while she slept. That was how the day went, with very little conversation and almost no thought on my part.

A few times I wondered about Amy and her phone call, but that only gave me a headache.

She awoke at four-thirty, bubbling with conversation. She talked about herself and asked questions about me. She revealed her childhood ambition to be an actress and philosophized about the funny things people do with their lives. For a long time she seemed preoccupied with losing control of her own destiny, dwelling on "most people" and how they lose control of their lives and can never get it back. Abruptly she shifted to my life, asking questions about my home and Judy; I answered them briefly but, I think, politely. By six she was getting hungry again; we pulled into a restaurant in East St. Louis.

"This time I'm buying," she said.

"Forget it."

"Look, I want to buy your dinner, okay?"

She did, too. She grabbed the check with an expertise that surprised me and paid it before I could stop her. Dusk had fallen when we got on the road again. For the first time since I'd left home I looked at a road map. Interstate 70 dropped into St. Louis from the north and ran due west to Denver. I stopped for gas and again consulted the map; the big interstate went almost in a straight line to Denver, and was partly completed through the Rockies. Route 50, on the other hand, dipped to the south at Kansas City, ran across southern Kansas and into southern Colorado. The highways parted for about a hundred miles before joining again at a town in western Colorado called Grand Junction. I did not want to get too far away from Route 50, but I knew there could be nothing of interest between St. Louis and Kansas City, and the interstate might save me a couple of hours' driving time across Missouri. I asked the attendant for directions to I-70, signed for the gas, and in a few minutes we were turning onto the interstate ramp.

"I think I'll sleep awhile," Amy said, buckling her seatbelt. "These big highways always make me nervous."

She closed her eyes; I accelerated and blended with traffic. We crossed the Mississippi River and passed around the great arch. Soon the city fell behind us and the rolling country spread out ahead. It was dark now, and I wasn't sure how much farther I wanted to drive tonight or what I would look for in the way of accommodations. I didn't feel at all tired; surprising, considering how little sleep I had had in the past thirty-six hours. I didn't worry about it, just pushed on in a half-blind stab at getting through it. Interstate highways are concentrated monotony, and they weave a hypnotic curtain around my brain. An interstate in California is the same as an interstate in Ohio; both are the same as an interstate in Missouri. Interstate 70 is, if anything, worse than average. The road stretches into infinity; the miles roll on and nothing ever changes. I pushed the car along at sixty-five and tried to keep my mind active. But soon I became aware of that dull sensation, that growing aggravation, that compelling urge to get off the interstate and find Route 50 again. I cannot explain how it began; one minute it was not there and the next minute it was. Dull, gnawing, not unlike my experience in West Virginia, only far less intense. It grew in intensity as I pushed on, and I fought against it with the logic that the interstate was my fastest link across a state that couldn't possibly matter to me. Again, logic lost out. When I grew tired of the struggle I turned off the highway and stopped to consult my map.

I was in a little town called Kingdom City, just off Interstate 70 and Route 54. I saw at once that Route 54 slashed southwest, joining 50 at Jefferson City. So I drove perhaps fifty miles out of my way, got on 50 again, and pushed westward toward Kansas City at a slower, easier pace. The road seemed to turn continuously after the smooth straightness of I-70, and I had to pass through a dozen small towns along the way. I found that irritating—a fine crash course in how to make a four-hour trip take six hours and more—but it was the lesser of the two evils. I was on Route 50 and that was what mattered.

We were more than an hour out of Jefferson City when I felt the first wave of fatigue. I looked at my watch; ten past nine, and I wondered again what to do about accommodations. Amy was sleeping soundly. Her head had rolled to one side and her eyelids had opened slightly, but there was no question in my mind that she was in a deep sleep. She slept like she ate: passionately and intensely. I wondered if she did everything that way. Twice I hit deep chuckholes in the road and she never stirred. Once a trailer truck came roaring past with such force that the car shook. Amy never moved.

I passed through Sedalia, a town with at least a dozen lighted motels, but I did not stop. With the lights behind me, the second wave of fatigue came, and I knew I could not go on. I looked for a spot where I might pull over and take a short nap, but there was nothing until I found a side road some twenty minutes later. The road was dirt, and it ran past several lighted farmhouses, dipped and turned for about four miles. There was a fork. The right fork looked to be an older road, little used and poorly maintained. I turned in there and parked under a large tree.

A chill was in the air as I opened my door, got out, and looked around. I seemed to be in the middle of a large farm, with this fenced road cutting between two fields. There were no buildings or lights in sight. I walked down the road for a short distance and reassured myself that the car could not be seen unless someone came directly past us along this narrow, rutted road. I thought that was unlikely and, feeling better, I returned to the car, opened the trunk, took out two blankets, and tucked Amy in.

It was just enough movement to chase away my fatigue and leave me, for a long time, sleepless. I have never been able to sleep well in a car, especially when I am sharing the seat with someone else. Amy was not in my way; she was curled up in a small ball in the corner, but her presence was disturbing. For a time I thought of the back seat, of perhaps stretching out full length with my feet dangling out of the open window. But I have never been able to sleep in back seats either. So I stretched out across the front as far as I could go without disturbing her, leaned against my door, and closed my eyes. My right leg cramped at once. I moved it quickly and kicked her leg. She sat up, looked around, and said something to me in a heavy, sleepy voice.

"It's okay," I told her. "I've just stopped for a rest."

If she heard that, or comprehended it, there was no change in her idiot expression. She fumbled with her seatbelt, unhooked it, shifted her position, and lay back across the seat. Her head dropped against my chest. She draped her arm over my shoulder and slept that way for the rest of the night.

For me, that meant little more than four hours. I was very much aware of her body pressed against mine, and increasingly bothered by the cramps in my lower legs, so I slept irregularly. Once I awoke fully aroused, my arm across her breast, and I was at least thirty minutes getting over that and getting to sleep again. Through it all she never stirred.

At three-thirty I sat up and looked at my watch. Both my legs were fuzzy from lack of circulation. I pushed Amy into a sitting position and let her down gently against her door. Again she said something senseless; I folded my blanket and put it behind her head. I pushed the button locking her door, got out to walk around, and relieved myself on the left rear tire. By that time I was fully awake, and I knew there was no use trying for any more sleep.

I was well past Kansas City before Amy woke. I had beaten the rush hour and, as I suspected, ended up in the same place that the interstate might have brought me hours earlier. No matter now. Route 50 petered out for a while but picked up again where Interstate 35 left off. The highway struck into Kansas from the southwest edge of town, and the land changed almost immediately. Gone was the rocky brown hill country, and in its place came the endless miles of prairie. The road straightened and stretched to the west in long sections unbroken by towns or crossroads. I had just reached the town of Emporia when Amy yawned and stretched and looked me over, her eyes still glazed with sleep.

"God almighty." Her voice was full of sand. "Jesus, I slept like a ton of bricks. Where are we?"

"Somewhere in eastern Kansas. Hungry?"

"Sure. What'd you do, drive all night?"

"I pulled under a tree and got about four hours."

"I don't remember; Jesus, I must have been out of it."

We found a restaurant near Emporia. After a trip to the ladies' room Amy began to function. While we were waiting for our orders, I went out to the car for the map and saw that she was using the telephone. I went to the men's room and splashed some water in my face and thought about it. She would know I had seen her when she returned to the table and found me gone. It might all be very innocent, her frequent use of the phone; she might be checking on a sick aunt, for all I knew. In that case she would feel no need to justify any of it to me, but I was betting otherwise. I came out into the dining room and saw her sitting alone in our booth; the waitress was just leaving our food. She looked up at me as I came toward her and her eyes never faltered.

"These goddamn country phones," she said; "you never can get anything out of a stupid country operator."

"You trying to make a call? I didn't know you had anybody around here."

"Long distance," she said. "Just try to get long distance from here." She shrugged. "Yeah, I thought I'd better call my friends in L.A., at least warn them I'm coming. Yesterday I couldn't get through and now today I can't get through either."

"You're just impatient. I've always found it the other way around; it's the city operators who don't know anything."

But her point was established and she let that pass. I paid and she didn't protest; we were on the road again. I drove all day, averaging better than sixty including stops for gas. Now I could feel the end; I could almost taste it, and my foot rested heavy on the gas. I drove sixty-five and seventy with a feeling of perfect safety on this long Kansas road. Traffic was light; I guessed that most cars were using the interstate. The windswept towns rolled past: Peabody; Hutchinson; Zenith; Macksville.

Dodge City. Tumbleweeds rolled across the highway just outside the town, adding to the cowboy imagery. We passed a rebuilt western street with saloons and wooden sidewalks and a Boot Hill cemetery. Amy wanted to stop, but I dismissed the town as a tourist trap and drove on through. Colorado was drawing me on; its effect was almost magnetic, and I was testing the law in my determination to make it by nightfall. We crossed the state line late that afternoon, but if I expected the Rocky Mountains to suddenly jump up

and engulf the car, I was mistaken. For many miles
there was only more of the same monotonous, rolling
prairie; when the country did change, it became even
more dreary. Now there were more tight bends and
the land was one of washed-out gullies and dried river-
beds and sunbaked plants. That lasted for more than
a hundred miles. Just before dusk I got my first look
at the Rockies, through the smoke and haze of Pueblo.
The lights of the city stretched across the plains ahead
of us; beyond—how many miles I couldn't guess—
were the mountains, black against the velvet of twilight. Darkness came very fast, and as the lights of the
city came up to me, the mountains blended into nothing behind them. Then the city engulfed us.

Pueblo is a small city with old, run-down buildings
and factories that constantly belch smoke into the air.
I found it dismal but a decided relief from the long
drive behind me. The city had an air of finality about
it; at least it created that for me, and that made up
for most of its physical shortcomings. I was damned
tired and looking forward to a shower and a bed.

"This is where we part company," I said; "I think
this is as far west as I go."

"Oh? I guess I should say something like it's been
fun, then, and thanks. It really has—been fun, I
mean."

"Even if I did give you a bad time that first night.
I'd like to apologize for that, by the way."

She smiled. "I knew right away you really weren't
like that. You're actually a nice man, you know that?"

I laughed out loud. "I'm a peach." We kidded
around some more, thoroughly enjoying each other in
our final moments. Of course, that was all a game too.
I did not for one minute think that I was finished with
Amy, but we would have to see about that. I almost
wished it could end here, with good feelings on both
sides, and for a moment I felt that she was wishing

that too. We enjoyed the play acting; going through all the bittersweet emotions of two people who become good friends overnight and never meet again. It filled the hour and made that night's meal the best of the lot. The food was terrible, but neither of us cared. It was just part of our arrival in this smoky little city on the brown plains of Colorado.

"I probably won't go on till morning," she said over dessert. "I hate thumbing, like I told you before; especially at night."

I nodded toward the telephone. "Maybe your friends are home now."

A strange, sad expression came into her eyes then and worked down to her lips. She moistened her lips with her tongue, started to say something, and thought better of it. What she did say was, "The hell with them. If they're really my friends they'll be glad enough to see me."

"I guess that's right."

"I always get by."

"Yeah, I know."

"Tell me," she said thoughtfully, "do you keep in touch with your friends? Do you write letters?"

"Not much."

"I'd write you if you'd answer."

"I'd like to hear from you. I'd really like to know how you make out in California."

"I'll do okay."

"Sure, but I'd like to hear about it."

"Then I'll write and tell you."

"Good." I stood and felt in my pocket for change. "Well, if you're not going to use that phone, maybe I will." She looked at me suspiciously, but I turned away from her and walked to the phone without explaining. For a minute I wondered about the time difference, then decided to take a chance. The Coughlins' phone number was in my wallet; I had an operator place the call and was delighted when Judy answered.

"I'm babysitting for them," she said. "Where are you?"

"Are you ready for this?—Colorado."

"Colorado?"

"I'll tell you all about it when I get home, okay? I just called to hear your voice. How's it going?"

"Fine. You got a call yesterday."

"At the Coughlins'?"

"Some guy in New York. He wouldn't leave his name; just said he'd get in touch with you later."

"How'd he know to call the Coughlins?"

"I think he called your office first and Darlene told him he could reach me here."

"Did he say anything?"

"Just asked where you were. I told him on a fishing trip."

"Well, did he say what he wanted?"

"No; I asked for messages, but he said he'd catch you later."

There was a long silence. Finally Judy said, "Daddy?"

"Yes?"

"Is it okay?"

"Sure, it's fine. I just can't figure out . . . well, it's probably business. Al Harper can handle it."

We passed the usual words of love and hung up. For a long time I stood there, bothered by this New York development and wondering if I had made a mistake. There was no answer for that one, so I went back to the table to find that Amy had paid the check and left. But I found her sitting in her customary place on the passenger's side of the car.

"Say, why don't we save all this goodbye crap for tomorrow?" she said. "I'm getting too tired to appreciate it."

We drove around for a while; Amy settled back with her head against the headrest. "God, the road can be a lonely thing," she said after a time. "It's funny how sometimes I love traveling alone and other times it drives me up a wall. Tonight's one of those other times."

We found a place near the western edge of town. She dashed in to register us. When she returned, the two rooms had become one, and we were in as Mr. and Mrs.

"It's cheaper this way," she said, tossing me the single key.

Showers felt good for both of us. And afterward I learned that Amy did have an intense, passionate way of doing just about everything.

6

WHAT THE HELL; IT SEEMED HARMLESS ENOUGH. Two days on the road, a roll in the hay, and *adieu,* if that was to be it: a far cry from the stuffy conventions of my youth, but this was the new youth with its new set of values. Once Amy decided to play the game, she played with class and expertise, bringing to bed a restrained hunger and joy that I found flattering and exciting. Afterward I lay awake wondering how I could have thought of her as a child.

But sex always changes things. It opens new doors and closes the old ones, loosens people up, crushes protective barriers, and creates assumptions on both parts. I had learned that with Sharon, and now I expected it with Amy. I was enjoying her, but I had reservations; still, I did not know the final price of all this. I slept soundly, and when I woke there was light behind the large venetian blind that covered the motel window. Amy lay naked, face up and uncovered, on the bed beside me. Her eyes were closed, but they fluttered as I stirred. She looked at me alertly, as though she had been awake for some time.

"I was just thinking," I said.

"Thinking what?"

"What a crazy damn fool your husband is."

That compliment got me a backrub; light massage along my shoulder blades; soon, fingers along my thighs; ultimately, more sex, but different—easier and friendlier, until her fingernails gripped my neck in her final struggle. We showered together, and when I came out of the steamy bathroom she was drying her hair at the dresser mirror.

"You still going home?" she said.

"I didn't say that. All I said was this is as far west as I go. I'll probably fool around in the mountains for a few days; do some exploring and maybe some fishing. Then I'll go home."

"Too bad."

"Too bad how?"

"Too bad we can't have more time together. You're sure I can't talk you into driving me on to California?"

I smiled. "I'm sure."

"I do have friends there."

It was a curious thing to say, and I looked at her curiously as I answered her: "I believe you."

"I guess we could still have some good times. *If* you asked me to go along with you, I mean. That's not a hint, by the way, but it looks like you're going to be around, and I'm not in any big hurry anyway."

"What about California?"

"It'll still be there."

That's what I mean about assumptions. From the start of our little sexual adventure she had assumed that I would want her along and I assumed that she would want to come. In this case both were reasonably correct, so that made things easier. Over breakfast I looked at a road map while she visited the ladies' room. This time she did not even look at the telephone, which was in plain view across the dining room, and I hoped that the whole nasty business—whatever it meant—was over for her. When the time was right I would ask her about it, and maybe she would have some answers. I still had a lot to find out. The New York phone call was annoying, but nothing could be done on that angle from here; I put it aside and played the hand I had dealt myself. I studied the road map, with particular attention to the area west of Pueblo, and the first thing I noticed was that Route 50 continued on through the Rockies and across Utah. More interesting at the moment was State Highway 96, which ran due west to the mountain range, then curled north and made a rendezvous with Route 50 about a hundred miles farther along. I followed 96 with my finger, looking for the road called 12, which would complete the trio of automatic-writing numbers; but either the map was not detailed enough or Highway 12 wasn't there. The state road ran a fairly uncomplicated path, curving along the mountains, intersecting 50 and dying at that point. There were a few unmarked roads along the way, thin blue lines on my road map that led to small towns in the mountains, and all of them would be worth checking out. Amy returned and I folded the map and put it away.

We left the smoky town in a rush, heading into the high country. I found 96 an easier driving road than 50; there was no traffic to speak of after Pueblo had been put behind us. The highway straightened and went in a beeline across a broad plain; the foothills rose up ahead and the few clouds broke and drifted away to the south. Amy asked for my road map and I gave it to her, but she put it aside immediately and stared out at the passing landscape. Her light mood of the morning had vanished; in its place had come an uneasiness. Twice I asked her what was wrong, but she brushed it off with a shrug. The road twisted sharply and began to climb; soon we saw snow-covered peaks in the distance, a great expanse of mountains that seemed to stretch north and south forever. I said, "God, look at that," but she nodded her head only in politeness and not with any interest. I had the feeling that she had seen it all before, so many times that it was old to her, and it was an uncomfortable thought that I couldn't shake.

It was partly confirmed later, as we passed a federal wilderness area and came upon a mountain development called Sangre de Cristo Estates. The developer operated out of a trailer just off the highway, and his roadside sign was an annoying intrusion into the unlittered drive. But it did bring my attention for the first time to the words *Sangre de Cristo*. The name had a faintly familiar ring and I said it to myself.

"It means 'blood of Christ,'" Amy said.

"What?"

"Blood of Christ—that's what it means. These are the Sangre de Cristo Mountains."

"Have you been here before?"

"Sure. I told you I'm from Denver; that's only about three hours from here. Anyway, I took Spanish in college. *Sangre* means blood. Sangre de Cristo, get it?"

I got it all right, more than she could know. But I swallowed my surprise and said, "Why are the mountains called that?"

"I think the Spanish named them hundreds of years ago. They say the morning sun gives a red tint to the whole range, so the Spanish called them 'Blood of Christ.'"

"You seem to know a lot about it."

Her answer to that was impatient, not quite sharp but getting there: "Oh, hell; look, I read it all somewhere once and it just stuck. Anyway, I told you I've been here."

"Well, have you ever heard of a Route 12 that branches off from this highway?"

She reached for the map.

"It's not there," I said.

"Then I guess there isn't any. If there was, it would be here, wouldn't it?"

She turned away from me again; I wrote it off as bitchiness and my inability to understand it and make it right. The mountains loomed ahead of us; I knew that these were the real vanguards of the Rockies, and all before them had been mere foothills. From the last of the foothills the road ran across the valley to the mountain base in a slow arc. There were a couple of towns at the bottom, and I stopped for gas and, I hoped, directions to Road 12. Nobody at the gas station had ever heard of it, and Amy took in my repeated queries without a word. I pushed on north, passing a few dirt roads and giving them all the same careful scrutiny. In the end, I thought, I would have to go to the end of 96, then come back slowly and explore each side road. Then I came to one road that was different from the rest. It wasn't quite a physical difference; just a tantalizing familiarity that had been missing from all the others. There were mailboxes and indications that the road had recently been snowplowed. I did not react well; even as I was passing it by, I jerked the wheel and turned in. The sudden movement startled Amy; she sank back against the seat and glared at me.

The road ran concurrently with the highway for a short distance, then turned west toward the mountain range. Just around that first bend we saw the sign; very old and hand-painted, it said: GOLD CREEK, 12 mi. I was so elated that I shouted, "This is it!" Amy only sat, stony-faced. Not until the silence between us became strained did she force herself to speak.

"What on earth are you talking about?"

The temptation was very strong to throw it all up to her, all the inconsistencies of her sudden appearance and subsequent behavior, with a few tough questions of my own. But that might do more harm than good. Amy wasn't stupid; she would know, if she was involved, that she was under some suspicion, so I had lost any element of surprise I might once have had. Anyway, it was hardly likely that she would lose her cool under any circumstances and blurt out all she knew. So I continued in my role of blind dupe, at least for a while longer; I said, "I'm just glad to be alive, Amy," and started to let it go at that. But that sounded as phony as it was, so I filled in the gaps with some back-home ramblings. I talked about how there wasn't much country like this, even in western Virginia, but she showed no interest or emotion and my voice trailed off in a half-finished sentence. I checked my odometer reading and pushed ahead. There were still patches of snow on the road, and where the snow had melted off it was washboard. I took it slowly and kept both hands on the wheel. As the road rolled up into the mountains there was more snow, and I could see by the tracks that at least one car had been through here either today or yesterday. The tracks were small and close together, indicating recent use by one of those foreign economy cars, possibly a Volks. The road dipped, cutting into a long canyon, and suddenly there was a rushing stream to our left; a sharp turn and we were climbing above it along the mountain face. Another turn and we dropped into an adjacent canyon. But the drive was surprisingly easy and the road was good. Only once did we get in a tight squeeze, when we met a jeep coming out. The jeep was piloted by a bearded man and occupied by three other bearded men. I was vaguely aware that Amy had turned to look at them after we crept past; I tried to focus on them in my rear-view, but there was too much bumping for a clear look. At the bottom of the canyon a wooden bridge crossed the creek; obviously new, it was freshly painted and well maintained. Someone had sanded it, maybe as recently as this morning. On the left bank the road began another slow climb. It was almost a straight climb to the top of the ridge, and from there we could see a long valley with the remains of an old town at the bottom.

It was exactly as I had pictured it. The one road wound down the mountain, through the town, and dead-ended at the stream. I started down and came soon to the worst part of the road, a hole where the melting snow had left a pool of mud. I sloshed through it and we came to a rim just above the town. My odometer showed that we had come almost twelve miles from the highway.

From here the town looked dead. The buildings— even though we could not see all of them yet—looked old and ruined. There were about four square blocks of rotting frame structures and a wider array of buildings, built without any kind of organization, on the other side of the stream. The town had evidently been a mining camp; the rusted remains of crude mining apparatus still clutched the mountainside. Then I saw movement and blinked twice; there were people here. Smoke curled from several of the chimneys across the stream, and as I looked closer I saw some men working on a house.

Amy had seen it all before I had: "It's a hippie camp."

"How can you tell that from here?"

"There's nothing wrong with my eyes. And I've been in hippie camps before. Didn't you see those four guys in the jeep? That wasn't the governor of Colorado driving."

I put the car in gear and we started down. As we came closer I saw that she was right: The area across the stream had become a haven for bearded men and long-haired girls. Many of the old shacks had been patched and propped; we could see perhaps two dozen people working in the sunlight. Some of the houses across the river seemed to be new; the workmanship often was shoddy but the wood had a still-green freshness. Most were unpainted; a few were wrapped in tar paper.

The road leveled off on a final ridge before dropping the final hundred yards into the town. Here, still somewhat above the town's rooftop, we came quite suddenly upon an old house. It stood alone, above the town, a giant old mansion of stone and glass perched almost at the edge of that final rim. In its own way the house was as out of place as the makeshift shacks across the river; obviously it had some age behind it, which the shacks did not have, but in no way was it of the same era as the mining town. Its appearance, unexpected and brief from the road, was startling, but heavy underbrush prevented more than a glimpse. In those few seconds I saw that all its windows were covered with either shades or heavy curtains, and a long row of flowerless flower pots lined the front porch. There was scaffolding at the sides and around back, indicating a huge renovating job in progress. The road wound among the trees to a double-door garage behind the house. I blinked and the image disappeared behind the trees and shrubs as my car began its slow descent toward the old buildings of Gold Creek.

Had it been slightly higher in the mountains, the town undoubtedly would have been a ghost. But nestled between great peaks, it was protected from high mountain storms, and the midmorning temperature was pleasant despite the snow. Large mounds of snow lined both sides of the street, and the street itself had thawed to a sticky mud. But there was virtually no wind, even though I could see snow blowing furiously off the mountaintops in the distance. The lower part of Gold Creek, where the business district must have been in the gold-rush days, was deserted. In the whole of the mining camp I saw only one building with any sign of life: a large frame store of some kind at the end of the main street. It faced me as I drove toward the hippie camp; obviously the main street had dead-ended here, at the junction of the main north-and-south street. Parked outside the store were a jeep, a Volkswagen, and a late-model Buick. The side street ran directly to the stream, where perhaps ten older vehicles were parked. The stream severed the valley here, leaving a crude rope walking bridge, the only apparent access to the hippie camp at the other side.

The store at the end of the main street turned out to be an inn called the Mother Lode, lighted on the inside and apparently open for business. "They've got to be kidding," I said as I stopped the car behind the red Volkswagen. "They can't possibly do any business in a place like this. Does this place look open to you?"

She nodded. I got out for a better look. This entire block was like a page from the 1880s, but on closer examination I saw that most of the buildings were props: all front and no insides. Someone had taken the trouble to restore this side of the street, right down to the wooden Indian and the candy-stripe barber pole. But it was all show: behind it was nothing but two-by-four braces. It was a dramatic contrast to the opposite side of the street. There the buildings were rotted out and crumbling, just as you might expect to find in any mountain ghost town. A few doors across from the inn was the old theater, obviously the town hotspot during the gold rush. The roof had caved in, filling the interior with light, and I could still make out where the stage and bar had been. Behind the stage were some flimsy rooms, dressing rooms for sure, but the walls had long ago rotted away. Next to the theater was a saloon, sagging and crushed by the snows of ninety years. A tree had grown up through the floor and its branches jutted through a side window. Farther along a side street I saw the crumbling remains of an old corral and something that might have been an outhouse.

I saw something else: the face of the old mansion on the ridge, unprotected from this angle and offering a view even more sinister than I got from the road. I turned away from it and called to Amy.

"Hey, what do you think of this place?"

"Not much, if you want to know the truth."

"I think it's fantastic."

She said something that sounded like "you would," but by then I had moved away from the car. I shelved the temptation to tell her that, after all, she had invited herself along, and after a time she got out of the car and joined me on the street.

"You just going to stand here all day?"

"No, I think I'll go inside and see if this inn's for real."

"That means you're staying?"

"For a while."

She sighed in painful resignation: "Okay, I guess I'll browse around across the river. There might be some people I know in the camp."

Amy trudged away through the mud. I locked the car and turned for another look at the fine old Victorian gingerbread that laced the outside of the inn. What I saw instead was a woman standing in a second-floor room, looking down at me. The instant our eyes met she stepped back and drew the curtains closed. I saw her only long enough to know that she was young and her hair was dark. Her fingers appeared briefly between the curtains, straightening the wrinkles, then she was gone. I shrugged and clattered up the boardwalk, kicked the mud off my shoes, and went into the inn.

The lobby was empty. It was very western, with oil

paintings of Indian raids and stuffed animal heads and ancient rifles adorning the walls. A long bar stood just to the right of the door, with a mirror behind it and a few bottles arranged neatly beneath the mirror. A beautiful old cash register stood at the end of the bar. Beyond was a social room, where eight or ten chairs were arranged in a semicircle. Across the lobby, near the back of the building, was a small kitchen with a refrigerator and a stove, and beside the stove a door that I guessed must lead to a storeroom. I walked along the bar toward the kitchen and noticed that the inn register lay open at the end of the bar. There were only two names: Jill Sargent of Bridgeport, Connecticut; and Willy Max of Philadelphia. I was thinking that the girl I had seen must be either Jill Sargent or Mrs. Max, and what a strange gathering of Easterners this was, when a man came out of the storeroom and crossed the lobby toward me.

He must have been forty-five, with hair that was graying and one day would be a distinguished white. He walked with a distinct limp, balancing himself with a cane that apparently had been cut and hand-carved from a tree branch. He smiled as he came closer, and the smile was wide and toothy and noncommittal.

"You can't be another customer." He said it as a fact, not a question.

"Don't tell me you're booked solid."

He laughed heartily at that. "God, I've never had three customers at once in all the years I've been coming up here."

"I probably shouldn't ask you, but how do you stay in business?"

He laughed again. "It's not a business; it's a hobby. I bought this whole town twenty years ago when mountain land was so cheap you could get it for boxtops. I wish now I'd bought the other side too. But at least I got this side. I fixed up the inn myself; now I come up every summer. I'd spend the winter too if I could get the county to keep the road open."

"But seriously, you do take guests?"

"Sure, if they come. I enjoy having them around."

"How much are your rooms?"

"Whatever you can pay. We're rustic as all getout. No room service, so you got to pick up after yourself. Five dollars sound okay?"

"Fine."

"That includes run of the kitchen. We got no cook here, so you just pick up your own supplies—whatever you want to eat—in town, and store 'em in the fridge. All I ask is just leave the kitchen like you find it."

"Great. I'll get my things."

I took everything from the car that I might need—all my clothes, the travel kit, backpack with its snakebite ration, and the large manila envelope containing the mountain pictures and the scraps of automatic writing. I locked the car and looked up just as the curtain fluttered closed in the second-floor room. The dark girl fascinated me, and I hoped I would meet her later. Again I started up the steps to the boardwalk; then paused almost as an afterthought and looked over my shoulder at the old house on the hill. That was when I saw the car, the big black Oldsmobile. It was just coming into view on the ridge over the town. I watched, captivated in a cold, clammy way, as it dipped out of sight for a minute and appeared again on the rim. It traveled quickly along the slippery road, slowing near the entrance to the old house, then turning in and winding among the heavy undergrowth. A few seconds later someone opened the garage door and the black Oldsmobile disappeared inside.

7

"SOMETHING WRONG?"

The innkeeper stood in the doorway behind me. The black Oldsmobile was gone now, but for several moments I could not take my eyes away from the old house. The words brought me back to reality with a start.

"I was just intrigued by that old house," I said; "it seems so out of place here. Do you know who owns it?"

"Some fellow in Pueblo. I don't think he's ever been up here."

"Somebody's living up there now."

"Those people are tenants. The owner's one of those land tycoons; got so much property even he doesn't know what he's got. He's got a fine mountain cabin up near Taylor's Gulch, and never used that either. I think he rents the cabin out to a hunting club in season and the members keep it up for him. It's a crime to have property if you can't use it."

I followed him back into the lobby. "It just seems out of place," I said again; "almost as out of place as this inn."

"Nothing strange about either one. They were going to make a movie here once. Some Hollywood director moved a film company in here, paid me for the use of the place and fixed it up like you see it now. They were all ready to start filming when the star took sick. They waited around for a long time, but costs mounted up and they finally had to cancel the film. They left it like it is now."

"What about the old house?"

"It was built during World War One. I guess there was still some life in the old town then; but it couldn't have been much, because my research shows it was abandoned at the turn of the century. Anyway, the man who built it was the father of the one who owns it now. People say he was crazy, but that's neither here nor there."

"How about the people living there now? Do you know them?"

"Some man and his wife; I think they rented the place about two months ago. I guess part of the deal was that they would work on it, put it in livable shape again. At least that's how I figured it when I saw the scaffolding go up. I never see them doing anything with it, but the owner's so busy he wouldn't know anyway."

"Have you met them?"

"If you can call it a meeting. We had a storm in mid-March and we were all snowed in for the best part of a week. He came in here one day ranting like a wild man; said he had to get out and why the hell didn't the county plow the road? Before that, I went up to meet them, but I never got past the front door. They wouldn't even receive me. So I never have met her, and I only talked to him through a crack in the door. I thought for a while they'd checked out; hadn't seen any sign of life up there for almost three weeks. Then, one day last week, I saw her out back sunning herself. She was behind the garage, where you can just see for a second as you drive past; so I knew they were still here. And now you tell me he's back."

He shook his head and pushed the register toward me. I signed my name and home address.

"Jim Ryan, are you?" he said, extending his hand. "Harry Gould."

I took his hand. "There's a girl with me, a young hitchhiker. She'll probably want a room too."

He didn't say anything about that. I took my key, picked up my luggage, and started up the stairs. Halfway up, I stopped. "Do you know much about the history of this place?"

"I consider myself the authority. If you're interested, we can talk after you're settled in."

"I'd like that." I continued up to the second landing. The steps creaked and the hallway on the second floor was dark. I walked quietly past the rooms and paused at the door facing the street in the center of the hallway. This would be the room where the young woman at the window was staying. I stopped and listened. Inside the room a radio was playing, but there was no sound of movement. A board creaked under my foot and I hurried down the hall, looking for my room number.

The room was at the far end of the hall, adequate but rough-cut and western, like everything else in the inn. I noticed at once a fringe benefit—an extra window. One of the windows looked across the sagging rooftops of the town and offered a partial view of the hippie camp; the other faced the incoming road, giving me a fine view of the house on the ridge. I sat at the window facing the house. Outside, I noticed, was a narrow balcony that ran down the length of the hotel. Only one door opened to the balcony, a door from the hall at the head of the stairs. For some time I watched the house, wishing for binoculars; better yet, a telescope. My eyes are good, but from this distance I could not make out anything specific.

After a while my eyes tired; that brought thoughts of Amy, and the fact that I had had very little sleep the last few nights. I stretched out on the bed and fell asleep immediately. I was awakened at four o'clock by a gentle rapping at my door. It was Harry Gould.

"I'm sorry," he said; "did I wake you?"

I shook my head, but there was still sleep in my eyes.

"Accept the apologies of the house. I just came up to see if you'd be interested in joining me and the other guests for dinner tonight?"

"Dinner?"

"It'll have to be pot luck, since I've only stocked supplies according to my own taste. At least you won't be subjected to my cooking. Miss Sargent is doing the honors."

"What time?"

"Seven o'clock. Come down at six and we men can have a touch in the den."

"I'll look forward to it."

He turned away, but I called to him before he had reached the end of the hallway: "Has the young lady I mentioned shown up yet?"

"I haven't seen her."

I nodded and closed the door. Then I showered and changed clothes and returned to my perch at the window for another uneventful hour watching the house.

At six I locked my room and went downstairs. Already an odor of good cooking was in the air, and as I came into the kitchen area I saw the girl at work over the stove. She was busy and did not see me, and I did not introduce myself, deciding to leave that to Gould. The den that Gould mentioned opened from behind the bar. I walked in and found Gould stirring a fire and another man, tall and thin, standing nearby

84

with a drink in his hand. Gould heard me enter and came forward, hand outstretched.

"Mr. Ryan, come in. This is Willy Max. Mr. Max, Mr. Ryan."

We shook hands and Gould said, "Did you meet Miss Sargent?"

"She seemed pretty busy when I passed through. I thought I'd leave her be till later."

Max smiled. "Judging from the smell of that meal, I'd say she's an artist. Nobody should ever disturb an artist at work. You probably did exactly right."

"Mr. Max is a great believer in human ability," Gould said.

"I believe everyone has one talent that he does naturally better than other people in that same field who cultivated theirs," Max said. "The trouble is, most of us waste our natural abilities, and they deteriorate to nothing."

I found that line of thought interesting. "What's your talent, Mr. Max?"

"I climb mountains, and call me Willy. My wife finds mountains as big a bore as I find her damned opera. So once a year she goes to New York and I come out here. What's yours?"

I thought for a minute. "I'm not sure I have one."

"Please—there's no room for modesty in this crowd."

"It's got nothing to do with modesty, honestly. I just can't think of anything that I can do better than anyone else."

"What's your occupation, then?"

"I'm an engineer. But that's probably a result of circumstances, not talent. I try not to take it home."

"Interesting," Gould said.

Max pressed it: "Some people excel at hobbies. Take Harry here—best damned innkeeper in the state. That's probably because he doesn't do it for money. Do you have any hobbies?"

I thought long again. "Not really. You'll give me a complex, Mr.—Willy—you've made me realize how really ordinary I am."

"That wasn't my intent. Well, let's drop it and have a drink."

Gould moved toward the door that opened into the bar.

"Bourbon, please," I said.

While he was getting my drink, Max sat in a large comfortable-looking chair that seemed to engulf him. "I try to get up here for at least two weeks a year. Usually there's no one else here; nobody but Harry and those abominable goddamn hippies. I can even remember a time when *they* weren't here. Now the place is turning into another mountain city. But I suppose none of us owns this country, isn't that right— Jim?"

"Yes, Jim—and yes, I guess you're right."

"I'd own it if it was available; not the town, but higher up, near timberline. That's my country. I think this part of Colorado is one of the most beautiful spots on earth."

"Why isn't it available? I would think you could buy anything for a price."

"The best of it is national forest land."

Gould came in then with two tall glasses in his hand. He passed one to me and kept the other for himself, checked Max's glass for level and returned to his spot near the fireplace. For a moment there was a strained silence, as though all were trying to think of something interesting to say.

"Have you been climbing yet, Willy?" I said.

"Once. I'll go again in the morning. Care to join me?"

"That depends."

"On what?"

"On what you mean by mountain climbing. If you

mean hiking, fine. But if you mean the works, with spiked shoes and picks and ropes, forget it. Sheer drops make me nervous."

"There's all kinds of country around here. Everyone can do his own thing. That's what I like about it."

"What do you do—for a living, I mean," I said, wishing I had phrased the question differently.

"Nothing," Max answered evenly.

There was another long silence. "Oh," I said finally, and that was the end of that line of talk.

From the outer room I heard the sound of pots rattling. Harry Gould excused himself with something that sounded like "there's no reason this should be an all-male affair," and in a moment he returned, ushering her into the den. She was perhaps twenty-five, though she might have been thirty or as young as twenty-one. She was one of those people who for about fifteen years remain ageless, as unchanging as a painting. I thought she was beautiful, and it was obvious by the stiffening in Max's back as she entered that he did too.

"Miss Sargent," Gould said. "You know Mr. Max. This is Mr. Ryan from, ah, Virginia."

"Jim," I said, nodding.

"I saw you come in today," she said, offering her hand.

The hand was soft in mine. "I saw you seeing me," I said, attempting laughter.

And she laughed too. "Yes, I know. I was trying not to be rude; that's why I stepped back and closed the curtain. But I guess that might be considered as rude as simply staring."

"I didn't think anything of it."

"That's good. The reason I was staring is simply that I was surprised to see another guest arrive. I just got here yesterday myself; I was told in town that the place was completely deserted."

"Even I don't come up till March," Gould said.

"And now it's full of life," Miss Sargent said. "People are everywhere these days, aren't they, Mr. Ryan?"

"Willy here was just saying the same thing; I guess it's true. He's surely seen more of the world than I have."

Max fidgeted and lighted his pipe.

"Are you drinking, Miss Sargent?" Gould said.

"I might be coaxed. What have you?"

"Bourbon and Scotch—and a few other things I don't handle well. I'm not very good at mixed drinks, so you'll have to take your chances."

"If you will just mix a little Scotch with a lot of water, that will be fine for me."

Gould, still moving with his slow limp, went out.

"Where are you from?" I asked her.

"I'm a born New Englander without the accent. Now I live in Bridgeport, Connecticut."

"And what brings you way out here?"

"I'm a photojournalist. I have an assignment from a New York publisher to deliver a photo book on the last vestiges of the old West."

"I think you can still find what you want in the high country," Max said. "I've been coming here off and on for years. I know of several real ghost towns; I'd be delighted to show you."

She smiled in a way that was noncommittal.

"Who did you say your publisher was, Miss Sargent?" I asked.

"I didn't, but it's MacDougald and Barnes; they do a lot of picture books."

"And you've done books for this publisher—MacDougald and Barnes, is it?—you've worked for them before?"

"This is my third book. I have an advance which

should cover my expenses. That's the only way a professional writer can work."

Gould returned with her drink. "The bar should be in here. I miss more interesting talk by not having the bar in here."

"You haven't missed much," Miss Sargent said. "Now that you're back, we can get into something really interesting."

"Oh?"

"Mr. Max was telling me last night that you have some fascinating legends about these mountains."

"I do know a few yarns," Gould said, his eyes narrowing like a fox. "But you didn't all come out here to listen to me talk."

"That's part of why I did come—to get the feel of the country by talking to the people—you see?"

"I'll second that," I said.

Gould looked at Max, who simply smiled. "You know I always like your stories, Harry," Max said when it became obvious that everyone was waiting for him to speak.

"After dinner," Gould said; "that's the time for yarn-swapping."

The meal had a simple, backwoods flavor that we all relished; the main course was venison, which I had never tried, and it was complemented by a delicious plate of wild rice. Miss Sargent sat between Gould and Max, directly across from me, and once or twice I caught her staring at me with that same intense meditation I had first noticed when she was only a face in a window. She only smiled and shifted her eyes elsewhere.

Max began to loosen up after dinner and another drink. He told several stories of his travels in Europe. It was hard to say if Miss Sargent was impressed; she was a tough one to figure. At about eight-thirty we moved back into the den for more drinks, and the party got very cozy and friendly. Max insisted that once and for all we drop all the formality and use first names; everyone complied but Gould, who continued to maintain his proprietorial image. By nine o'clock I was feeling fine; I had not known such a homogeneous gathering of strangers in years.

Much later Jill said, "The night is going fast, Mr. Gould; are you saving your stories for midnight? Shall we all draw up to the fire?"

Harry Gould laughed. "We're having too good a time to spoil it with a bunch of stuffy old yarns."

"We insist," I said.

"If you put it that way, how can I refuse?" He got up and moved his chair closer into our circle. "Yes, let's do as Miss Sargent says—everybody pull up closer to the fire. Has everyone got a full drink?"

Everyone had. We made a semicircle around the fire and Gould turned off the lights.

"Probably no region on earth has more legends and stories than this part of the Rocky Mountains. The legends come from three main sources—from Indians, who lived here for thousands of years; from the Spanish conquistadores, who raped the land and the people in the sixteenth century; and from the pioneers of the late eighteen hundreds. All of them left something here. Often what they left was gold, treasures more valuable and vast than anything ever invented in fiction. Let me tell you about a few of them."

The red-orange light of the fire flickered on his face as he told us his first tale. It was an absorbing little drama about an old miner of the 1880s named Jeremiah Horn. After twenty-five years of poverty-level grubstaking, Jeremiah struck a fat vein of rich ore. Every spring after that he took a pack mule into the mountains, disappeared for three months, and came back in late summer with enough gold to carry him through the winter. Many people tried to track Jeremiah to his mine, but the old man was an expert tracker and backtracker and he always lost them.

One spring Jeremiah Horn rode away into the hills and never returned. "Nobody knows what happened to him," Gould said; "and nobody ever found his mine, either. My guess is, Horn either got bushwhacked or was lost in a spring storm."

"Is that likely? About getting lost, I mean," Jill said. "If he was such an expert tracker . . ."

"The weather in these parts can change in a minute, Miss Sargent. Even an old-timer can lose his way in a high mountain snowstorm. People still get lost, a few every year. In the case of Jeremiah Horn, who knows? Maybe he fell from one of those early mountain trails you see in pictures. Maybe someday somebody will find his bones in the bottom of a ravine, and that might open a clue to the location of the mine."

Gould moved on. His tales were short and earthy, and he knew just enough about each to whet my appetite for more. Next he told us about a train robbery, when gold worth more than two million dollars was stolen and stashed somewhere in the mountains. Within twenty-four hours of the robbery the bandits were captured, but the money never was found. "It's out there somewhere, buried under some rock," Gould said; "it's just waiting for somebody to find it."

He sipped his drink. "What I'm telling you now are stories based entirely on fact. Some of the legends are really wild, but everything I'm telling you now actually did happen. There are records proving that Jeremiah Horn lived, and that he made a fantastic strike. We know the loot from the train never was found. All three of the robbers were dead within a year, and all of natural causes. None of 'em ever told where the money was. Call it coincidence or fate or whatever, but that's what makes these mountain tales so fascinating. You look at this country and you know that *anything* can happen here. There must be two or three dozen documented cases of treasures found and lost again."

"Why?" I said.

"Pardon?"

"Why were they lost? You'd think anyone who found something like that would be careful to map it out."

"You'd think so, but it wasn't that way. This territory was a melting pot in those days, Mr. Ryan; not at all what TV has made it out to be. There wasn't often a face-to-face gunfight; it was far more ordinary to find someone shot in the back. If people knew you had something valuable, why, they just took it away from you if they could do it. So when a man struck it rich he kept his map in his head and he kept his mouth shut. When he died—and that was usually at an early age—the location of the mine went with him.

"There's another factor too, and that's the land itself. This country changes all the time. We get heavy snows here every year, and landmarks have a way of disappearing from one winter to the next. I know of several reliable stories of miners who struck it rich, marked their claims, and came back the next spring only to find the whole landscape different. I can see you find that hard to believe, but ask Mr. Max; he's seen it."

Max nodded. "Tell them about Caverna del Oro, Harry. You were talking about wild legends, and that's the best of them all."

"Please, not tonight; I'm not used to talking so much. Let's save Caverna del Oro for another time."

The party dissolved quickly after that. Gould turned on the lights and Max excused himself. Jill stepped outside for a breath of air and I followed her out.

"How long will you be here?" she asked.

"A few days; maybe a week. How about you?"

"Until I've finished my work. I want to hike up into the hills. . . ."

"I was thinking of going out tomorrow too. Will you come with me?"

"Yes, I'd like that. Right now I'd better get up to bed."

But we stood there for a few more moments, listening to the mountain noises and feeling the sting of the cold air. I did not say anything. I was thinking again of Amy, and now I had to admit it: I was beginning to worry. Jill sensed my preoccupation and soon turned away to go in. I escorted her upstairs. At her door she turned to me and said, "What time tomorrow?"

"Let's go early. Six o'clock?"

"Fine."

"And maybe tomorrow night we can hear the rest of Harry's tales. His Caverna del Oro interests me."

She nodded slightly. "Good night, Jim."

8

LONG BEFORE FIRST LIGHT I WAS AWAKE, BUT I DID not get up. I forced myself to lie still until I heard the sounds of birds outside. It was five-fifteen. The air was pale, with a foggy predawn glow that I used to love but have grown to hate. I swung my body out of bed and looked through the window toward the rim. I was surprised to see a man standing in the front yard of the old house. He stood so still, watching the inn with such obvious intent, that I almost passed over him in my quick scrutiny. From my perch he was fully two hundred yards away, and I could not make out his features at all. I saw that he wore a red shirt and dark pants, but the facial characteristics probably would have been blurred at that distance in broad daylight, let alone the gloom of early morning. A telescope was mandatory; that was unquestionable now. I would get away to Pueblo in a day or two and bring one back with me.

While I was watching, the front door of the old house opened and the vague form of a woman appeared behind a screen door. She remained in the darkness, coming only to the door to speak briefly with the man before stepping back and closing the door. He remained outside for perhaps another ten minutes, and I watched him for as long as he was there. He went in just as the sun was breaking the sky in the east.

I was full of insane notions these days; now came the wildest yet. For all of fifteen minutes I calmly weighed my chances of prowling around the old house without being caught. Of course it was mad; something like that always is to a man who has lived his life within the law. Yet somehow I would have to clear up this matter of the black Oldsmobile, and if that meant employing unconventional methods, so be it. The telescope would be a first step in countersurveillance. Beyond that, I did not know at this point how far I would go. A lot would depend on what *they* did, and when.

I came down into the lobby at exactly six o'clock. Already Harry Gould was up and on the job. He stood behind the bar, grinning broadly, as if anticipating another flood of guests. "I thought you might be going out this morning," he said quietly. "I wanted to give you some pointers about the country before you go."

"Great." I pulled up a barstool.

He poured coffee from a pot simmering behind the bar. "People who have never been in the high Rockies can't appreciate how fast this weather can change. I know I told you that last night, but I could see then that it didn't make much of an impression. Don't ever make the mistake of underestimating it, Mr. Ryan. Right now it looks like summertime outside. That can all change in an hour; we could be buried under snow again by tonight. We're due for a few more good snowstorms before summer really comes anyway. I've even seen it snow in July."

"So I should watch the weather?"

"You bet. If it starts to cloud up, get on back here. Don't fool around with storms in this country. Up there, when everything is white, it's so easy to wander off the trail and get lost. If that does happen, don't walk around. Find some shelter and build a fire, if you can; wait it out. We'll find you."

I nodded and sipped from the steaming cup.

"That's the sermon," Gould said. "There's just one more thing: Stay out of old mines."

"You don't have to tell me that."

"Yeah, well, you never know what might attract people. Some of these old mines have been here for ninety years. A lot of them are half filled with water. And watch out for shafts."

"Shafts?"

"That's a hole sunk straight down into a mine to give it air. Some of them are a hundred feet deep. I don't have to tell you what would happen to a man who fell into one."

I shivered. "Jesus, does that really happen often?"

"Once is too often. Sure, I run across a newspaper story now and then about a hiker who's fallen into a mineshaft. It's easier than you think. Some of them are boarded over with rotten wood; some are overgrown with weeds. Once in a while a man just disappears in the high country and never is found. When that happens, I figure he probably fell into a shaft."

I heard Jill's soft footsteps and gulped my coffee as she came down. "My hiking partner arriveth. I appreciate your help."

He nodded amiably. "Coffee, Miss Sargent?"

"I had some instant in my room," she said. "I think my heart is beating now."

"You'll need some breakfast and a lunch," Gould said.

"I'm not big on breakfast," Jill said.

Gould insisted. "The mountains are high and the day is long."

Over eggs and toast, I asked where we might hike.

"Are there any ghost towns nearby?" Jill asked.

"There is an excellent ghost town called Taylor's Gulch, about three hours from here. I told Mr. Ryan something about it yesterday—that's the town where the owner of the mansion keeps a cabin. There is a jeep road up there, but it's a fairly steep hike; it might take you half a day if you're not used to the altitude." He took a pencil from beneath the bar. "I'll draw you a map. Use it if you want; if not, you'll have it for another time."

He explained the landmarks to us as we walked outside. I put the map away in my pocket and hoisted my backpack up on my shoulders. Jill had a smaller bag, which she carried in her hand, and she had brought two cameras, slung around her neck. The weather was beautiful; neither of us wore heavy coats. We splashed along until the muddy street became a dry path that turned upward along the stream's bank. Jill led the way between the vehicles parked at the stream's edge, and one at a time we crossed the rope bridge. The sight of the hippie camp brought back my worry about Amy, even though in the warm sunlight her disappearance did not seem nearly so sinister as it had last night. Now I thought it quite possible that she was playing musical beds; she might well be shacked up with someone in the camp. I decided to have a closer look at the camp and its people.

"Would you mind if I stopped here for a minute?" I asked Jill.

"Do you know someone here?"

"I might; I'm not sure."

She followed me down the path. At the first cabin a man was cutting wood with an ax. He looked up as we approached; his expression was neither friendly nor unfriendly. A partly clad girl came out of the cabin and for a few seconds I thought she was Amy. But she stopped and looked directly at me and I saw that she was not. This girl might have been her sister. She stopped in her tracks, turned around, and went back inside. The man, meanwhile, had put aside his ax and was waiting for us to approach him. He was older than most of the kids you find in these groups; at least older than my preconceived idea of what a hippie was. This man was at least my age, possibly even in his early forties. His shoulder-length hair was streaked with gray and so was his beard. From the neck down he blended perfectly with the others; his plaid shirt was full of patches and so were his jeans. A brute of a Great Dane stood nearby, growling menacingly and following us with his eyes. It was a relief that the dog was chained to a heavy tree.

The man never made a move. He kept his eyes on me and did not offer any greeting, spoken or gestured, until I spoke.

"I'm looking for somebody; a girl who was riding with me. She came up here last night to look around and didn't come back."

He shook his head. "She must have changed her mind. I haven't seen anybody new for three, four days."

"She was young, looked a lot like the girl I just saw come out of this cabin."

Again he just stood there, offering nothing.

"If you see her, would you ask her to come down to the inn?"

He nodded and terminated the conversation by turning away and taking up his ax. We climbed out of the hippie camp and were well above the rooftops before Jill said anything. Soon we were above the hippie camp and the town proper; the path climbed steeply for a few hundred yards before leveling off in a slow ascent along the mountain face. It went like that: long and straight for the first hour. At the end of the trail we could still see the town; a few specks and occasional flashes of light against glass far below. We were at the top of a small mountain, with the entire range ahead of us. There were snowcapped peaks that dwarfed this one, and a stiff wind whipped the snow from the peaks into swirling white mists. But that was perhaps two thousand feet higher; here the wind died to a fine spring breeze.

We rested there and shared some talk about ourselves. But each of us wanted to learn about the other, so the talk didn't go anywhere. From the top the path dipped a bit and the town was lost to view; we began the tough climb that Gould had promised. We tackled it with gusto, but soon I had to stop and rest.

"How come you're in such great shape?" I asked. I was blowing hard and frankly jealous of her stamina.

"I play tennis every morning. It helps build my wind."

"And I work out three times a week. So what? None of that seems to matter in this altitude."

"Oh, I feel it too, but I like it; let's go on."

"Oh, please!" I was still gasping. "Sit down, will you?"

She laughed cheerfully and sat beside me on a rock.

"I'm sorry," I said, "it must be old age."

"Yes, yes, you must be all of what? thirty-two?"

I didn't answer her. My eyes had picked up some movement on the trail far behind us and I was scanning the slope for signs of life. I saw a brief flash of light, as though the sun had reflected against metal, but again I could not pinpoint it. I looked until my staring became obvious, and when she too began to look I shrugged it off. We climbed higher. Gould's estimate was almost perfect; it took us all morning to reach Taylor's Gulch. Jill alone might have done it in three hours, but I stopped once more before we reached the town. The path rose to a plateau, and even before we reached the top we found remnants of what must have once been a boomtown. It was built on three levels, much rougher than Gold Creek but of about the same era. The mountains rose all around us, leaving the town in the bottom of a giant cup. The buildings were badly weatherworn, much worse than those in Gold Creek; many had been completely crushed by the heavy mountain snows. Often only a heap of rotted wood remained to show that a building had once been there.

Like Gold Creek, the town had only one main street, but there the resemblance ended. The street twisted its way up the plateau to the top, crushed and crumbling houses and piles of rotted wood following it up. I tried to imagine what life here was like, but I could not. At the top the street widened and leveled off. This had been the town's business section, where the saloons and gaming tables and whorehouses were, while the section below probably had been residential. At the head of the plateau another road joined the street, a jeep trail that wound down the opposite side of the same mountain we had just climbed. The land sloped upward on both sides as the plateau blended with the mountains; built into the slope about fifty feet up was the cabin Gould had described to me. It was new and obviously well maintained, with fresh paint all around. The opposite slope was dotted by two semiboarded holes in the rock, dark mines that once had played a major part in the town's economy.

Jill already had taken several pictures. She mumbled something about needing another lens and a tripod and wanting to shoot the place in the early morning when the sunlight would be pouring in and everything would be pink and wet. It was an impressive performance to someone who had never watched a photographer at work. It impressed me, anyway. Jill worked as if she knew her business, and I felt good about that.

But it was easy to believe in anything up here. It was even easier to brush aside all my thoughts of intrigue; of Robert Holland and the mountain pictures; of Amy; of the man of the black Oldsmobile. There were a lot of things to consider before making any character judgments of the people who had suddenly come into my life. The last of those considerations, I told myself as I watched her, was a beautiful face and a vibrant personality. It seemed to me that I was the star player in some unfolding melodrama, and everyone had a script but me. They had all been waiting, banded together like a pack of vultures, for my arrival, and perhaps nobody was what he seemed to be. In Jill's case it was easy to check. I made a mental note to call her publisher in New York the next time I got to a telephone.

For now I was content just to watch her. Either her infatuation with Taylor's Gulch was real or she was a talented actress. Until I knew better I assumed that she was just what she claimed to be. She fitted it so well. She must have taken fifty pictures in thirty minutes. Everything she did looked genuine to me. Soon I forgot about it and moved deeper into the town for a closer look. As I walked through the ruins I felt the same stirrings of old ashes that I had first noticed opening those mountain pictures: *I had been here.* Then a funny thing happened, that experience you read about but never expect to go through yourself. People call it ESP, but I had never had anything faintly resembling ESP and never expected to. I came to a corner where all four buildings were partly standing. Three boulders as large as houses lined the crossstreet to my right, making it an effective blind corner, yet I *knew* what was there before I turned it. There were deep ruts in the alley, and two buildings faced each other from opposite sides. One of the buildings was stone, still standing and in good shape; the other had been a saloon. The saloon was a frame building and, like the others, had surrendered to the elements. Inside was the wreckage of a platform that had been a stage, but the roof had caved in and the stage was piled high with rotted timbers. The alley became a trail leading off into the hills.

I saw all these things in my mind in that second before I turned the corner. It was all that way, exactly. The saloon was in worse shape than I expected; the stage had crumbled and only parts of it remained. The alley was badly rutted. The stone building, which might have been a jail, had no roof, but the walls were solid. Part of what had once been a wooden roof hung down into the structure, which was about ten feet square. If there had ever been a floor it had long ago rotted out; grass and weeds grew high inside the building. There were two windows, gaping holes now that all the woodwork was gone.

Then the second strange thing happened, and suddenly and finally I knew that I had been brought here for some real purpose and was getting very close to the end of it. I went to the doorway of the stone building and ran my fingers over the smooth surface. Cut into the stone were the initials RH. It could have been anything, or it could have been Robert Holland. But there was no denying it: I had known they were there; I'd known exactly where to look for them. I went inside. The broken rafters above my head filtered the sunlight and cast a gloom over the inside of the building, but again I knew just where I was going and what I was looking for. I began to examine the walls. There was more graffiti; near the west window someone had written "joan is a lousy lay" in paint. Beneath it was the name Jake Walters. Even in the gloom I could read it easily, for the letters were large and the cutting was deep.

I cannot say I was surprised, but somehow the lack of surprise only heightened the shock. It had a numbing effect. Finally I forced myself to move to the window and touch the lettering. It was a carving to last for the lifetime of the wall. The letters were half filled with dirt, giving them a three-dimensional appearance against the gray whiteness of the stone. Most of the initials around it were dated either 1972 or '71 and, I guessed, had been made by hippies who had hiked up from the camp. The Jake Walters cutting had been there for a much longer time; whether eight years or eighty I could not guess. My speculation was interrupted by a noise outside, and I saw Jill move past the doorway. "I'm in here," I called, and she stopped and peered in through one of the windows.

"What are you doing in there?"

"Just looking around. How's the work going?"

"Lousy. I'm going to have to come back and catch the morning light."

"You'd have to hike up at midnight to make it."

"It would make more sense to camp up here for a night. But right now I think we'd better get back." She looked at her watch. "It's after one already and it's a long climb down."

If I had expected the trip down to be easier, I was wrong. You use a different set of muscles climbing down a mountain trail; by the time we reached bottom I was exhausted. Even from there the hike back to Gold Creek seemed interminable. Dusk had come when we arrived, the kind of dusk that falls over mountain country when the sun slips behind the hills but is still an hour away from dark. Jill had had a good workout too, and she went straight upstairs for a shower. I suggested that we meet later in the lobby for dinner and we set an approximate time of eight o'clock. I sank with a sigh into a large chair in the lobby, closed my eyes, and dozed for a time.

When I woke the windows all around me were dark. Harry Gould was standing behind the register, a smile on his face. "Did you have a good hike?"

"Great. But it made me realize what a tenderfoot I am. The ghost town is fantastic."

"Isn't it? I'm afraid it won't last much longer, though. The winters take a heavy toll up here. And then those hippies are forever carving their stupid initials into things."

"Yeah, I noticed. Is Max around?"

"He went out climbing and hasn't come back. Sometimes he stays overnight, and since it's dark I really don't expect him back tonight. But I don't worry about Mr. Max; he's an expert and he knows the country."

"Good." I rubbed my eyes and got up. "Any sign of the girl who came in with me?"

"There's been nobody here all day. She must have moved on without telling you. Did you say she was a stranger?"

"Yeah, that's probably it. Thanks."

I wanted to stay under the shower all night, but fifteen minutes later I stepped out and got into some fresh clothes. Jill was cooking something when I came down, and it turned out to be a simple meal thrown together from her supply bag. She apologized for its shortcomings, but I found it delicious. Gould did not join us; in fact we saw him no more that night. We talked little while we ate; both of us were too tired for words. After dinner we had a short walk around the town, which Jill recommended as a relaxing exercise for stiffening muscles. Then she excused herself and went up to bed.

Despite my physical weariness, my mind was now restless and I knew that sleep would be elusive. For a long time I sat in a chair just outside the inn's front door. Again, Amy's disappearance was bothering me, and I decided to walk while I pondered it. By this time it was very dark, but I knew the town and I knew where I was going. I crossed the rope bridge and climbed along the trail toward the hippie camp. In the distance a campfire was burning, and I could see the black forms of people moving around it. But that was fully a hundred yards away; if I was careful there was no reason why I should even be seen. I approached the first cabin, where the man with the gray-streaked hair lived, and crept around it toward the rear. A light was burning in the window facing the mountains; I could see its reflection against the trees that surrounded the house. I moved closer and turned the corner. The window was covered with an old burlap sack which was almost transparent when you got close. I got very close, pressing my nose against the cold glass.

The light inside was bad, cast by lanterns which stood in each corner. There were five people in the room; at once I saw that Amy was sitting on the floor, her back against the door, facing the window. The gray-haired man sat next to her; the girl I had seen this morning sat next to him. There were two others, both men, and I had never seen either of them. They were smoking grass, passing the joint from one to another with a clip. Even in the semidarkness I could see that Amy's eyes were closed. The man on her right nudged her and she took the joint, dragged long on it, and passed it to the gray-haired man without opening her eyes. He passed it on without taking any of it.

I waited a long time for any conversation. When it did come it sounded like a continuation of an argument that had been simmering for days.

"Look, let's get it over with, okay?" the gray-haired man said.

Amy's eyes fluttered open, then closed again.

"I'm talking to you," the man said.

Intense irritation showed on her face. "Listen, goddamnit, I told you I'll handle it my own way. How many times have we got to go through this?"

"We're all one here," the man said; "you knew that when you came. Somebody had to hold up your end while you were gone."

"Yeah, just get off that crap. I'll tell you something, Arnie, you are becoming one big fat bore."

"Amy, Amy, will you ever grow up and stop being a Vassar brat?"

"Up yours, Harris." She thrust her middle finger up almost to his nose, and for a moment I thought he was going to hit her. But he checked his hand in mid-air and took the weed as it was passed to him. This time he dragged deeply and settled back against the wall. I waited a long time for more talk, but that was the end of it. Someone lighted a new joint, and the five of them got stoned in silence. Eventually the girl who might have been Amy's sister got up and staggered into the other room. She moved around in there for a minute, then another door opened and I realized with a sudden flash of terror that she had turned out the Great Dane. The dog began barking, and Arnie Harris, the man with the gray hair, struggled to his feet.

"Somebody's outside." He started toward the door. I took off across the clearing, but the dog caught me before I made the underbrush. It tore at my legs with its teeth. I twisted and kicked out hard, crushing the dog's nose with my foot. I scrambled up the hill toward the path, and in the distance I could hear the man yelling, "Get 'im, boy, chew 'is ass!" The dog loomed up in the darkness and its body hurled forward and knocked me off balance. First I tried to cover my head, but its huge mouth ripped away at my arms. In desperation I grabbed both jaws and tried to tear its face apart.

There were some bad moments after that, when the dog's howling and the cries of the man blended together, and I wasn't sure where the dog or the man or the path had gone. I was running again. I felt the bouncing rope bridge beneath my feet and I slipped and almost fell into the stream. But I did not stop running until I reached the inn.

9

I DID NOT USE THE OVERHEAD LIGHT IN MY ROOM, BUT
worked instead by flashlight. I washed and dressed the
gashes on my arms and legs and across my forehead
that way, propping the flash on the end table and
bringing a basin of hot water in from the bathroom.
When I was finished the water was a deep red. One
leg of my pants was in shreds, so I balled up the pants
and threw them into a paper bag for disposal later.
All the bloody rags went in there too. Then I turned
off the flash and sat in darkness at my east window.
Nothing moved outside; there was no flash of light and
no sound within the inn. My mind churned actively for
an hour, and sometime in the middle of the night I
fell into bed.

When I opened my eyes the clock on the dresser
said nine-thirty-five. I felt heavy-headed and miserable
and sorry I had wasted so much of the day in bed.
On the way down I stopped at Jill's door and knocked,
but she was out. I found Gould in the lobby, standing
in his customary place beside the register.

"Where are the others?" I asked.

"Miss Sargent went with Mr. Max for a walk along the creek. I doubt they'll be very long. What happened to your head?"

"It's nothing; I just bumped it. Is there a telephone?"

"Not here. You'll have to go into town for a phone."

"I think I'll do that."

"Have some breakfast first."

"I haven't even bought any supplies yet."

"I guess you'll have to raid the fridge then. You can buy some things in town and replace what you take later, if you want to."

I did have some breakfast, and it brought me back to life. Gould joined me for coffee and idle chatter. I had bigger things on my mind, and possibly Gould could help me fill in the blanks. But I have never excelled at handling multiple problems, and now too many factors were playing hell with my imagination to allow any meaningful talk. And the thing foremost in my mind at that moment was personal. The fact that Jill and Max were out together bothered me; I felt a stupid flush of teenage jealousy that was annoying and at the same time intriguing. No woman had roused that green-eyed monster in me in more than fifteen years. I decided to walk it off. The walk took me along the back streets of Gold Creek, past the crumbled remains of the corral, and along a trail below the mines. I felt like a man under a microscope. Quickly I looked up at the house on the ridge and saw that I *was* being watched. The man was standing in the shadows of the two big trees, looking my way intently. I raised my arm and waved to him, but he did not acknowledge my greeting or move in any way. I hurried along the path toward the ridge, but by the time I reached the top he was gone.

The house stood less than fifty yards ahead. From

this perspective it was even more impressive than the alluring glimpse from the road. There had been some obvious recent window work; some of the frames had been painted and the broken panes replaced, and the scaffolding still stood at the sides and rear where someone had been painting. The yard was thick with trees and undergrowth; *good cover for anyone who wanted to get in for a closer look*. I climbed the four steps, which were new, and crossed the porch, which wasn't. The boards creaked under my weight. The door was ornate and old-fashioned, with intricate carvings and a beveled oval glass in the center. A set of flimsy see-through curtains were drawn across the glass, but a set of heavier drapes remained open. I looked into the hallway. There were no people anywhere in sight, so I tried the large brass knocker set into the door just below the glass. The sound echoed inside but brought no response. I tried again, and when no one came I pressed my face against the glass and peered inside. Beyond the hallway, I saw an old-fashioned room heavily furnished with period pieces and a mantel lined with potted plants. Closer to the door was a flower arrangement. That was all I saw of the inside; I suddenly became uneasy and looked away. I tried the knocker again, not really expecting a response and not getting one. Then I walked down the steps and moved away from the house. At the rim I turned and gave the place a final look, and in an upper-floor window I saw the slight but unmistakable movement of curtains.

It was disturbing, but there was nothing that I could do about it. I couldn't have the people arrested; I couldn't even prove that they were my trackers, though I was sure that a close look at that black Oldsmobile would verify it. At the inn I looked around for Gould but couldn't find him. I drove in to the nearest town and wandered along the streets, looking for a good telescope. There were no telescopes, good or otherwise, so I had to go all the way to Pueblo. In one of the large department stores there I bought a deluxe model, which cost me more money than I like to think about. I visited a supermarket and bought some food. As an afterthought I called New York information, who could not find any listing for MacDougald and Barnes under any possible spelling of the name or under book publishers.

I remembered that it was Saturday. No school today. I called Judy from some gas station on the way back, told her where I was staying, that I was having a good time, and would be home in a few weeks. I arrived in Gold Creek in late afternoon. The place was as deserted as I had left it. I took the boxed telescope out of the trunk and hurried through the lobby. I thought I heard Gould moving around in his den, and I crept past the open door and up the stairs. Somewhere on the upper floor a radio was playing; as I reached the second landing I found that it came from Jill's room. I moved quietly past her door to my own room and immediately set up the telescope in the window facing east. I adjusted the tripod and placed a chair before it. After some experimenting I focused on the house. With the telescope I had about the same view as a man standing at the top of the ridge. I moved it slightly to my right, to the spot where I knew the garage opened from behind the house. The scope was going to work out great. I could probably read the numbers on a license plate, and at least I could tell if it was a Florida plate. But I knew I had let myself in for some long, boring work.

I proved that by sitting down and watching the house for more than an hour. In all that time nothing moved but the grass on the hill, stirred slightly by the wind. I tried switching my surveillance from the house to the garage and back, but that got boring too; by the end of the hour I was wondering if buying the expensive telescope had been a good idea after all.

Footsteps came along the hall and stopped at my door. I jerked open my closet door with the first knock and called, "Just a minute," while I was grabbing the telescope and pushing it—tripod and all—into the small compartment. It did not fit; the door would not quite close, but I let it go at that and went to answer the knock. Jill, standing alone in the hall, smiled as I opened the door.

"Dinner tonight?"

"Great," I said. "I bought some things. . . ."

"Yes, I found them."

"You seem to be getting stuck with all the cooking. I can't do anything about it but be sympathetic. I'm a lousy cook."

She shrugged and smiled. "Come down any time," she said.

I closed the door and began to change clothes. All the time I kept my eyes on the east window, but my thoughts were on Jill. The telescope would not help me there; that would take action of another kind. I had no idea how to handle it. I had to admit it: She had become far more important to me in a very short time than I had ever expected her to be. Now that I knew she was lying about her purpose here, my uneasiness with her was compounded. Somehow I had to find out. I thought of the balcony connecting our windows, and I opened my window and looked out. It looked very shaky; a few of the boards were missing entirely and some of the others obviously were loose. I sat in the windowsill, swinging my feet over the edge and touching the balcony with my toes. It creaked, like everything else in the hotel, but it might support me if I stayed near the building, where the braces were. I leaned out of the window and looked down the length of the building. A shade was drawn at Jill's room, but the window was unlocked and in fact was cracked open slightly. It was almost an open invitation, but my nerve failed me. I ducked back inside, finished dressing, and went down to join the others.

I avoided Jill, moving quickly through the lobby and seeking out the men in Gould's den. But the den was empty. I saw Max pass the window, then Gould came by, and the two of them stood in the little yard behind the inn, talking. I went to the fireplace, which was cold and half full of ashes. Gould apparently had been fussing with it; some of the ashes had been scooped out and there were some papers and fresh logs on the floor. He had done everything but arrange it and light it. I started to do that for him, but some of the papers looked like discarded mail, so I did not. It was mostly junk mail—circulars and advertising, and there was something from a Denver goldsmith—but I did not want to burn it without checking with him first. I looked around for an old newspaper, but in another minute Gould came in through a side door.

"I thought I'd light the fire," I said, "but I wasn't sure you intended to burn this mail."

"Go right ahead," he said, and I fired it up. In another minute we had a good blaze going.

"Where's Max?" I asked.

"He's got a headache. Went to his room till dinner."

In a way I was glad that Max would not be around before the meal. That would give me a chance to pump Gould about the high country and some of the mountain legends. Having heard it all many times, Max would only inhibit Gould, as he had the other night. Gould poured my drink, making it bourbon without asking, and joined me at the fireplace.

"Your tales really add something to this place," I told him. "The other day when Jill and I were hiking, I thought about those old miners all the way up."

He smiled, trying without success to hide his pleasure. "I always do too—or used to, before my leg went bad and stopped my climbing. Now I have to go by jeep when I go. There is a jeep trail up to Taylor's Gulch, you know; did I tell you that? I try to get up there two or three times a summer. But you're right, I never go up without thinking about everything that's happened here."

"The other night you started to tell us about a cave of gold."

"Caverna del Oro. It's one of Colorado's most famous legends, maybe the most famous of them all. It has all the elements. To begin with, it's really colored by time. Most of these mountain yarns go back at least eighty years, but Caverna del Oro dates from the time of the conquistadores, three hundred years ago. I'll tell you the legend first and then the fact.

"The legend: Somewhere in Colorado there is a fabulously rich mine located at the bottom of a very deep cave. The cave is a straight drop of a thousand feet, and at the bottom, two great oak doors mark the entrance to the mine. Behind those doors is a storeroom where the Spanish miners hoarded the gold they found. As the legend goes, the gold is worth thirty to fifty million dollars, though there's no way of telling. All we can do is guess, using whatever knowledge we have of Spanish mining. This legend was passed down by the Indians, who were enslaved by the Spanish and forced to work in the mine. When the Indians revolted, most of the Spanish were killed and the mine was lost. The few survivors either could not find the mine again or never tried.

"Now the fact: Many scholars in this state are convinced that Caverna del Oro does exist. Treasure hunters have been trying to find it for years; they've looked all over the state, but in recent years the search has centered in the Sangres near here. We know there was a lot of Spanish activity here. We know the Spanish made large gold discoveries here. Finally, a three-hundred-year-old journal found a few years ago in a Madrid junkshop pinpoints this area as the location of the mine. There is some question about the accuracy of the journal, but at least some explorers are taking it seriously. There are other things that point this way too."

"Other things?"

"Early in this century explorers found a deep cave, just like the one described in the legend. They were led there by an old Indian woman who told them the story as it had passed down among her people. The cave turned out to be a shaft. Several scientific parties explored it in the 1920s and '30s, but no one from those parties ever reached bottom. But they did find plenty of evidence of Spanish activity. An old skeleton in Spanish armor was found near the mouth of the cave. One of the explorers claimed he found other skeletons on the way down, but it was never verified. They did find old tools and other undeniable evidence of Spanish mining. And the mouth of the cave was marked with a Maltese cross."

"A . . . what?"

"It was an old Spanish symbol, the mark of a Maltese cross."

I waited for him to go on.

"So when they found this cave—in 1905, I think it was—they found this cave with the mark of the Maltese cross, there was quite a bit of excitement. But two or three expeditions failed to reach the bottom. It wasn't until much later that anyone actually got to the bottom."

"What happened then?"

"Nothing. There was no gold; no mine; no skeletons. A lot of these yarns get colored along the way, and it isn't until a scientific party checks it out that we know the truth. Whether Caverna del Oro even exists is still very much up in the air. But we're pretty certain now that it isn't at the bottom of the Marble caves."

"How far are those caves?"

"From here? Oh, thirty, forty miles, as the crow flies. More by car and jeep. Not too many people go up there any more. But that's the way those legends go; when they're hot, the hills are full of treasure hunters. When they cool off, so do the treasure hunters. Sooner or later somebody will find another cave and it'll start all over again."

"I guess there are a lot of caves in this part of the country."

"More than anyone can guess. The so-called experts figured they had all the caves mapped out, then they found another one that may be the biggest of them all. They haven't even finished exploring that one yet. That's fine with me; it keeps them away from here. I just wish I could still climb."

"What happened—to your leg?"

"Arthritis. I've had it ever since I was a young man, but the damn thing has really gotten bad the last couple of years. I probably won't be able to walk at all before long."

I was about to ask if doctors were making any headway on arthritis when Jill came to the door. "Willy won't be joining us tonight," she said; "his headache's worse."

The subject of Caverna del Oro had been exhausted anyway, and I was ready to eat. After dinner Gould joined us in the den for a touch of brandy, but the light atmosphere of our first evening together was missing. Gould obviously felt like an awkward third party, although it wasn't true and I rather wished he would stay. But he excused himself, and his departure did not change anything. Jill and I sat about eight feet apart. For a long time neither of us said anything. The fire burned down to red embers. Somewhere in the inn

I could hear someone moving around, but then that too stopped and everything was quiet and dark. Now we could not even see each other.

"I guess I'd better go up too," she said from the darkness. Still she did not move out of her chair. "It's so easy just to sit here; I think I could sit here all night."

But she didn't. In another five or ten minutes she stirred and moved toward the door. I walked her to her room.

"See you tomorrow?"

"Perhaps," she said.

She leaned forward and kissed my cheek, then went quickly into her room. I still had no idea how to handle her, and I was determined not to lose sleep over it tonight. In my room I took the telescope out of the closet and set it up again in the window. At night I knew it would be useless, but I was not yet tired and I wanted a diversion from the problem of Jill. In the valley the darkness was almost complete. I guessed that the old house had heavy drapes or darkened shades that allowed no light seepage, and I did not figure to get much use from the telescope at night. I watched the ridge anyway for about thirty minutes, and in that time I could not make out any movement or shape or light. I could not even see the outline of the house.

Finally I gave it up. I lay on my bed and the pillow felt cool and comforting under my head. It was about fifteen minutes later when I heard the noise. I had no idea what kind of noise it had been, only that it was sharp and had aroused me from the initial stage of sleep. I sat up in bed and listened. For a minute I heard nothing more, but when it came again I knew that it was the sound of a stone striking the window. I got up and looked down into the street; a black form moved beneath the window. I dressed quickly and opened the door to the hallway. As I passed Jill's room I saw that a steady light shone under her door. A board creaked under my foot, and I heard a movement inside her room, and the light went out. I moved down the stairs and through the lobby, being careful not to trip over any chairs. At the door I stopped and looked outside. Nothing. I went out on the boardwalk and pulled the door shut behind me. Amy stepped out of the shadows and came close to me. I stiffened, on guard for new tricks, but she held her finger to her lips and motioned me toward my car.

The only sounds we made the whole time were two gentle clicks of the doors closing. But I saw that Jill's window was up and both the curtain and the shade were open.

"Let's get out of here," Amy said.

I only sat, staring at her.

"Please . . ."

I could not keep the sarcasm out of my voice: "Running away from your husband again?"

She covered her eyes with her hand and swallowed hard. "Okay, so I lied."

"You want to tell me about it?"

She did not say anything. I started the motor, aware that I would wake everyone in the inn. The hell with it. I drove out of town, using my parking lights until I swung past the house on the ridge. Then I turned on my headlights. Soon we were over the hill and she began to relax.

But I pulled off in a little clearing just over the hill. "What are you stopping for?"

"I told you; I want to know what it's all about."

"Can't we do that while we ride?"

I did not say anything.

She too was quiet for a long time. Finally, in a voice that smacked of defiance, she said, "Okay, okay, so I was hired to watch you."

"That much I've figured out for myself."

She was surprised. In the light of my dashboard her face showed confusion.

"It wasn't that hard to figure," I said; "I'm abnormally suspicious of people anyway. Besides, you weren't all that good."

She was stung by that, and I drew a petulant satisfaction from her discomfort.

"So what made you decide to throw it in now?"

"I had a fight with my sister. That's a long story and I don't want to go into it, okay?"

I shrugged. "Who hired you?"

"I don't know. Some woman I've never seen before. She gave me two hundred dollars and a bus ticket to Virginia. I met a man there, and I rode with him until he decided to plant me. I'm supposed to get another two hundred now that it's finished, but . . ."

"But . . . ?"

"I don't want it; I won't take it."

"That's nice. Do you want me to make it up to you?"

That brought back her fire. "I didn't say that. Listen, goddamnit, I've put up with that kind of crap till I'm sick of it. I was just doing a job. I didn't even know you, okay? So get off my goddamn back."

I thought it over. "So you were to spy on me. Only when you found out how nice I am you changed your mind."

"Jesus." She looked at me with moist eyes. "You sure aren't making this easy for me, are you?"

"Why, was I supposed to?"

"Just why do you think I came back tonight?"

"Hell, how do I know why you do what you do? Maybe you always lay the men you spy on. Tell me, was that part of your bag of tricks too?"

It was a cheap shot and I knew it, but it was out and I couldn't get it back. Amy said, "Oh, you sonofabitch," pushed open the door, and lunged out of the car. She turned onto the dirt road toward Highway 96, walking briskly and never looking back. I caught her in less than a minute, slowing the car so that it rolled along with her as she walked.

"Look, I'm sorry," I said through the open window. "No more games, okay? I promise. Now get in and I'll take you anywhere you want to go; you tell me what you know and no more name calling. Fair enough?"

She got in without a word. I drove out to the highway in silence. We were still, after all, playing games. She was looking for a deeper apology and I was determined not to give it. We didn't say anything until the scattered lights of the small town appeared ahead.

"You can let me off anywhere along here, thanks."

"This is where you're going?"

"It'll do till I get there."

"And where is there?"

"Where I told you the first time."

"California? I don't think you can get there from here." My attempt at humor was weak; she didn't even smile.

"I'll run you on to Pueblo," I said; "at least you can get a bus there."

"Don't do me any favors. I've got no money for a bus anyway."

"What about the two hundred dollars?"

"Arnie took most of that before I left for Virginia."

I didn't say anything about Arnie or her friends. Now it occurred to me that there was a real danger of losing whatever information she might have. I tried to recoup. Almost kindly I said, "Why don't you tell me about this woman?"

But that was phony and she saw through it immediately. "I think I've told you all I want to tell."

There was another long silence; she withdrew, leaving me to ponder another opening. It never came. Soon we were in the small range of mountains, then we were heading downhill and across the wide plain toward Pueblo. I tried a couple of things but she did not respond. We came into the outskirts and passed the motel where we had stayed together; she did not even blink as we passed it. I stopped for gas. I apologized, sincerely this time. I asked her to talk with me. We were good over breakfast; we could have breakfast now, and have our talk, and afterward I would put her on a bus for California and it would be all over.

I went into the restroom. When I came out Amy was gone. Across the road a truck was just pulling out, heading west, toward the California that she was so anxious to reach.

10

I HAVE HAD MY SHARE OF POOR JUDGMENT, WHEN STU-pidity reigns and ego gets in the way of reason, but I honestly believe I have never handled anything so badly as my final confrontation with Amy. She had been almost eager to tell all, but I had driven her away with my dumb display of male ego, and without learning much more than I already knew. An incredible performance! I stood at the crossroads, watching the truck's taillights until they disappeared around a bend. Incredible! Bitterly I started back to Gold Creek. The ride was miserable. Only as I turned into the canyon did I begin to feel any relief.

Actually, the Amy thing had not been a complete waste. I now knew that someone *had* followed me across the country; that was no longer outside the realm of established fact. Someone cared enough about my movements to hire a girl, pay her four hundred dollars, and give her passage to a strategic point on my trip. Even then it was a calculated risk; they had no way of knowing for certain that I would pick her up. But that was a risk they had been willing to take; whatever the reason, it was that important to them. No matter now; it had worked and it was finished. I could assume that they would be watching my next step as well.

The next logical step was a careful examination of the ruins where I had found the initials of Robert Holland and the name Jake Walters cut in stone. And this time I would go alone, though that probably meant going at night. Gould had mentioned a jeep trail to Taylor's Gulch, but I doubted that I could find it in daylight, let alone at night. So I would have to risk a night climb along the mountain trail from Gold Creek. The prospect was not so frightening as it might have been; I knew the trail now, and though it was fairly steep in places, it was uncomplicated and there were no sharp drops. All it would take was a good flashlight and a little nerve.

By the time I reached the hill near Gold Creek it was after two. The events of the night had stirred my senses and I was not at all tired, physically or mentally. Already I had decided to try the climb tonight, partly a penance to myself for having blown it with Amy. I parked in the same clearing, but deeper, where my car could not be seen from the road. Then I hiked over the hill and down to the ridge, closing in on the old house from the south. I did not go any nearer to the house than necessary to get down into Gold Creek; the last thing I wanted was to be seen by anyone living there. Instead I cut directly over the ridge and down into the valley. Now the moon was high; I could clearly see the buildings below me. I walked in a long arc, joining the road at the edge of town. I came straight up the street toward the inn, thinking how easily I could be seen now from my bedroom window. Knowing that there was no one watching from that window made me feel better. But I noticed that Jill's window was now closed and the drapes were drawn. The red Volkswagen was gone too. Softly I walked up the boardwalk, opened the front door, and stepped inside. The inn was as quiet as a tomb; in fact, I had a strong feeling that the inn was completely empty. I fought down the urge to shout, "Is anybody here?" and got on with my business. I found a pencil beside the cash register and wrote a note to Gould, saying that I had errands in Pueblo and would be gone for perhaps two days. The die was cast. I recognized the dangers inherent in such a plan and I accepted them. If anything happened to me—be it broken leg, snakebite, or whatever—there would be no search, at least for several days. There would also be no interference. I crept upstairs to my room, dressed for the part, and slung my backpack over my shoulder.

A tremor moved along my spine as I crossed the rope bridge and moved up the trail past the hippie camp. Clearly I was not cut out for this game. But I pushed ahead; the trail began to climb and the rocks loomed up, and then I was over that first great hump. The security of knowing that the town was just behind me dissolved. I was alone and now I knew it. That fact bothered me more than anything else. My flashlight batteries were good and the darkness did not worry me at all. As I climbed higher, there was more light from the moon and stars, and in some places I didn't even need the flash. The climb seemed shorter, though I know it must have taken me as long as the first time. I only stopped to rest once, but my pace was slower now that I had no Jill to push me. The eastern sky was getting pink as I cleared the last hill and saw that final gradual rise to the plateau. Still, it was another hour before I reached the ruins of Taylor's Gulch.

I had timed it perfectly. The sun was up and the dew was melting off the grass, leaving a pink-blue haze over the place. I walked along the twisting road to the top, past the jeep trail, past the cabin, and for future reference I tried to get a fix on where the jeep road came out below. It disappeared into a tall stand of timber and I lost it there. The road did not look too difficult, but I doubted that a car could make it. I moved into the upper part of town and felt a surge of anger. A jeep was parked just off the street. Someone was here.

I had never seen the jeep and had no idea who the owner might be. Slowly and quietly I went through the streets, looking in each building as I went. I wasn't anxious to meet my shadow, whoever he might be, suddenly and by accident in this lonely place. But I had no intention of turning back or hiding in the bush until he left. My eyes scanned each crack and corner for some movement, and with every turn I felt more edgy. By the time I reached the center of town I was so nervous that even a woman's voice made me jump.

"All right, Jim, what are you doing here?"

I jerked around defensively. Jill was climbing down a rough trail about thirty yards behind me. She was smiling, but there was annoyance in her smile, as though I had caught her in some very private act. For a moment I didn't know what to say. What I did say was, "I could ask you the same question. Where'd you get the jeep?"

"I rented it two days ago. It's been parked in town. And I've already told you what I'm doing."

"Oh, you mean shooting pictures."

"That's right. You just spoiled my best one, you know. I told you I want to show the desolation of this place; that means no people."

"I didn't know you'd be here. I'm sorry."

"Okay, I can still get it if I hurry. My camera is set up there"—she pointed up the mountain trail—"so if you'll just stay out of the way for a couple of hours I'd appreciate it."

She turned away from me and climbed up toward

her perch. Now I could see her tripod nestled among some mountain underbrush. I followed her up and paused while she reloaded the camera. Clearly she was in no mood for conversation, and I reasoned that the sooner I got away from her, the better for both of us. "I'll probably do less harm if I'm behind you," I said. She nodded.

"Maybe I'll just climb along the trails above town for a while," I said. "Do you know where they go?"

"Some of them just drift around. I think the main trail is maintained by the forest service. Mr. Gould told me it was built for hikers. It goes fifteen or twenty miles into the forest."

I brushed past her without another word and did not look back until I was about fifty yards away. She was working intensely over her camera, changing positions and settings and shooting all the while, and she never once looked at me while I watched her. It was a great display of authenticity, and it would have impressed me no end had I not just learned that her publisher, MacDougald and Barnes, was another part of the fairy tale. I found the forest path easily enough. It rose above the town and was marked with neat signs, white lettering against brown. The letters said MISSION, 4 mi.; HOWARD FALLS, 12 mi.; RANGER TRAIL, 17 mi. The trail dipped and turned sharply, running parallel with the town along the face of the mountain. From there Jill was visible for a long time. Only once did she look up. I waved to her, but either she did not see me or she was ignoring me. She huddled over her camera and went on with her work. I climbed above the stone building and the saloon, but now, strangely, I had no inclination to explore the town any more. Again I felt that magnetic pull, stronger than anything before it, but it led me along the forest trail and away from the town. I looked one more time at Jill and saw that she was still working. Then I climbed quickly along the trail, and both the girl and the town slipped from my sight.

Ahead was a panorama of untouched wilderness. The trail, lined with stones, climbed higher; the mountain sloped gradually away from it into a lush valley. Another range of mountains rose from the valley floor, running north and south until it was engulfed at both ends by swirling white mist. As I climbed higher and my breath came in heavy gasps, I became impatient to get wherever I was going, and I knew where that was even if I didn't quite know the way. The stones lining the trail petered out. Two paths branched away, one going higher up the mountain, the other dropping down toward the valley. I ignored them both. The main trail peaked and started down. I was on the other side of the mountain now, but I had lost all track of time. I had no idea how long I had been climbing or how far back I had left Taylor's Gulch.

I came to the place called Mission some time later. It was a natural rock formation, with all the appearances of a real mission from the top. As I came closer, the illusion dissolved and the rocks became just rocks. The path forked there, and for the first time I had doubts about going on. But I did go on, staying with the main trail, dipping below the mission rocks and below timberline. The trees closed in on all sides; small pines grew up alongside the path and partly blocked it in places. I was deep in the forest, where the trail was used only by hardcore hikers; signs of people, fairly common before, became scarce. There were no bottles or beer cans and only occasional remains of old campfires just off the trail. The path hit bottom and started up another mountain. It was hardly a path any more; just a thin line across the wild grass. Again I rose above timberline, and the bald dome of the mountain spread out before me.

I saw a flock of buzzards and wondered what had

died. My eyes shifted to the sun, high in the sky; to the north I saw an ominous formation of black clouds. I remembered what Gould had said about storms, but I knew I was getting close now and I pushed ahead faster. My breath preceded me in white puffs. I stayed with the trail across a snow-spotted clearing, then a tumbling stream caught my eye and lured me along it up the mountain's backside. The stream poured out of a crack in the mountain wall and plunged underground in a pile of stones and undergrowth. I clattered over the rubble and found myself on a stone trail that ran deep into the crack, concurrently with the stream. Soon the flowing water covered the trail, and rock overhead partly blotted out the sun. I was ankle-deep in the water before I saw the end. There the rock above broke away and the sun revealed a sandy bottom and a waterfall. The stone trail skirted the sand and wound among the rocks behind the falls, ending at the mouth of a small cave.

I did not know why I was so excited; I only knew that I was. I fumbled at my backpack for my flashlight and almost dropped it in my eagerness. I played the light into the cave and moved slowly ahead. The opening was tight; twice I had to crawl on my hands and knees. About fifty yards in, the hole opened into a large room and I could stand again. I was in a circular chamber, perhaps half the size of a normal house. There were signs of some habitation; an old fireplace, several yellowed newspapers, and two sets of initials spray-painted on the rock. Already the dampness was working the paint off, and I knew the initials would not last another year. I studied them, but they meant nothing to me. I followed the walls around to the passageway, then went around again, looking for any crack or hole that might be a continuation of the cave. There was nothing.

That was where it ended.

But it couldn't be!

I went around the walls a third time, feeling the rock with the fingers of my free hand. Nothing. I played the light higher, to the ceiling. That was the end of it. Suddenly a great weariness came over me and the strain of the long climb took its toll. I sank to my knees, a lump forming in my throat. The flashlight dropped to the floor with a clatter, rolled against the rock wall, and lay there shining at nothing. My hands trembled, and the shakes spread along my back and down my legs. I lay back against the wall, breathing hard, completely exhausted. I realized then how I had made the climb without stopping; it was a form of light self-hypnosis, and it had left me physically and emotionally drained. It was so easy to rest now, to forget it. But I didn't forget immediately. I lay with my eyes half closed, staring at the hazy beam from the flash, thinking, *so this is it, this is the end of it,* and wondering how my subconscious would react to that decision. I would leave this goddamned place in the morning. Tonight, as soon as I reached the inn, I would burn the photographs. The gold coin would go into the stream, no matter how valuable it might be. When I got home I would burn the Holland tapes and I would never again open any unmarked envelopes. If it persisted, I would see a doctor; plain and simple, that was how I would fight it. And if I never did any of those things, thinking of them now brought a small spark of relief. I thought it through again and tried to draw more comfort from it, but it was gone the second time. As I closed my eyes, the last thing I saw in my mind was Vivian, sitting in our old apartment telling Judy her vile code of life, while Robert Holland and I played poker with faceless men in a distant, darkened room.

I have no idea how long I slept. My eyes fluttered open, and I saw at once that my flashlight had dimmed to almost nothing. My head rested on my arms, and my legs were curled under me. I sat up with a jerk, grabbed the flash, and played it around me; there was hardly enough power left to show the walls. I got up. My legs were cramped and my muscles ached, but the weakness and trembles were gone. I felt my way along the wall to the passageway and crawled out to the opening. What I saw as I emerged under the falls was terrifying: snow blowing, swirling between the canyon walls, piling up against the rocks at the mouth of the cave. I struggled down the water-covered pathway and came out on the grassy mountainside. The pink morning light was gone; in its place was a gray nastiness that had settled over the mountaintops and was coming in like a giant rolling pin.

Already the mountains across the valley were almost obliterated by the mist. Snow swirled around my head, melted at once, and left my face slippery-wet. I stood there for a full minute, undecided about trying to reach Taylor's Gulch before it really broke. I would be safe in the cave if I just took Gould's advice; hole up and wait it out. In the morning it would be over and I could pick my way leisurely down the trail. That was the sensible thing to do, and I probably would have done it had I not remembered Jill. When I didn't come back she might well come looking for me; yes, she would come and risk being lost herself while I was safe in a cave. So that option was out and there was no use thinking any more about it. I was wasting time. I shifted my backpack and started quickly down the trail. Snow was just beginning to stick as I reached the bottom and started up along the face of the mountain. A wind had come up too; it was stinging my nose and ears. The thought of frostbite was sudden and alarming; I had no protection for my ears; my skullcap partly covered them, but I had no muffs or flaps, not even a rag that I could tie around my head. Like a man in a Jack London story, I had overlooked one tiny detail; I had misjudged the country despite the warnings. Now I tried to make up for it by running. I only slipped, losing more time than I gained. All the while that deadly looking white mist closed in around me.

I think I expected it to hit me with a frigid blast that would knock me to the ground. It wasn't like that at all. The mist passed over and around me like a great cloud, but there was no immediate increase in the snow or the wind. That came later, just past Mission, when the snow pounded me so hard that I could not open my eyes. I just stood and waited for it to let up, but for a time I was afraid there would be no letup. The wind drove the snow in a tiny cyclone around my head; the snowflakes melted as they hit my face, and the water seeped under my eyelids, blurred my vision, and ran down my cheeks. Then it passed and there was a time of almost total calm. That lasted less than a minute, just long enough for me to shift my backpack and start *the wrong way* down the trail. I stopped. How could I be going the wrong way? How could I have gotten turned around? But the canyon dropped away to my left, as it had all the way up; so waiting for the snow flurry to pass, I had somehow turned myself around during those minutes when I thought I had been standing still. I turned around and again everything made sense. That was another bad sign, another grim reminder that I was losing this deadly game with the mountain.

I did not have much time or energy left, so I pushed on at a steady pace. Twice I slipped off the path. The first time I went down only to my knees, but it happened again in a more serious place. The path had narrowed and the slope was steeper here. I fell fifteen or twenty feet down the mountain, pushing snow with me until a treetrunk stopped my fall. I braced myself against the tree and looked down; another mistake, because I couldn't see anything *down there,* and the vision that formed in my mind was of a sheer drop and only this tree between me and it. I moved my foot, and the tree gave slightly under my weight. That tightened every muscle in my body; my knees burrowed into the snow and my fingers clawed under it, feeling for a hold in the brown mountain earth. I gripped a clump of grass and cried out; the cry was lost in the wind. I moved again, and the ripping sound I heard might have been imaginary or it might have been roots tearing out of the earth. It didn't matter; I heard it clearly, and that was enough to bring another useless scream up from my gut. But the wind whipped my voice around my head, and even I could hardly hear it.

I lay there panting, hallucinating, dreaming that I had fallen into a silky bed somewhere and could sleep all day. I came back to reality with a jerk, the way a truck driver will jerk when he catches his head bobbing on a busy freeway. When I opened my eyes again I thought darkness had fallen. The mist had cleared away above me, but the mountains were black outlines beyond it. The thought of night falling while I was propped on that slope was too much to bear. I pushed down hard against the tree and there were more ripping sounds, but it did not give. I did not look down again; I kept my eyes on the path all the time I was clawing and pulling my way up to it.

Jill came along just as I had cleared the edge and flopped over on my back onto the path. I saw her from a strange perspective, my face pressed into the snow, and at first I thought she must be another hallucination. I blinked but she did not disappear; she came closer, then knelt beside me and asked if I was okay. I gasped out something, I don't remember what, and I felt her hands on my belt, pulling my legs over that final hump where they had been dangling. For a long time I just lay in the snow while she rubbed my cheeks and ears.

"You going to make it?" she asked.

"How much farther?"

"Thirty minutes. Maybe less."

I struggled to my feet. Now the walk was very tough; my left foot felt numb and I didn't make good time. She led the way, pausing occasionally to warn me of a slippery place. By the time we reached the bluff overlooking Taylor's Gulch a premature dusk had fallen and I could hardly see the outlines of the buildings. We crossed the flat above the town and started down. The trail from the bluff into the town was much steeper than I remembered and we slid most of the way, landing together in a pile of snow at the foot of the alley. Quite without warning I began to laugh. Jill lay on her back, breathing very hard and apparently unable to see the humor of it. Then she laughed too. She rolled a small ball of snow in one hand and threw it at me, hitting me squarely between the eyes. That set us both off; we laughed insanely for a full minute. Then, with a great effort, I got to my feet and pulled her up.

I stood in the desolate street of the ghost town and wondered what to do. Both of us must have been thinking about the long journey down to Gold Creek, but nothing was said. I assumed that it was out of the question and let it go at that. We pushed ahead into the town; I mentioned something about a place to spend the night and she didn't argue. By the time we reached the stone building the storm had settled in for the night. We crawled inside and I collapsed just below the window where "Jake Walters" was cut into the stone.

"We can't stay here," Jill said.

"I know it," I said, and I did. The snow filtered

down through the cracks in the timbers. The boards creaked, and all around us was wet and drippy.

"We could sit in my jeep," she said.

I didn't say anything, and for a time she was absolutely still beside me. A large lump of snow dripped from the boards and splattered against the back of my neck. I was too tired to reach up and scoop it off. I turned my head to look at Jill, and the water dripped down my back. She was not even a silhouette in the darkness.

"What about that cabin?" Her tone was impatient now.

"We'd probably have to break in."

"So what?"

"My flashlight batteries are about shot."

She opened her backpack and pressed her flash into my hand. The beam was strong, and that was the end of the excuses. We charged into the storm again, half sliding down the alley to the main street. From there it was a long walk through the upper part of town to the rim where her jeep was parked. In places the snow was knee-deep, and it was a wet snow that gripped our legs and could not be kicked aside. The walk took at least ten minutes, and even when we had reached the jeep I could not see the cabin for the blowing snow. "It's there!" Jill shouted above the wind. She took the light from me and led the way to the slope. The path was completely snowed under, but she found it as though she had committed its location to memory. She plowed through the unbroken snow, slipping twice, and both times I tried to push her from behind and slipped all the way down from the effort. At the edge of the cabin was a narrow level spot, and Jill had a long wait for me there while I struggled up the hill for the third time. The cabin looked strong and impenetrable. Of course the door was locked. There was a window on each side and Jill easily found the latch.

She broke a pane nearest the latch, reached her hand in, and flipped it open.

"Hold the light and boost me through," she said.

"I've just got two hands."

"Then put down the light."

She held up her leg for my hand, but she wouldn't fit until she took off her backpack. The second time she went through head first and hit the floor with a thud. I passed the light to her through the broken window. In another moment she had the door open and we were both inside.

11

THE CABIN HAD EVERYTHING BUT RUNNING WATER.
Somewhere, I reasoned, there was a generator that
would start the pump working, but I had no intention
of looking for it. There were two Coleman lamps,
which threw all the light we needed, and a stove that
operated on gas. That was enough for me. The gas
bottle was either empty or turned off, but that didn't
matter, because we didn't have anything to cook anyway. There was a wide double bunk, a couple of roll-
aways, and an old sofa that probably made into a bed.
A bathroom opened from the one large room. Later
I could melt some snow and bring in a bucket of
water, so we could at least flush the commode. We
would be here awhile.

Already Jill had collapsed into the bottom half of
the double bunk. She lay absolutely still, and just
when I thought she had either passed out or was
asleep, the lamplight flashed in her open eyes and she
raised her arm to her head. I went to the back door
and looked out. There was a woodpile, small but suf-
ficient if we used it carefully. It was covered and most

of the wood was old and dry; it had been here since last year, I guessed, and it would burn well. I took several small sticks and a few logs into the cabin and knelt over the fireplace to light them. Jill sat up as the flames began to warm us.

"Lovely," she said.

I nodded. "This cabin is better than the Hilton Hotel."

"We should pay the owners for the broken window at least." She came close to the fire and knelt beside me, warming her hands. "Are your clothes wet?"

"Probably. I'm so frozen it's hard to tell. My ears are really bad."

She was taking off her coat and feeling the sweatshirt beneath it. "Soaked through," she said. "God, listen to that wind."

"I can see why people get lost up here."

"We were lucky. What on earth made you climb so far?"

"Just got carried away, I guess. I can't say I wasn't warned."

Jill pulled off her sweatshirt. Under it she wore a flannel shirt, which almost came up with the sweatshirt. It stopped just short of her breasts, then flopped down over her stomach. She felt the arms and body of the shirt. "It's pretty damp, but maybe it'll be okay if I stay near the fire for a bit. How about you?"

I hadn't even started yet. "I'm still in shock," I said. I did take off my coat then and moved closer to the fire. I had worn only two layers of clothing, and my shirt was very damp and cold.

"Did you bring any extra clothes in your pack?"

"Just a couple of T-shirts and shorts. How about you?"

She shook her head. "I didn't plan on spending the week. Maybe you better get out those T-shirts and we'll put them on. It's probably best to have something dry next to the skin, don't you think?"

I did not think anything. I opened the backpack and took out the T-shirts, revealing the unopened bottle of bourbon beneath them. I passed one of the shirts to her and played perfect gentleman while she stood, turned away from me, stripped to the waist, and pulled the T-shirt over her head. My eyes never left the fire, but I sensed every movement. When she turned, so did I, and my eyes moved quickly up her body and met hers. She was smiling with her eyes, that alluring, concealing way she had. I saw at once, and so did she, that the shirt was almost twice her size, and she crossed her arms in front of her breasts as she came close to the fire.

"You'd better get yours on too," she said.

Mine fit snugly. Jill hung our clothes over chairs near the fireplace. She took a blanket from the bunk and wrapped it around my shoulders, then got the other one for herself. The blankets were very heavy and warm. For a long time we sat like that, without saying anything. Then she said, "Did I see a bottle of something in your backpack?"

"You might have. I packed it for emergencies."

"Wouldn't you call this an emergency?"

"I would." I threw off the blanket and rummaged in the cupboard until I found two glasses. "Water?"

"I guess I better. Scoop up half a glass of snow; that'll be fine for me when it melts."

The melted snow made less than a quarter of a glass of water. I poured her a stiff one and made mine even stiffer.

"How long since you've eaten anything?" she asked.

"I haven't even thought of food. I don't know when it was—last night's dinner, I guess."

I saw her point. Obviously she had not eaten during the day; the liquor would affect us both quickly. I savored mine; she finished hers first. She declined my offer of another, but when I had one she had one with me. We began to loosen up and both of us knew it and neither of us cared. She was taking her drink slowly now; I sipped mine steadily. We were feeling good.

"I don't even care any more," she said. "I am hungry, though."

"I wish I had something to give you."

She smiled and touched my cheek. "It's all right."

I poured her another half shot. The stinging taste of the first drink had long since worn away and the liquor was smooth and mellow. Jill was a little dizzy and clearly enjoying it. She laughed easily and her laugh was deep and sensuous. We began to talk about ourselves, but I tired of that because I could never be sure that what she was saying was the truth, and here, tonight, I didn't even want to think about that part of it. I listened, but when she asked about me I begged off until a time when I was more sober.

"You're too cautious when you're sober," she said.

"Yeah, well, so are you."

"I know it. I wish I could do something about that. I inhibit men. I really do, really; I always have. Men won't even tell a dirty story when I'm around."

I looked at her. "I would."

"Go ahead and tell one, then."

"What for?"

"Just for the hell of it. You tell one then I'll tell one. Then you tell another one and I'll tell another one. You ever played that game before?"

"What game?"

"It's called gross. The jokes get worse and worse and you see who grosses who out first."

I laughed. "You're high."

"I think I'm a little more than that."

I poured each of us a small, final shot and put the

cork back in the bottle. We played her game for a time, but in the end she was right: She did inhibit me. The jokes got gross to a point, and did not cross that point. My grand finale was a five-line limerick that I remembered from my college days:

A disgusting young man named McGill
Made his neighbors exceedingly ill
When they learned of his habits
Involving white rabbits
And a bird with a flexible bill.

She threw back her head and her rich laughter filled the room. Her head hit the floor and she was sprawled helplessly, laughing like that, for almost a minute. The shirt was up to her ribs, and it was the simplest, most natural thing at that point to reach over and touch the firm flesh around her navel. I did, and her laughter stopped at once. She looked up at me and her eyes were wet and unclear. She was not focusing well; she was not handling it at all. She covered my hand with hers, and I knew then that it would be all right, that there would be no problem unless one of us passed out. She tried to rise, but it was too much effort; she sank back and her head hit the floor with another dull thump. She giggled and I rolled my blanket and made a pillow for her head. She liked that; I liked her liking it. My hand touched her breast softly and she said, "Do you know the one about the man from Nantucket?"

"Yes, I know that one."

"Tell it."

"Not tonight."

"I'll tell it, then, except I can't remember the words. . . . There was a young man from Nantucket, something something, whose . . ."

"Hush."

"I told you I intimidated men." She rose and kissed my hand through her shirt. "This must be the new Parker Brothers' game."

I smiled. "It's called fondle."

I tried to carry her to the bed, but the John Wayne bit didn't become me. I slipped, dropped her, and knew that I wasn't in any better shape than she was. We each made it under our own power. A fitting end for my most strenuous day in years.

Sometime during the night my eyes fluttered open and I was wide awake. Jill stirred, and I felt her warm flesh next to mine and her head under my chin. She was breathing deeply. Across the room one of the Coleman lamps was still burning; it cast a semiglow over our bed. I shifted my body, and my hand dropped, only partly by chance, into her bare lap. I moved my fingers softly but she did not stir again. But before I could begin to think about it my attention was drawn outside by something else. What else? I don't know. I listened for a long time and the sound, if in fact it had been a sound, did not come again. All I heard was the wind and the unbroken rhythm of Jill's deep breathing. I decided to look around, though I truly hated to pry myself away from her. She rolled over and mumbled, "Where are you going?" as I got up, but I didn't say anything and she was asleep again at once. I poked the fire and added more wood and watched the flames lick at it, aware of a dull pain— the early effect of a hangover—behind my eyes. Then I moved to the opposite end of the cabin and put out the lamp.

With sudden darkness inside, I saw a light outside. I moved around the table and chairs for a closer look through the front window, but it was gone. I watched for perhaps fifteen minutes, but it never did come back. I went to the fireplace and felt my clothes; they were still damp. I dressed anyway, pulled on my boots, and went outside. The storm was as bad as ever; I moved a few steps away from the cabin and the snow swirled around my head. My visibility was limited to about thirty yards, though occasionally the snow flurries died away for a few seconds, allowing a good view of the dead buildings below. It was during one of those lulls that I saw it again, a quick flash of light somewhere up the mountain on the other side of town. Just a flashlight, perhaps, but who would be there in a snowstorm at this time of night? I half closed my eyes and peered into the misty gloom, and as it swirled past I saw a very faint glow directly across from me. The glow of a campfire? The mist covered it again, and for a time I considered crossing the valley to check it out. All things considered, that would be a damn fool idea, so I shelved it. But I wasn't satisfied.

Much later I went inside and undressed. I warmed myself by the fire before crawling in beside Jill, and she snuggled against me, sharing her warmth. But it was a long time before I could doze off, and I woke several times before falling into a heavy sleep just before dawn.

When I woke again Jill was gone. I heard the sounds of water splashing in the bathroom sink, and near the door I saw the dripping bucket she had used to carry it in. I lay still, and soon the bathroom door opened and she came out. She walked naked past the bed and turned away from me as she bent over and felt her clothes. Satisfied, she began to dress. I wanted to reach out to her, but some instinct stopped me. Instead I lay quiet and still while she dressed and went outside. When she was gone several minutes I got up. My muscles were sore, my head throbbed, and even dressing was a pain. I pulled on my boots, opened the door a crack, and peeped out. The sun was just breaking over the mountaintops and the light was harsh. It actually hurt. Everything hurt. I closed the door for a minute and went around the cabin, looking out of windows. I couldn't see anything, so I went outside.

During the night the snow had drifted high against the cabin, but now it had stopped and the sun was breaking through. There was still a slight wind and the morning was cold. I pushed through the snow to the rim and looked down at the town. Jill was directly below me, unloading equipment from her jeep. She took out her cameras and a large leather bag, then hiked up to the bluff where I had first seen her yesterday. And she began shooting pictures. I watched her for a few minutes, then stumbled back to the cabin and lay on the bed. My hangover was reaching its peak and I certainly did not feel like solving any mysteries. But the thoughts persisted. Maybe I *was* wrong; maybe there was a MacDougald and Barnes somewhere in New York. I very much wanted there to be, and that opened a whole new bag of problems. I knew then that I was letting her get too close to me; that couldn't happen until I knew what she really was. But it was happening, and there might not be anything, at this point, that I could do about it.

I fell asleep, still in my wet clothes, and I slept until I heard a thump outside. She kicked the snow off her boots and came in, whipping off her knitted hat and her coat in what seemed like one motion. "Get up, sleepyhead," she shouted, throwing open the window.

I dragged myself into a sitting position. "Holy Christ, what time is it?"

"Nine o'clock; time to be moving on. I am so hungry I don't think I can stand it another minute."

"Where do you get all your energy? Don't you even have a hangover?"

"I don't have hangovers. Ever. Hey, come on, get up and let's get back to town."

"Oh, listen, I'm not even alive yet."

"Come on, you've already got your clothes on. We can be back in one hour. You can have some aspirin or bicarb and I'll have some ham and eggs. That's all I need right now."

There was a pause while she regarded me and I gathered my wits. "Sleep well?" I asked.

She smiled. "Extremely."

We put the cabin in order, locked up, and climbed down the slope to the jeep. But leaving was another matter. For me it wasn't yet finished. Again I felt that magnetic pull, back to the cave, and I knew that once more I would have to play it out. A final try, and even I could not ask any more of myself than that. Nothing about it would be easy; I too was hungry and the temptation to drive away with her and forget it was strong. I knew too that she would argue with me, as she did.

"You must be crazy," she said; "the lack of food has affected your brain. Maybe it was the alcohol . . . or something else?"

"The combination of the three."

She was incredulous. "You can't be serious."

"My legs are cramping up," I told her. "If I don't walk the crinks out I'll probably be miserable all day."

"Well, I'm leaving; you do what you want to do. You know the way down."

She got into the jeep, started the motor, and gave me one last chance three more times. Finally convinced, she started down the road, pushing snow out of her way as she went. At the bottom of a short ravine she paused and blew the horn, but I did not respond and she moved ahead toward the bottom. I watched her until she was out of sight. The jeep handled the snowdrifts well, and far below, near the long strip of timber, the snow had already melted off and the road was clear. I climbed along the mountain opposite the cabin to a point almost directly in line with my lookout point in the early morning. I moved along in a straight line until I came to a half-concealed mine opening. It was the first one I had seen up close, and just what I expected: a black hole bolstered by roof and wall timbers. The hole became blacker as it went deeper, and I had no intention of going in. But just inside the mouth I saw a sign of human activity; it lured me in just enough for a closer examination. Yes, there were footprints, one clear set made by a man's shoes, and a concave place in the soft earth where, apparently, he had been sitting for a long time. At the mouth of the mine I saw the ashes of a fire burned so completely that I had walked through them without noticing. I held my hand to them and felt faint warmth. I guessed that they were between five and six hours old.

So someone had been here. But where was he now? I peered deeper into the mine and saw only a number of rocks and the rusted remains of a rail where miners had once driven ore-filled carts. There were no footprints leading any deeper than the makeshift camp. The place gave me a chill and I got out of there. I stood on the hill below the mine and watched the cabin, with no question in my mind that he had been able to see me much better than I had seen him. I felt watched even now. My eyes scanned the slopes around me, trying to pick out any movement; there was none. Quickly I moved down the mountain, and almost blundered into one of those deep shafts.

It was completely concealed by snow, underbrush, and rotted timbers. The first warning came when I stepped on a snow-covered timber and felt it give under my weight. I jumped back in panic, and my buttocks hit a slimy mixture of snow and mud and loose rock just as the earth seemed to open around me. I was sucked toward it; only by twisting around on my stomach and gripping a clump of underbrush close down, near the roots, was I able to save myself. All of the timbers and snow slipped into the hole, leaving my kicking feet dangling over the edge.

That left me emotionally drained. I pulled myself clear and got down the mountain, though later I never could remember how. When I opened my eyes I was sitting in the stone building, with "Jake Walters" cut into the wall just above my head. I was breathing hard, trying to force thoughts of gaping black holes out of my mind. But the gloom of the stone building only encouraged those thoughts, and that forced me again into the sunlight. I began to climb the north face, taking care to stay on the path, and soon I was on the stone-lined walk high above the town. The cold air helped clear my mind. Dwelling on near-escapes and men who watched me in the night would only stop me from doing what I had to do. It was a much longer climb than I remembered; even the trek to the Mission rocks seemed to take forever. Afterward there was still a healthy piece of ground to be covered. But I climbed steadily to the cave, stopping to rest only as I neared the canyon of the rushing stream. I waited there a long time while my eyes scanned the trail behind me. Nothing moved anywhere; even the wind was gone now and the mountains looked like a fine still photograph. The hell with it. I moved boldly into the canyon; if anyone wanted to follow me there he damn well would anyway. The water covering the canyon floor seemed colder today, but I splashed through it and moved straight up to the cave.

I took Jill's flashlight from my backpack and played it along the walls, crawling through to the big room. I went through the same motions as yesterday, feeling around the circumference of the chamber without finding any crack that might go deeper into the rock. The room was almost a perfect cylindrical chamber; the walls had been worn smooth, perhaps by some ancient water flow, and there was no indication that there had ever been more to it than this. But it followed that if flowing water had formed this cave there had to be someplace for the water to flow from. I moved the light beam across the ceiling. It was, I judged, thirty feet above the floor, and again there seemed to be no imperfections. Near an edge I saw it: a flat-looking rock jutting out from the wall. The rock was so close to the roof that it blended with the ceiling and seemed to be part of it. I took my rope from the backpack, tried to make a lariat, played out a long loop, and threw it up toward the rock. The rope collapsed inward and fell around my head. I tried again, with the same result. I tried perhaps fifty times and never came closer than the first time.

I was looking for a different approach when I saw a large oblong rock near the embers of the old fireplace. I tied the end of the rope around the rock and propped the flashlight upward on the floor, fixing the beam directly on the overhang. I threw the rock at the ceiling, letting the rope stream out behind. It hit the wall and bounced back. A dozen throws also went that way before, on the thirteenth try, the rope looped the overhang and dropped on the other side. I lowered the rock into my hands, made a slipknot, and pulled the rope tight. It felt solid. I snapped the flashlight to my belt and started to climb.

Nothing in this project was easy, but that climb was hell. After five minutes of intense struggle I hauled myself over the top of the rock and lay there, exhausted, in a flat space just large enough for a man's body. Ahead of me, through a tiny hole, the ceiling opened into another cave.

12

I CRAWLED TOWARD THE HOLE, HOLDING MY LIGHT out ahead of my body. The tunnel curved up from the ledge, and for a time all I could see was a curving wall of rock. I eased my body into the hole and, using both legs and my free arm, pulled myself slowly upright, sliding over loose rock and filling the narrow passageway with dust. When I was standing erect I clipped the flash to my belt, beam pointed upward, and began to climb. I was climbing straight up, using deep notches in the rock for footholds. On both sides of the hole the notches continued at regular intervals, spaced perfectly for my hands and feet. I had no doubt that they had been cut there. The rise was about twelve feet, curving gradually all the time, and at the top I crawled out into another large room.

It was almost a duplicate of the cylindrical room below, but this time the passage continued at floor level. It continued as a narrow crack, widening slightly, then narrowing and widening again. I heard water running beyond one of the walls, but I could not tell which one even by pressing my head against the rock.

I moved deeper into the cave, along a low passageway where the floor was very rough. Tiny stalagmites peppered the place, and once I came to a huge column of rock that extended from ceiling to floor. There was just enough room for me to squeeze past, and again I saw that there had been some cutting of rock; someone had been through here and had notched out the rock column so that *he* could pass. I stopped and played my light across the floor. The cuttings were still there; large chunks of rock obviously battered down by an ax. I picked up the pieces and looked at them, but there was no way of knowing how long they had been here. With the rock column behind me, the passageway started up again, gradually at first, then sharply. Soon it was another climb. I found some more broken rock, and about halfway up I picked up six old flashlight batteries. The ends were rusted out and I guessed that they had been here at least several years. I dropped them where I found them and moved ahead. The passageway turned abruptly and climbed even higher, but there at the turn the left wall was broken away and an immense cavern opened before me. My light was lost in it; there was no floor or ceiling or walls that I could see, just an endless pit of black space. The sound of falling water was very strong and at the same time distant, and a spray came up from the black depths. I cringed back against the one wall and edged past it, breathing hard as solid rock rose up around me again. I came to a crest and started down, and the walls pinched tighter around me. Twice I had to squeeze through very narrow cracks, and once I tore a layer of skin off my right arm getting through. But the cave squeezed itself off and at the next turn came to a dead end.

But there was no stopping me now. I found the crack that I knew was there, again a very small hole opening in the ceiling, and I pulled myself into a small tunnel of crawling room only. I was worming my way forward in a near frenzy, my sense of danger almost totally replaced by my urgent need to get to the end of it. The tunnel went like that for about twenty yards and ended at a wall of packed snow.

A great excitement came over me, much as I had known yesterday with my first discovery of the cave. I pushed against the snowpack, but it had frozen on this side, and it held fast to the rock. I bent my head and got my shoulder into it, heaving upward with my legs until it broke away and sent me sprawling into the raw sunlight.

And there, not five inches from my face, was a sheer drop, hundreds of feet down. I had fallen out onto a ledge and was so close to pitching over the edge that I screamed out in terror. My voice came back at me as a hideous echo. The canyon yawned up at me; far below I saw a stream and rocks and trees blending together in a sickening, reeling blur. I was frozen to that spot; I literally could not move. Only gradually did my eyes focus, and then I saw a waterfall and another rushing stream. I could see too where the mountain turned and blocked the canyon from the trail to Taylor's Gulch. I saw all those things encompassed in that sheer drop, and I reacted instinctively, pushing myself back from the edge. But my hands pushed against air. I knew then that I had been stunned by the fall; my hands had missed the edge completely and I had hit the rock ledge squarely on my face. I felt my mouth; it was sticky with blood. The blood ran from my nose and from another cut somewhere on my forehead; I took out a handkerchief and tried to stop it. With my eyes closed I lay that way until the bleeding seemed to stop. I turned my head then, without moving my body, and opened my eyes. A second shock spread through me. Without doubt, I was looking down the trail of the photographs.

This was it, but it was the end of it for me. Somehow I eased backward from the cliff and squeezed my body into the hole. The cave swallowed the sunlight quickly, and I used the flashlight to guide my feet down the tunnel to the larger cave below me. Once I almost dropped the flash; it slipped from my fingers and banged against the wall. In near panic I rescued it before it could roll down to the lower level. I was a fool, a goddamn amateur fool, to come here alone with only one light. On the lower level I rested until I could stand without holding the walls. Then I scrambled down to the ground and got the hell out of there.

Another dusk over Taylor's Gulch, and the gloom of early evening had settled into my soul as well. During the long trek back I consciously weighed it and made my decision: to leave Gold Creek in the morning. Enough was enough. *They,* whoever they were, could fight it out, whatever it was, without my help. Coming along the trail above the town, I saw Jill's jeep parked in the same spot below the cabin. A light bobbed behind the cabin, and in a moment she came around and looked in through the broken window. She saw me as I started down, and she came down to meet me. At the jeep she waited for me to come to her. She had changed her clothes and tied back her hair; she was fresh and lovely, and angry.

"Just don't speak to me, okay?" She hurled that at me across the valley floor. Softly she said, "I'm not talking to you."

I came close to the jeep; she opened the door for me and I fell into the passenger's seat. "Thanks for coming," I said; "I couldn't have gone much farther."

"You deserve to get lost. What happened to your face?"

"I took a spill; nothing serious. What I need now is a bath and something to eat."

She was still quite indignant, but she closed the door gently and got in on the driver's side. "There are some sandwiches and a thermos of soup in that bag; you eat while I drive." With that we left the ghost town for the last time. By the time I thought to look back, the last light of day had gone and there was nothing to see. She drove the jeep with skill, following her own tracks into the long forest at the bottom of the mountain. There the snow had partly melted off and the potholes gave way to a heavy growth of weeds which threatened in places to choke off the road completely. A stream ran across the road and she plowed through that without hesitating. Then the road straightened and smoothed slightly and she used her bright lights.

"I guess you're not going to tell me about it," she said.

"About what?"

"Please don't play stupid. It doesn't become you and I don't like it."

I thought about that for a minute. "Then I guess I don't have anything to say right now," I said.

"At least that's honest."

"Say, are you mad at me?"

"I'm a little upset, yes. I guess it never occurred to you that I might worry when you didn't come down."

I was surprised. "No," I said; "it never did."

The road twisted for another five miles and we took the rest of the drive without speaking. The jeep road dropped sharply and joined a graveled automobile road, which in turn hit State 96 just west of the Gold Creek turnoff. As she figured it, the total drive was just over an hour; it was after eight when we arrived at the inn. Jill got out of the car and walked briskly to the door, waving to me as I went quickly past her, through the lobby, and up the stairs. There was nobody around, and for that I was thankful. A shower took off the caked blood, but the nosebleed started again. I rested with my head down until it stopped. My head injury was a small but deep cut at the hairline; it too began to bleed and I covered it with a bandage.

Soon Jill came to the door, carrying a tray of food and apologizing for the sandwiches. She sat with me while I ate; an uncomfortable silence fell between us. I took my meal slowly because I wanted her with me and I couldn't think of any other reason to keep her here. The events of the day had washed out the effectiveness of the night before. In my mind we had regressed; we had not slept together, and now that first-line communication had to be done again, the words said over, without the stimulations of a snowstorm and a bottle of bourbon. The bourbon was still in my backpack, but now it seemed so inappropriate that I did not mention it. That was just as well, for Jill did not share my need for communication. She took the dishes away when I had finished, but fifteen minutes later she returned, put out the light, and slipped into bed beside me.

The contrast between this and our first time was remarkable. Now she just lay beside me until I fell asleep, and it was warm and good in an asexual way. She did not even undress. Sometime during the early evening she left me; she was gone when I awoke, and I could see by my clock that hardly two hours had passed. The hands stood squarely at ten-fifteen. I went to the doorway, looked out into the hall, and listened. Downstairs I heard voices; someone laughed. I moved to the head of the stairs, where I could hear them clearly. The three of them were there, having a nightcap in the den. I resisted the temptation to join them and returned to my room. I got out the telescope and for a time tried to scan the valley, but even the full moon helped little in this place and I gave it up. Bored with that but still restless, I thought of the balcony. I got the flashlight from my backpack, opened the window, and sat on the sill. Again, for a long time I contemplated the walk across the shaky boards to Jill's room, and this time I decided to try it. The balcony creaked under my weight but held fast. Once committed to it, I walked the thirty feet to her window quickly, keeping to the inner edge and watching my step. I found the window cracked open slightly; I lifted it, parted the curtains, and stepped inside.

The room was completely dark. I debated risking lights, decided against it, and brought out the flash. A quick look around showed that her bed was made and the room was in generally a neater state than mine. The layout, other than the fact that I had two windows, was identical to my room. I moved to the dresser and played the light across the top. There were a few bottled cosmetics, a lipstick, and a hand mirror; nothing else. I eased open the top drawer and saw a variety of undergarments. The other drawers contained clothes, and I felt them without disturbing their arrangement, to be sure that nothing was hidden beneath them. Then I moved to the closet. It contained her hiking boots and some photographic equipment, an extra pair of shoes and a dress coat that I had never seen her wear. I closed the door softly and felt my way around the bed. I was kneeling on the floor when I heard the footsteps. They came so quickly that trying for the window was impossible. I ducked under the bed, pushing aside a large suitcase, and waited for her to enter. The steps stopped outside and I held my breath. A key turned in the latch and I realized that it was Max, going into his room across the hall. He was there for less than a minute, then he came out and returned to the lower part of the inn. I pulled myself from beneath the bed and dragged the suitcase out with my free hand. It was not heavy; I guessed that the clothes it bore were stored in the dresser. Still, it was locked, and that fact was enough to send me searching for the key. I felt under the dresser doily and along the closet shelving but finally found it in her purse in a drawer of her night table. The main storage compartment of the suitcase was empty, but in a slip pocket I found some papers and a little leatherbound book. The book was so familiar that I put it aside habitually, as though I had read it many times before. I looked through the papers, letters addressed to Jill either at her Bridgeport home or at some New York firm called Smith and Lorenzen. All of them had been slit open, and I was about to examine them when I heard another noise on the stairs. Quickly I put them in order and placed them in the suitcase pocket. Again, for an indecisive second I held the book in my hands. It was *so* familiar . . . and then I had to know. I could tell by the creaking boards that she had reached the top of the stairs, but I flipped open the book and scanned the first page from the bottom up. In the upper right-hand corner I saw the handwritten name *Robert Holland*.

The fourth Holland journal.

Her footsteps passed the door and continued down the hall to my room. I knew she would return at once, but the Holland book worked a momentary paralysis on me and I was slow to react. At last I dropped it in with the letters, locked the suitcase, and pushed it under the bed. I heard Jill's muffled voice call my name, then she came back up the hall toward her room. I tiptoed around the bed and replaced the key, then the purse, closed the table drawer, and hurried across the room to the window. I must have closed the window just as she opened the door, and I flattened myself against the outer wall as she turned on the light. There was a moment of indecisive silence; she was absolutely quiet, and I wondered if I had left everything in order. Then I heard a bottle drop; she said, "Damn it," and a few minutes later the light went out and she sat on the bed. There was a dragging noise, as though she had pulled the suitcase out from under the bed, then more quiet, for what seemed an interminable time. It was broken only when the front door of the inn opened, directly under my feet, and Gould and Max came out on the boardwalk.

They stood there for a moment without speaking, and I held my breath. Finally Gould breathed deeply and said, "Well, it's your decision, Mr. Max, and I know I can't influence it. But you won't find nights like this back in Philadelphia."

"I know it," Max said.

From inside I heard the sound of the bedsprings. She came to the window and I pressed my body as flat against the wall as I could get. I saw her fingers on the sill, then touching the bottom of the window frame, as though she intended to raise it. I braced myself for a confrontation, but instead she moved back into the room.

Softly I let out my breath.

"My time here always goes too fast, Harry," Max was saying. "I wish I could have got to know your other guests better. Especially Miss Sargent."

"She's lovely," Gould said.

"Ryan too," Max said. "I'm afraid I put him off that first night with all my talk of extraordinary achievement. Now that I look back on it, that all sounds stuffy and pretentious."

Gould laughed. "Always a student of people, aren't you?"

There was another short silence, then Gould excused himself, with more regret at Max's planned departure. For a time Max stood alone on the boardwalk; when he did move, it was not back into the inn but out along the street. He stopped at the old corral, still sipping his drink. His back was turned to me and I took advantage of the break, quietly crossing the balcony to my window.

My mind was so full of the discovery of the Holland journal that I hardly thought of my narrow escape. I flopped into bed, but an all-consuming restlessness forced me to the window again. Max was gone, but that hardly mattered now. The Holland journal was the most startling break I had had; it dominated my thinking. And yet my mind could not settle on any single aspect of it or on any possible answers. My thoughts just churned around it and gave me no rest. At last, still feeling miserable from the long day, I went downstairs and rifled the refrigerator. Before I could settle on anything Max came in.

"Jim," he said from the doorway, "I'm glad you're here. I have to leave tomorrow and I was hoping you'd join me for a nightcap."

I could not refuse him, though I did not feel at all like making small talk. A quick one, then, and I would beg off and try to somehow get some rest. I mixed myself a very light drink, not really wanting that, and Max adjusted the den lights at a very low level. That suited me perfectly. We sat facing each other in the same chairs Jill and I had used two nights ago, and I waited for him to say something.

"You got a bit banged up."

I brushed that off.

"Climbing can be like that. I'm sorry we didn't get to talk more. I'm afraid I make a poor first impression."

"Not at all," I said.

"Be that as it may, I wanted you to know that I'm not really the stuffed shirt I sometimes seem to be. You asked what I do for a living—I'm an architect."

I shrugged and smiled, wanting to put it aside. "And now—you're leaving?"

"Early tomorrow. I can only justify this for so long,

then I have to get back to my life. Christine—my wife—is planning some social thing in Philly next weekend, and I think she'd be unhappy if I stood her up." He puffed at his pipe. "I take it you're not married?"

I shook my head. "Not any more."

Almost to himself he mused, "All things considered, I'd rather be here than in Philadelphia. There's an old story that W.C. Fields put that on his tombstone. If it's true, I think I understand it."

"If you feel that way, why don't you move here?"

"It would mean the end of things that I'm not prepared to give up. My marriage, for one. Children, civic responsibilities, things like that. Things I enjoy until I'm around them too long. Besides, if I lived here, where would I go for my two-week getaway?"

I saw his point, and I decided that after all I did like him. His initial coldness wore off quickly as our second talk progressed. His smile, on a one-to-one basis, was friendly and warm; in a group of strangers it had been somewhat disarming. Willy Max was not a man of crowds; I understood that now and I knew why his mountains were so important to him.

"I'm leaving too," I said softly.

"But you just got here."

"I know, but the country is a bit too much for me. I had a few narrow escapes today."

His eyebrow arched and he sat forward in his chair.

"I almost tumbled into a mineshaft," I said.

"Jesus, didn't Harry tell you about those?"

"Oh yes, he warned me, all right; I just forgot."

"That's a bad mistake—but I guess you realize that, now." He emptied his glass and stood. "Well, it's too bad anyway; you're going to miss a lot of fine country by leaving so soon. Now I guess I'll turn in. I've got a long trip tomorrow." He offered his hand and I took it. "It wasn't much, but I'm glad we had this talk, Jim. I hope I'll see you again sometime."

He walked out of the room and up the dark stairs. I returned to the refrigerator and made a ham sandwich, then sat in the dark at the bar and ate it and drank a cold beer. I tried again to think through my options. Clearly there were only two: to stay or to go. Both seemed inconceivable. That old depressed restlessness came over me, and I knew that I could no more turn away from it now than I could have long ago in West Virginia. It was a clear choice of the lesser of two evils, and now that I had made the commitment, now that I had found Robert Holland's fourth journal, now that I had reached the trail of the caves, there could be no double-cross of that commitment. There were several beachheads to attack, and I did not know which one to handle first, or, in fact, how to go about any of them. Strangely, it was not the Holland journal that bothered me now; that would be there when I wanted it, and I would have another go at Jill's room as soon as I saw an opening. What was bothering me was the trail of the caves. That was the one part of it that I could not handle alone. Sometime after midnight I made that commitment too. I felt my way upstairs and stopped just outside Jill's door. There was no sound anywhere in the inn. I turned to Max's room and rapped three times lightly. A bedspring creaked and a light went on. In a few seconds Max opened the door, looking very sleepy and slightly annoyed.

I held my fingers to my lips. "I need help," I said in a whisper. "Can we talk?"

13

"T HAT'S QUITE A STORY," MAX SAID.

We were sitting in the darkness of his car, the one place where I knew we would not be overheard. The two photographs of the mountain trail were in my lap. I had not intended going quite this far with it, but once I started to tell it I had to fill in the gaps to maintain credibility. Piece by piece, then, it came out, the whole story of Robert Holland and the cave and the man of the black Oldsmobile. The one thing I did not tell him was Jill's part in it, partly because my story did not need that for credibility; mainly because, even after finding the Holland journal in her room, I was not sure of the thrust of her involvement. There was another factor, of course: my reluctance to admit, in the face of cold proof, that she *was* mixed up in it and had been for some time. Whatever the reason, I avoided mentioning her. Max sat through it without reacting either way. When I had told it all, he held the pictures and the gold coin under the dashboard light and examined them closely. "Do you mind if I take this tape loose?" he said. "We should probably look this coin over on both sides."

I nodded and he peeled back the tape. The coin dropped in his hand.

"I don't think there's any doubt that this is Spanish," he said after a time; "it's damn old and probably worth a bit of change too."

"That's what I thought."

"And you say this ledge you found is the same one shown in these pictures?"

"I'm sure of it. The pictures were shot from another part of the ledge, farther along. I couldn't see the cave from where I came out, but I know it's there."

"Could it be that the pictures were shot looking back toward you? Maybe the cave showed here is the one you came up through."

"No, there's another cave; I'm sure of that. The tunnel up to the ledge was just a hole at that point, just big enough for a man's body. I can't be sure, but this cave with the Maltese cross looks like a walk-in cave, and it's at the end of the ledge near the base of the mountain."

He studied the picture some more. "I think you're right. It's an exciting thought. What are you going to do about it?"

"I don't know."

He looked at me curiously.

"I'd just about reached the end of my rope with it," I said. "First I almost fell into that mineshaft, then I almost fell off the goddamn ledge. If I keep on with it, it's just a matter of time till I get killed. Yet . . ."

"Yet you can't leave it."

"Not this way."

"I can understand that, all right. Why did you tell me?"

I shrugged. "You're a climber. I assume you've got the technical ability to get across that ledge, and I haven't. I had to trust somebody."

"I'm flattered," he said dryly. Another pause, then:

161

"Assume the cave does exist and that we can get to it along that ledge. You have any idea what we might find there?"

"I can't begin to guess."

"I can," he said.

I knew what he was thinking; I too had thought more than once of Harry Gould's mountain tales, but the possibility seemed too remote to consider seriously. I wasn't interested in that anyway, not while there were so many personal questions unanswered. Max had lapsed into deep thought. Once he glanced at me and said, "You know my wife will kill me, don't you?" Wife or not, there was no doubt that he was going with me. Somewhere in the middle of a thought he stopped talking about Philadelphia and Christine and started talking about climbing equipment. He had some equipment in the trunk, but he would need a day in Pueblo, perhaps Denver, to get the rest. We could plan a trip to the cave day after tomorrow at the earliest.

"It might be just as well for both of us to go through the motions of leaving," he said. "Everybody knows I'm going anyway, and if you clear out too maybe the heat will be off. Is there any chance you were followed up to the cave today?"

"Anything's possible," I said. "I thought I was being careful, but I'm no woodsman."

"Even so, if it's as tough a climb as you say, they'll have as much trouble getting in as you had. I think we'll have a day to get ready. Anyway, that's what it'll take."

"I could use the day—to rest."

"Yes, you do look run down. Listen, let's sleep on it, both of us. I'll get up and leave as I planned. You pull out sometime tomorrow afternoon. Tomorrow night we'll meet in town—there's a motel there called the Sangre East—and we'll see how it looks then."

We parted on that promise. At Max's door we shook hands, and I went to my room hoping that at last I would find the peace of mind to sleep. It didn't happen. I sat at my window until thick black clouds covered the moon, then I lifted the window and pushed my head through the crack. The valley was so dark that I could not see down the balcony to Jill's room. The street was a black presence below me, felt rather than seen. I looked toward the hill and remembered that my car was still parked there, in the forest above the house. I would have to get it early in the morning, before anyone was up. I went to bed but tossed restlessly for half an hour and got up again. Just to be doing something, I decided to get the car now. I looked again at the hill and saw a blaze of light. Surprised almost to shock, I groped for the telescope, sat behind it, and adjusted the eyepiece; I turned it until the light came clear. What I saw was the porch of the house, with light pouring through an open door. At first there were no people, but then the woman came to the door. She was only a silhouette to me, and she stood there for no more than ten seconds. The man appeared in the circle of light, walked up the stairs and into the house. The door closed and the hill was dark.

I watched for another ten minutes, but there was nothing more to see. Lightning flashed and the house and grounds were revealed in a staccato white light. Rain fell against my window; my restlessness increased with the patter of the raindrops and I felt a need for some strong, positive action. I dressed quickly, slipped into my coat and went quietly out into the rain. Already the street was turning to mud again. The rainfall was steady, soaking through my hat and trickling down my face. I stumbled off the road and into a patch of briars, realizing then that I had forgotten the flashlight, but I did not turn back. I moved ahead by memory, blundering around until I came across the path that led up the hill from the valley floor.

I climbed in almost total darkness, looking back once at what must have been the town. I could not see even the outlines of the buildings. From the ridge the old house was a mere shadow; black on black. Lightning flashed again and I saw the porch about thirty yards ahead. I climbed the steps and crossed the porch to the oval glass, but the drapes had been drawn tightly and I could not find a crack of light between them. I had a sudden terrible vision of the door being jerked open, strong enough to send me scurrying down the stairs double-time. On the bottom step I fell and went belly first into the mud.

I got up and moved around the house, feeling my way along toward the rear. There was light there, but dim and high, coming from a third-floor window. I did not know if the window had a shade, but the hill behind the house was steep and I guessed that I could move higher until I could see better. But the higher I went, the thicker the forest was. I did reach third-floor level, but the view was lost in a mass of tangled branches.

There was more lightning, prolonged and jagged. It lighted the whole area. I saw the garage at the rear of the house and the scaffolding that was still there from the work project. The lightning had quit then, and I felt my way down the hill. The only light for a long time was that steady flat yellow of the window on the third floor. I probed the texture of the house bricks with my fingertips, moving along toward the garage until I bumped into the scaffold. Looking up, I saw that it was perhaps as high as the house itself; it went beyond the lighted window, possibly to the roof. There were small two-board platforms at each level, with skinny crossbars holding it together. Taking hold of the outer bars, I started to climb. On the lower level the scaffold was sturdy; it became shakier as I went higher. Once, between the second and third levels, I thought it was turning over. I gripped the side of the house with my fingernails; the nails scraped against stone and the thumbnail broke. I shifted my weight forward, toward the house, and that helped stabilize it. As I climbed above the second landing I saw the woman's figure pass across the windowshade. There was another lightning flash and I saw the windowsill just above my head. But again the scaffold shook, this time clattering against the house.

The shade came up and the woman peered out. I flattened against the scaffold boards and froze there. The scaffold was still swaying; she could not miss that if she looked carefully. But the shade was up for only a second, then it was jerked down and the silhouette moved away from the window. I did not waste time wondering if she had seen me; I pulled myself to my hands and knees and reached up for that final level. My feet found the crossbars and I pulled my face up to the windowsill.

I was looking into a bathroom. The woman stood naked less than two feet away. She was drying her body with a bath towel. The shade had been pulled almost to sill level and I could see only the lower half of her body. She bent over once, but her face was in shadow. She dried her toes carefully, then opened a medicine cabinet built into the wall near the window. I got a full view of her pubic area; a long hysterectomy scar stretched up from the thick mound of hair. Suddenly the light was out and, still nude, she walked out of the bathroom and down a semilighted corridor. She put out the corridor light and went into a room at the head of the stairs.

I climbed down, undecided about what to do next.

But I had no time to consider it. A noise from the front of the house sent me stumbling through the darkness toward the garage. I heard it again, closer now, and my groping fingers found a small side door in the garage and pushed it open. I left the door cracked slightly so that I might watch, if I could see, what happened in the backyard. Nothing happened and no one came. The inside of the garage was, if possible, a deeper black than the outside. Only a flash of faint bent light came through a window somewhere and reflected from the glass of the Oldsmobile. With that, I knew that someone had turned on lights in the lower level; because of the angle, I could not see who it was or what he was doing. The hell with it; I turned my attention to the car. I moved around it, feeling along its length and kneeling at the front, at the license plate. I felt the words *Florida* and *Sunshine State,* and the numbers 38–3414.

More noises, closer now. A scraping noise just outside the garage and the sounds of someone coming. Keys falling on a keychain, then a man swore, as though he had just remembered that he had not locked the door after all. I ducked behind the car, near the right rear tire, then flattened on the floor and rolled under the car as the door opened and the man came in.

He was dragging a heavy chest and talking to himself. Obviously he had been drinking, but I heard the words *whore* and *bitch* and figured that they had been quarreling. He dropped the chest and turned on a light, which shocked me into a muscular freeze. I held my breath as he came partly around the car and stopped. His foot was inches from my face.

"Goddamn cunt," he said.

He leaned on the car and looked out of a window; the car dipped slightly under his weight. A movement off to the side caught my attention and I shifted my eyes just as a puffy black rat crawled out of a ragpile and moved toward my leg. It moved slowly, staggering as though it was sick, but its eyes were wide and its nose, wiggling, pointed right at my leg. It stopped to leave some droppings in its path, then moved toward me again. The man kicked at something, and there was a clatter as a shovel fell to the floor. The rat held still and so did I.

"Bitch," the man said.

The rat pricked its ears but did not move. The man opened the chest and began to unload climbing gear; spiked shoes and coiled ropes, heavy picks and a pointed ax. There were shovels too, three of them, with heads of different shapes. He walked to the rear of the car, opened the trunk, and began to load the gear. I felt something soft brush my leg and I clenched my fist and closed my eyes. Then the trunk was slammed shut and the light put out; the door opened and the man was gone. I kicked out with my foot, but the rat had moved on to other things.

I blundered out into the rain, and the light from the lower room fell full upon my face. I saw the woman's silhouette pass the window, then the man came in and there was some shouting. I moved closer. Between the angry outbursts from the man came the soft voice of the woman. I was close enough now to touch the window; I did touch it, but their voices were muffled beyond understanding. The shade was pulled tightly against the sill, but the lower edge was torn slightly. I pressed my face against it just as the man walked past. The water flowed down and blurred my vision. I rubbed the glass with my sleeve, but the water ran down faster than I could get rid of it. I was getting only occasional glimpses of the man's back; the woman seemed to be sitting in a chair beyond my vision. She sat there for a long time. When she did move, she went to the fireplace, directly across from my window. She turned and regarded the man with a look of scorn.

That face . . .

That face . . .

Judy . . .

No . . .

It was my wife, Vivian.

14

SHE MOVED AWAY FROM THE FIREPLACE AND I DID
not see her again. Then they both left the lower room
and went upstairs; the flat light of the third-floor window came on again and a shadow passed the window.
I watched the house for another ten minutes; the
upper lights went out too, and I crawled into a dry
place under the rear of the building to try to plan my
next move. For a while I was full of doubt; self-ridicule
set in, and I doubted what my eyes had seen. I tried
to brush it off, but it was too strong, too vivid. The
woman was Vivian, all right. I waited under the house
for about fifteen minutes, but the wind shifted and
blew the rain into my face anyway. I walked away
quickly toward the road. Lightning flashed and I
looked back at the house; it was ghostly white against
the hills and trees, but there were no lights anywhere.
My night's work, I guessed, was over; Vivian and her
tinny-voiced lover were in bed.

Soon I intercepted the road, turned east, and
walked up the hill toward the clearing where I had
left the car. As I climbed higher the walk became very

difficult; the trees closed in around me and the darkness was like a weight. With each turn I blundered off the road, cursing my stupidity in not bringing the flashlight. I slipped to my knees repeatedly, stumbled, and once fell into a water-filled ditch. But I found the clearing easily enough; just over the hill the trees fell away and I saw a slight breakup of clouds far to the north. I crossed the clearing, tripping over roots and stumps; at the far end I found my car, still hidden among the trees as I had left it.

The headlights were a great relief, but I turned them off and used my parking lights as I crossed the hill and started down into the valley. That meant slow going; the one thing I did not want was to slip off the road into the ditch. I inched past the house, and there, where the road led into the old place, I saw the headlights of another car. It seemed to be in the backyard, just coming out of the garage; without question it was the Oldsmobile. I stopped and put out my parking lights. Something was happening. The Oldsmobile stood idle behind the house, lights aiming at nothing, for a long time. I was about to move in for a closer look when a form passed in front of the headlights, someone got in on the driver's side, and the car lurched forward. I pulled my car just out of sight, got out, and stood behind a tree while the Olds came nearer. The car turned east, heading out toward the highway. I could not see who was driving, but there was only one person in the car and I thought it was the man. That meant that Vivian was alone in the house.

Alone.

Did I dare do it? I watched the taillights of the car for as long as I could see them. It was a half hour's drive from here to anywhere; that meant he would be gone for at least an hour. I was intrigued with the thought; it led me back to the road and along the right rut to the house. I still could not see anything, and I was groping ahead with my hands. Before I realized how close I was, I walked into the yard and stood again under that scaffold at the back of the house. I came close to the garage and noticed that the door had been left open. The back door of the house was open too; apparently it had been left slightly ajar, and now it was swinging in the wind. I climbed four steps and found myself on a small rear porch, looking into a black hallway. The wind blew water into the house; the hallway was slick with it. After a long moment of indecisiveness I stepped into the hall and pulled the door closed. It clicked shut and I tried the knob to be sure that it had not locked. I crept through the hallway, feeling my way along the walls with my fingertips. A board creaked; I froze still for a full minute. Nothing moved anywhere in the house. I let out my breath slowly and moved forward again. There was a light somewhere; a nightlight perhaps, upstairs. I was standing at the bottom of a long, winding staircase, and I strained my senses to pick up anything—sound, vibration, instinct of presence—from the upper part of the house. Nothing. My eyes moved ahead to the living room, where I had seen the potted plants through the glass in the door. *Flowers.* It all fit so well with what I remembered of Vivian.

I did not stop to think about it; otherwise I never would have done it. I started upstairs, and the top of the staircase opened into a hall on the second landing. The nightlight was at the end of the hall. I moved toward it, stopping at each door and peering inside. The last door on the right was a narrow staircase to the third floor. I took it to the top and looked into that same dark hallway I had seen from the scaffold less than an hour ago. The bathroom door stood open, just as Vivian had left it, and a flash of lightning illuminated the bathroom and part of the hallway ahead of me. I walked softly to the door of the room that Vivian had entered and tried the knob.

It opened easily but stopped halfway. I pushed against it, but it gave only slightly, then stopped again. Something heavy . . . something on the floor . . . was stopping it. I pushed my head and shoulders inside the room, and the thing blocking the door rolled over; the door swung open freely, and I was standing above the body of the man of the black Oldsmobile.

I think I knew it even before I turned on the light. A leg dangled grotesquely over the bed and the leg was obviously that of a man. The lamplight fell directly upon what had been his face before someone fired a shotgun into it. The shotgun still lay on the floor beside the body. Blood was still oozing, so I knew he had been dead less than fifteen minutes. There was blood on the bed too; the sheets were soaked with it. So this was how it ended for the man who had followed me. He was wearing that same red shirt I had first seen on him from the window of my room. *But where had Vivian gone?* That was the prize question, and a question frightening in its implications. As if on cue the car door slammed and a rumble that obviously was the garage door closing spread upward through the house. I jerked open the hallway door, but the footsteps already were on the stairs. Frantically I felt around for a hiding place. The sounds were in the hallway; she was coming to this room. I rolled the man against the door and ducked into a closet. The closet door would not close and I had to hold it; even then there was a crack between the door and the jamb. Another door opened, across the room, and there was the sound of a chair being knocked over and more footsteps and heavy breathing. The footsteps hesitated, then came to the foot of the bed, around it, and to the closet door. The light went on; there was movement inches from my face. I turned my face away from the light as the figure passed the crack and bent over the body. All I had to do was turn my head to see it all; it was that simple. I kept my eyes looking away, into the dark. It was better that way, better and easier. The movement and the heavy breathing continued. The body was rolled over and the door opened, then there was a grunt and more struggling and a dragging noise. I felt a great weakness in my knees; I closed my eyes and braced both walls of the closet for support. I knocked something over; it fell with a dull thump just as the closet door swung silently open.

I came up with a jerk, prepared to attack. But there was nothing to attack; the room was empty. The sounds of struggle were now coming from the outer hall; she was wrestling the body down the stairwell, I thought. There followed a steady, dull bump, bump, bump, the sounds of something dragging on the stairs. I waited until the sounds were well below me, then I stepped over the mass of red matter on the floor and moved quickly to the head of the stairs. There was quiet for a long time, then the footsteps, coming up again, and I ducked into one of the side rooms. The steps came close and passed me, stopped at the door across the hall and went in. I heard a clatter; probably the shotgun being moved and dropped, and there were more steps and the sound of water running in the bathroom. In a few minutes the gore would be gone, and *so would I, friend, so would I.* I slipped out of the room while the water ran in the bathroom and walked boldly to the stairwell. I never once looked back or thought about the noise I made. I just got out of there. By the time I hit the backyard I was running. And I ran without stopping through those black woods, branches tearing at my face and arms, until I stumbled out on the road near my car.

* * *

I actually roared up to the inn. I left the motor running and the lights on and rushed into the lobby. Now I didn't give a damn how much noise I made; I *wanted* to raise someone. I ran up the stairs to the second floor and pounded on Max's door.

There was no answer.

I called out to him.

Nothing.

I tried the door and it swung open. Max had already gone; I looked at my watch and saw that the night too had gone. It was morning, almost five o'clock; soon the sun would be breaking in the east, and by now Max might be halfway to Pueblo. I left the room, took the two steps across the hall, and knocked on Jill's door.

Nothing.

I listened. The inn was absolutely still.

Her door was also unlocked. The inside of the room was stuffy, and my eyes went at once to the window, which she always kept open but now was closed tightly. I crossed the room to the night table and turned on the lamp. The key to her door was in plain view on the table; the bed was neatly made and the room had a strange, dismal look about it. A vacant look. I opened the closet; it was bare. I pulled open the bureau drawers; all empty. I dropped to my knees and looked under the bed. The suitcase was gone.

Empty. As vacant as if she had never been here.

I threw open the window. Down in the street my motor was still running and the headlights flooded the doorway; my car was the only one there. The town looked as deserted as the inn. I closed the window and went into the hall, feeling an almost desperate need to talk to another human being. I went downstairs, into Gould's den, turning on lights ahead of me as I went. No one came. I called Gould's name loudly, and still no one came. I knew then that the inn *was* deserted; I had no idea where Gould slept or how to find him. Never mind; I was joining the crowd. I was getting the hell out of here, right now.

I ran upstairs to my room. I didn't bother to pack; just threw my clothes together in a ball and dumped them that way into the back seat of the car. On my second trip down I brought the heavy clothes and the folder with the mountain pictures. I went up once more, for the telescope. That was when I saw the paper on the floor, where it had been slipped under the door.

Jim,
I must go. I can't explain it now and won't even try. Call me when you get home and we'll talk. My home number in Bridgeport is at the bottom of this note. It's unlisted, so don't lose it.
    Take care.

                                        Love,
                                        Jill

I read it through three times, then I sat on the bed and lingered over the words *take care* and *love* and her name. I read it again. It didn't make sense. I folded the paper carefully and put it away in my wallet. None of it made any sense at all. I dropped to my knees beside the telescope and began to loosen the nuts that held it to its tripod. That was when I saw the headlights of the car on the hill; the Oldsmobile, still parked outside the garage. The telescope brought the scene into focus; two white globes against the black. Then I saw that shadow pass in front of the headlights and the car lunged forward, just as before. This time it came very fast, and instead of turning left it came right, over the ridge and down toward me. The burst of speed terrified me: *coming after me,* I knew, and I reacted in panic. I bolted for the door, knocking the telescope to the floor. I covered the hall in ten leaps, full speed, and took the stairs three at a time. I reached the front door just as the Oldsmobile cleared the ridge and straightened out for that long run across the valley to the town. *Hurry.* I could hear the car now, splashing through chuckholes in the road, and I lost sight of it for a moment as I jumped down into the street and behind the wheel of my car. I killed my lights and eased the car out of the street, behind the false fronts of the buildings, just as the Oldsmobile came to a stop in a flying spray of muddy water.

Through one of the windows I could see part of what was happening. The driver had left the motor running and had gone into the inn; that was my break and I took it. I backed my car into the street, turned on my lights, and gunned the motor. My car rumbled past the idling Oldsmobile, and in another minute I had cleared the ridge, leaping it like a San Francisco cop on a chase. I started up the hill, looking over my shoulder at the black behind me. An animal ran across the road and I crushed it under my wheels. I didn't slow up; I was in the middle valley now, and the car clattered on the washboard road and the dirty water filling the ridges splashed up from my tires and coated my windshield with a thick brown film. I used my windshield washers until the bottle ran dry; then, at the top of the last hill, I had to stop and wash the windows with a handful of snow.

Light was breaking in the east as I turned into Route 96. I brought the car up to seventy. On a long, straight stretch I looked over my shoulder and saw headlights far behind me, and I eased the speedometer past eighty. The scattered, abandoned buildings of an old ranch flitted past and I knew I was nearing the town. Now the sky was pink and the land was purple; a few lights appeared in houses ahead. I slowed the car and turned into a gas station. It was closed. I parked in the shadows of the building and waited. After a time an old Plymouth passed, then a pickup truck. I stayed there, trying to unwind, but a bad case of nerves settled over me and I lay back on the seat, trembling. I fell asleep and was wakened by the sound of a car hood slamming. The station had opened for business and two men were working the islands. One of the men scowled at me and I pulled into the bay area and filled the tank to pacify him. I turned again into the eastbound lane of Route 96, and soon the Sangre East Motel loomed on my left. It was a cheap place, nestled off the road among the trees, and there were signs out front that said TV, cafe, and six dollars. I parked behind the row of rooms, where my car could not be seen from the road.

The proprietor was an old man with white hair. I had to wake him to get a room, and he was none too happy about the business. He grumbled about tourists who don't sleep at night, like normal people, and he was still grumbling as he handed me the key. I got the room on the far end; I went there without unloading anything from the car and collapsed in sheer exhaustion into the bed.

15

It was a lousy way to sleep. Sometime during the day I must have roused myself and taken off my wet clothes, but I never remembered it afterward. I slept without any other interruption for ten hours. When I opened my eyes the window was the same pale shade of early morning gray, and a full minute passed before I realized that the morning had gone; I had slept through the day. My watch was still running; if it was right the time was six-thirty. I lay on the bed for a time, feeling heavy-headed; when I did get up I went to the window and parted the curtains.

Snow flurries were falling and the highway was slick. The motel sign was on; it was one of those flashing red signs that always remind me of three o'clock in the morning, and I did not want to think about it. My stomach growled and I realized that I was a full day past my last meal; I crossed the room and found to my great surprise and delight a hotplate, a pot, and a package of instant coffee. I put on some water to boil and sat at the window to wait for it.

It was a long wait. The hotplate, like the man who

owned it, was old and slow. I was awake and functioning long before the coffee was ready. I splashed water on my face and again sat at the window to think. There were things to be considered and decided; the game was hardball now, and I had to react accordingly if I was to survive. The thought of Vivian cutting down a man with a shotgun was too much for me to handle; somehow, even after all the hate was out, I couldn't imagine her doing something like that. Then I touched the lumpy scar on my neck and it all came back. Yes, she was probably capable of anything. Had I forgotten that once she considered smothering our daughter?

Judy. There was a comforting thought. I would give a pretty penny to hear her voice now; it would sweep away this insanity and perhaps give me a better grip on what I must do. I went out into the blowing snow and crossed the courtyard to the office. The old man eyed me suspiciously as I entered.

"You got a phone?"

He nodded toward the phone at the end of the counter. "Calls is ten cents."

"I want to make a long distance call."

He shook his head.

"You can get the charge from the operator and I'll pay it now." I did not wait for his answer; I picked up the receiver and dialed it. No answer. I looked at my watch: seven o'clock; nine there. Well, they weren't home and there would be no Judy for me tonight. Bitterly I hung up and turned to the old man.

"You stayin' another night?" he said.

"I haven't stayed this one yet."

"Your money went on yesterday's rate. The day starts at noon in the motel business. Technically you owe me for another day anyway."

He brightened somewhat when I paid him. "Listen," I said, "has there been a man named Willy Max looking for me?"

"Nope."

"You sure of that? You been here the whole time?"

"There ain't nobody else to be here."

"Well, look, if he shows up in the next half hour, tell him I'm in the cafe, will you?"

"Cafe's closed."

"Closed?"

"George Hawkins—he's the man that runs it—George always closes for a week in springtime to go fishin'."

Frustrated, I faced the cold reality of my empty room. The water was boiling and I mixed the coffee strong and black. As an afterthought I added some of the powdered cream; at least there was some food value in that. I covered old ground in new thoughts: There were a lot of changing factors in the game now; a body, a killer, my ex-wife. Basically my decision still centered on the same two alternatives, but with complications. Legally I had a duty to perform; I grappled with that and rejected it consciously on the same grounds that my subconscious had rejected it earlier. In their own way, police represented only a new threat. I visualized myself trying to explain to some local sheriff about a murder in the big house, and the house had fingerprints all over it, and some of them were mine and I had been an intruder—no, a prowler—when the murder was committed. All I drew from that imagined encounter was a big zero. When the law learned, as it had to sooner or later, that the woman of the house was my former wife and that I had come here in a beeline from the East Coast after months of "acting funny" in my job and home life, the conclusion would not be a good one. Leaving, under the circumstances, might be even worse in the long run. Nothing but bad news came out of any imagined contact with the police. I tried to remember if I had touched the shotgun; looking back on it, I couldn't be sure of anything.

Thankfully I was past the point of blind fear. I examined the problem from several different angles, and if I did not come up with any easy answers, at least I didn't panic. I sat at the window, sipping my coffee and taking each part as it came to me. Then I tried to analyze it and act on it. My first move had to be one of self-defense; I needed a gun. I went outside and found my car, incredibly dirty and streaked with mud, where I had left it. The drive into town was short and futile. The only hardware store was closed; there were two cafes, both closed. I returned to the motel feeling frustrated and just plain unlucky.

By then it was dark. The snow flurries had stopped and the streets were slush; the town, dismal even without the snow, took on a sinister appearance. In my room I drank some more of the coffee and tried to think, but I still came up empty-handed when I groped for answers. The only answer seemed to be *stay loose and let things happen.* That hadn't worked so far, but there was always tomorrow.

Maybe, but I couldn't quite buy it. I lay back against the propped-up pillow and tried to watch some TV. The only clear station was showing five-year-old *Bonanza* reruns, so I turned it off and turned off my lights and lay in the darkness. *What the hell?* More than anything, at that moment, I was bored; wanting something to happen and at the same time fearing it. I closed my eyes, but my entire sleep cycle was off and I knew I would not rest easy this night. I thought wild thoughts: of sneaking back to Gold Creek and prowling the house again, to get some line on Vivian and what she was doing. But I had a hunch I wouldn't find much there; just a dark, empty house and an empty garage. Possibly she was in another state by now. In that case she would dump the black Oldsmobile and disappear and that would be the end of it. But I couldn't buy that either. It was inconsistent with her character, as I remembered it. Vivian was here for a reason, and her purpose hadn't yet been fulfilled. I could never write her off.

I heard a noise just outside my door, then a gentle tapping. It startled me; I jumped up from the bed and knocked my empty coffee cup to the floor. I waited. The rapping came again, louder.

"Jim?"

It was Max. I opened the door a crack.

He was alone. "For Christ's sake, open up."

I opened the door and went back to my place on the bed.

"Can we have some lights?"

"Sure."

He turned them on and sat on a chair across from the bed. "What's the matter with you?"

"Is something the matter with me?"

"We're just going caving, not scouting behind enemy lines. I thought you were going to ask me for a password before you let me in."

"Sorry; I'm just jumpy. Coffee?"

"Is it any good?"

"Not much. It's instant. All I've got, though."

"I'll take it." He poured as I stretched out on the bed. "You act like you've been cooped up here all day."

"What makes you say that?"

"Because you're so jumpy. You look like a man who's been waiting for a reprieve from the governor."

"I came over here too early, I guess. The inn was getting on my nerves too. When I got up this morning there wasn't anybody around."

"I know. Miss Sargent was leaving just as I got up. We just passed a few words and she was gone, just like that. Strange girl."

"I couldn't find Gould either."

"Harry's often up before dawn. Sometimes he likes to drive up in the hills and watch the sun come up. So if you got the feeling that you were alone, you were probably right."

"Well, I didn't like it."

He looked at me curiously. "Jesus, you really are jumpy, aren't you? You been having second thoughts about our expedition?"

I thought about that. "A few, I guess. I'm having second thoughts about what the hell I'm doing here anyway. I don't relish the thought of tackling that goddamn ledge again."

"You won't have to; just point me to it." There was a long pause, then he said, "Listen, it's up to you, you know. If you've changed your mind we can forget it here and now with no hard feelings."

"What about all the equipment you bought?"

"That was a drag, but I can use it sometime. You call the shots and let me worry about the equipment."

I ended the pause that followed with more stalling: "I don't know; let's sleep on it and see how it looks in the morning."

"All right." He looked around the room. "I guess I'd better get a room for myself."

He went out and I turned off the lights. Soon I heard him unloading some things into the room next door. The walls between the rooms were very thin and I could hear most of his movements; I heard it when he dropped a glass and when he sat on his bed and later when he showered. It was after nine when he came again to my room.

"Let's get an early start, either way," he said; "I've got a lot to do if I'm going to ship this stuff back to Philly, and if we do go I'd like to be in the high country by sunup."

"What time?"

"Leave here at four."

I nodded and he left me. I heard the cracking of ice and the tinkle of a bottle against a glass. The springs of his bed squeaked as he got in. For a long time he watched TV; he turned it off at ten and there were no more sounds from his room until his alarm clock went off at three-thirty. By then I was awake anyway. I had slept intermittently, for no more than an hour at a time, and now I dressed as though the place had caught fire. At three forty-five Max came to my room, fully dressed for the climb.

That was the curious manner in which my decision was made for me. Max took charge of the day from the beginning, and he ran it like a gentle taskmaster. "You better eat something," he said; "it's going to be a long day and we're not going to find any open restaurants this time of morning. You'll find some milk in an ice chest in my room and I bought some corn flakes last night. It's not much, but you'll be glad later you had it."

I was glad now. There was no sugar, but I ate three bowls of the corn flakes anyway. I was washing the bowl when he came in again. We exchanged almost no conversation on my indecision of the night before; he brushed it aside as though he had never taken it seriously and neither had I. "I assume that crud last night was just a mood talking," he said once; "to tell the truth, you'd surprise the hell out of me if you backed out of this now."

I looked at him. "Why?"

"No reason, except I've got you pegged differently. Your curiosity is a lot like mine; it would never let you rest till you satisfied it."

We got out quickly after that. I took my boots and parka and locked my car; Max put out the lights of both rooms and we were off. We took a jeep parked near my car behind the motel, and I had to squeeze in among the equipment piled everywhere. The morning was cold though the snow had stopped. Max worried that the weather in the high country might be bad, and I remembered all too well how bad it could be. We passed the turnoff to Gold Creek and some of my tension dissolved. It settled in again as we turned into the graveled road to Taylor's Gulch.

"It could be a bitch," Max said; "if it's snowing we'll have to come back some other day."

Clearly I did not want to spend another day in that motel. I shook my head and Max caught the movement out of the corner of his eye.

"Even if it's not snowing, the road over the top might be snowed in."

"What road?"

"There used to be an old road over the top. It was used by forest rangers and lumber men about twenty years ago. Now it's used only by explorers. It can be hairy in places, but I've driven it. I was counting on it to get in close with the equipment; otherwise we'll have to pack it in from Taylor's Gulch. And from what you tell me that's quite a hike."

I did not say anything. Soon we turned off the gravel road and started up the jeep trail. As we climbed higher the moon broke through the clouds and the cold, pale light spread across the bald mountains ahead. Max stopped the jeep and got out. I waited there while he walked along the trail and looked for his lumber road. The wind came up suddenly, and Max was clutching his hat when he came back.

"I think maybe we're in luck," he said; "it doesn't look like there was any more snow up here than we had in town. I think there'll just be a light crust on the road."

"Did you find it?"

"Not yet; I think it's up ahead somewhere."

We went through that long stand of timber at the base of the Taylor's Gulch plateau, and on the other side Max found what remained of the lumber road. It wound behind the plateau, running along the foot of the mountain.

"The trail is on the other side," I said.

"I know it; I told you, this road goes over the top. I'm hoping we'll come down somewhere near your cave without too much of a hike."

I had my doubts, but I didn't burden Max with them. Trees closed in around us and cut off the road ahead. Max used his low gear and pushed through them. In one place the six-foot pines were so thick that they blotted out all windows and the windshield. Max crushed them under the wheels and emerged at a stream. We splashed through it, and for perhaps five hundred yards on the other side there was no road at all. At the base of the mountain Max parked the jeep, sat back, and lighted his pipe.

"Okay, we're in good shape," he said between puffs; "now we'd better wait for sunrise."

That came about an hour later, and for most of the time we sat in silence. With the first light Max got out for another foot inspection of the area. He returned fifteen minutes later, saying that he had found the road; we had come too far. Max turned the jeep around and backed around a small growth of trees. We started up the mountain. I still did not see any road, but five minutes later I saw two faint ruts ahead: we were *on* the road. The weeds fell away and the trees became stunted and gnarled. Higher we went; soon sunlight flowed into the purple cracks below and lighted the world. I saw Taylor's Gulch as a shabby gathering of rotted wood far below. We went still higher. The road disappeared again as the ghost town slipped behind the mountain. We were riding along a flat grassy area; the grass was grubby-looking and there were huge patches of snow all around us. We reached the top; the mountain sheared away and became a glacier, dipping into the valley like a great white sliding board. Max drove along the rim until I got nervous.

"Can we get away from the edge?"

"Not much," he said, but he tried. He turned the wheel left and the jeep moved away from the edge but tilted at a sickening angle.

"It was better the other way," I said.

He dropped back into the ruts. "Your cave is probably over that next mountain range," he said, pointing.

I looked into the valley. We had come almost full circle around the mountain; far below I could see the trail where I had blundered into the snowstorm.

"I'm not sure; as you said, it was quite a hike."

"That *is* quite a hike," Max said. "I've walked up there many times myself. I've done some cave exploring around here too a few seasons back. I might have even been in your cave, at one time or another."

"You know that place called Mission rocks?"

"I know it well."

"The cave is up past that."

He nodded and we dipped toward a white canyon that brought us within five hundred yards of the footpath; then he turned upward again and we drove along the face of the next mountain. It was easy going even though we had completely lost the road, and we rattled along in good time. At the far side of the mountain we came to another dropoff.

"I guess we don't go any farther this way," Max said. "But I don't think we ought to try to climb down from here either. I know I remember the road almost meeting the trail at one point, but this doesn't seem to be it."

He had to back the jeep along the mountain for two hundred yards before we came to another grassy area where he could turn around. From there it was a sharp climb along the mountain's face to another level, where again we found the ruts of the old road. The climb was very steep and I took it with my eyes closed. At the top the road completely circled the mountain and dropped behind the Mission rocks.

"This is it," I said; "it's not far from here."

"Can we drive up close to it?"

I shook my head. "I doubt it."

But I was wrong. Max handled the jeep with ability that went beyond expertise; we clattered down an incline so steep that my stomach heaved and my gut shifted. At the bottom I directed him along the footpath, around the mountain to the rushing stream. We bumped over rocks for thirty minutes before I saw the gushing water, and Max stopped less than thirty feet from the crack in the mountain wall.

We climbed along the trail and under the waterfall, and Max made a quick examination of the lower chamber first. He played his light along the walls and ceiling while I pointed out the rock ledge where the cave stretched upward.

"We'd better unload the jeep and hide it somewhere," he said.

That took twenty minutes. I waited alone in the cave while Max camouflaged the jeep. When he returned he was breathing fire and ready to begin.

"I'm going on up," he said; "I guess you want to stay here."

"I think I will, yes."

"Whatever you like. Let's get the equipment up first."

He made a long loop in the rope and in one throw had it over the projecting rock. He climbed it effortlessly. At the top he dropped the rope to me and said, "First dig out one of those miner's helmets—in the green bag, yes. There's one in there for you too. Don't go anywhere in this cave without it."

I tied the helmet by its strap and he pulled it up. For a few minutes he disappeared into the cave, then he was back, lowering the rope. I tied each bundle securely and Max pulled them up. He struggled in the confinement of the ledge, pushing the equipment ahead of him into the cave. When there was no more room he packed the bundles up to the higher chamber. That took him an hour, and there was nothing for me to do but wait. He was breathing hard when he came down the last time.

"I'm going on through the cave to the ledge," he said; "I'll be back as soon as I know what's there."

He climbed out of sight. I replaced my hat with the miner's helmet and crawled out to the cave's mouth. I waited there for a long time, watching the trail. Satisfied that no one was coming, I went into the chamber. That old uneasy feeling, that insistent restlessness, came over me again. I fought against it for a time, but at last I gave up the struggle and began to climb the rope.

The climb was just as difficult as it had been the first time, but now I moved quickly through the cave, pausing only at the spot where the wall broke away in a sheer drop. As I pushed my head carefully through the opening to the ledge, I saw Max standing at the edge about twenty feet away. He was smiling.

"I thought you'd be along," he said.

16

"IT'S AN OLD MINER'S TRAIL, ACTUALLY," MAX SAID. He was standing with unshakable confidence at the edge of the cliff, looking into the canyon. "You can see what happened to it farther along, at this end. There must have been a landslide and the trail was buried from there on down, but at one time it probably went all the way to the canyon floor."

"How old is it?"

"I have no idea. But it's quite wide once you get used to it."

"It doesn't look so wide."

"That's because you're afraid of it. Stand up and hold on to the rocks until you get your courage up."

"No . . . not just yet."

He smiled patiently. "It's almost wide enough to push a wagon through; it was probably even wider when it was first cut through, but parts of it have crumbled off since then. See how uneven the rim is?"

"Yeah, I see. Christ, how can you stand so close? Get back, will you? You make me nervous as hell." I looked away from him when he did not move. "So what are you going to do next?"

"Check it out; see what's at the other end. That's what we came for, isn't it? You want to wait here?"

"Yes." But I shook my head no.

"You can't have it both ways. You think about it; I'll be back in a few minutes."

"Wait . . . just give me a few minutes. If I can make it I want to come with you." I eased my body out of the hole until I was sitting on the ledge, my back against the wall.

"Try not to look down, at least not at first," Max said. "If you can get comfortable without forgetting where you are, you'll be fine." He fidgeted while I struggled to overcome my jitters. Finally he said, "Look, why not let me check it out? I'll only be a few minutes and then we'll know if there's anything worthwhile."

"No!" My voice was sharp and I apologized for it. "I've got to be there, see it for myself." I got to my hands and knees, but that didn't help because I was facing the edge, looking straight over the sheer drop. I had to sit down again. After another short pause I tried again; I rolled the other way, facing the wall, gripped a rock, and pulled myself up.

"Just turn around slowly," Max said.

I did turn and a flush of confidence came over me.

"There's really nothing to it," Max said; "but we won't go on till you feel comfortable with it."

"I'll never feel comfortable with it, but I think I'm better now."

"The thing you've got to watch out for is loose rock under your feet. Watch every step."

We took it slowly. Max walked with ease in the center of the trail while I inched along, hugging the wall. My confidence came and went with the dips of the ledge. Max paused occasionally to wait until I caught up. The trail dipped out of sight around the mountain and he waited for me there. It climbed slightly to another point, where it curved inward again. I was moving faster now, more out of eagerness to be done with it than any newly found courage, and we reached that final turn together. And there it was, the scene of the photograph, exactly as I remembered it. The trail ended in a small flat spot at the base of the mountain, and the cave was there among the rocks. The only difference was that, since the time of the pictures, a large part of the trail had broken away, leaving only two feet of ledge for a ten-yard stretch.

"That's a bitch," Max said. "We'll have to use a rope to get across." He tied us together and positioned me in a sitting position well back from the break. "If anything breaks loose, all you have to do is hold my weight for a minute till I can climb out."

He walked across to the other side. "Looks good," he said. "You're a bit heavier than I am, but it shouldn't give you any trouble. Keep the rope tied to you, just to be sure."

Starting across was the hardest part. Once out on the broken rock, it was easier to go forward than back. I walked side-step, my back against the wall, but watching each step and unable to resist glancing beyond my feet into the yawning canyon beneath them. Max was waiting for me at the other side, his hand outstretched. I took the hand and pulled myself clear.

Max untied the rope and turned eagerly to the trail. It widened gradually from here; I felt better just looking at it. We walked together to the cave and I saw familiar objects just inside the mouth: a coil of rope, a backpack, a shovel. These things were in the pictures; they had been here undisturbed since the pictures were taken. Max knelt over the backpack and examined it with his fingers.

"It's falling apart; it's been here a long time."

"Any telling how long?"

"Years." He loosened the buckles. "I can't say for sure, but they weren't left here yesterday." He opened the backpack and took out a faded blanket and a canteen bearing the initials KB.

"Kenneth Barcotti."

Max looked at me. "Do you know him?"

"He was Robert Holland's best friend. Remember I told you about Robert; well, Kenneth Barcotti disappeared sometime in the mid-fifties. He was exploring . . . somewhere . . . in Colorado."

Max met my eyes and nodded. He turned on his headlamp and looked deeper into the cave. We were in that cove of rocks that protected the cave from sunlight and made the pictures so underexposed. The mouth opened between the rocks, and easily visible in the flattest part of the rock was the Maltese cross.

"There it is, Willy." I felt very close to him then and I wanted him to share what I was feeling, though I knew he never could. He was going through a range of emotions that had nothing to do with Robert Holland or Kenneth Barcotti. "I wonder," he said at last, "if those old tales Harry tells are maybe true after all. Did you ever get him to tell you about Caverna del Oro?"

"Yes, he told me."

He arched his head toward the cross. "Let's look a little closer."

The rock around the cross was damp; it had worn away in years of erosion. A slight hollow appeared in the face of the rock where the water flow was heaviest; it washed directly across the lower arm of the cross and had all but obliterated it.

"I think we'll find your Mr. Barcotti," Max said, "in there."

I felt a chill as he moved into the cave. Inside we found more supplies; another canvas bag, tools, and a box of canned goods. Emptied cans and their tops were scattered around, and in the center of the cave Max found the ashes of an old fire. We moved around the fire, and now the light from my headlamp joined his.

"Jesus," I said, "this could go on forever."

"Yes, it really could," Max said; "some caves run for ten, twenty miles. Some of the really big ones go three or four times that. This probably joins the other cave somewhere along the line. It sure would be easy to get discouraged if you stop and think about it."

He went deeper and I followed a few steps behind. The passageway turned and dropped sharply. "Careful," he called. He sat and wormed his way forward. About fifty yards in we came to a vast hole which consumed the entire width of the cave in a sheer drop. Max could not keep the excitement out of his voice.

"Everything fits," he said, as if to himself; "it's all here."

He slid on his belly to the edge of the hole. He dropped a stone; several seconds later we heard the clatter far below. He dropped another, timing the fall with the second hand of his watch.

"Six seconds—Christ, that's deep; five hundred feet, maybe more."

"Look at this." I had crawled up close to him and was examining the remains of an old rope. It had been fastened to a sturdy rock column and dangled over the edge. Max felt it and found it limp. He pulled it up, counting off about two hundred feet to the end.

"There's your answer," he said; "that's what happened to your Mr. Barcotti."

"You think so?"

"I'll bet on it. We'll find his body at the bottom."

There was a long pause while we reflected soberly on the dangerous journey to the bottom. "I'll have to go back along the ledge and get the equipment," Max said at last. "That might take a couple of hours."

"What about me?"

"Just sit tight and wait."

"Can't I help?"

"I doubt it; no, you'd just be in the way."

"At least I can carry the stuff from where the trail breaks off."

"Yes, you can do that. Let's get started, eh?"

The sun was high when we finished. Max rigged a pulley of sorts over the crumbled section of the trail; from there he attached the packs and I pulled them over and carried them to the cave. With the work behind us, we sat at the mouth of the cave thinking about the work ahead. Max suggested that we eat something. "We probably won't have much time for lunch once we're in there; it's almost noon anyway."

He cut the top off a can of peaches and that was his lunch. I ate a sweet roll and a candy bar. Afterward Max turned his attention to the two largest of the four bundles of equipment; I had thought little of them to this point, but I watched in fascination as Max unrolled a long ladder made of lightweight wire. He attached it to the same rock that held the rope and unrolled it into the pit.

We shook hands.

Then he fastened a safety rope around his body, knelt, sat, dropped his legs over the edge, and disappeared into the black hole.

He was gone more than an hour. Ten minutes after he started down he called to me; he had found a horizontal cave branching off from the shaft and he couldn't yet see the bottom. I guessed by his light that he was two hundred feet down. He stepped off the ladder into the cave; it went slack suddenly. He cast away his safety rope and was gone so long that I began to worry. I was about to call to him when I saw his light below. I had squirmed to the edge of the hole and was peering down as far as my headlamp would let me see. His lamp met mine and I took up his safety line as he came. He was breathing hard by the time he reached the top; he unhooked himself and we moved back away from the hole.

"What's down there?"

"There's a cave maybe a hundred fifty feet down. It's more of a tunnel, I guess; it goes straight in from the pit, like it was bored there a long time ago. It joins another one; hell, there might be a honeycomb of tunnels and caves down there. I found a set of steps . . ."

"Steps?"

He laughed wearily: "I knew you'd say that. I swear to God, there's a set of old steps cut into the stone. They go down to a lower level. I didn't get to explore down there much; I figured you'd be impatient as hell up here."

"You got that right. I'm about to jump out of my goddamn skin. Now what?"

"I think we can go all the way to the bottom from that middle level."

"Well, let's go."

"I should tell you now, Jim, it's a pretty hairy climb."

"Yeah, well, I've already been through some hairy climbs."

"Not like this. The mouth of the tunnel is set in about four feet from the shaft. It's very old and apt to crack. You've got to step off that four feet from the ladder to the mouth of the tunnel; there's no getting around that. I'll go first and help you get close. But don't go getting vertigo on me down there, friend."

My mouth was dry at the prospect, but there was

no stopping me now. I nodded and Max said, "Listen, you lower the stuff to me first, then I'll help you all I can."

"Do we really need to take all this stuff?"

"We can leave the food bag if you want to, but we'd better have most of the rope and the other ladder." He sat at the edge of the hole. "Watch me go down, watch how I play out the safety rope, and you do it just the same way. Just remember, you can't fall as long as you've got that safety rope around you."

Max eased over the edge and started down. "See what I'm doing? One leg behind, the other in front; you hug this ladder like it was a woman on a cold night, and keep your safety rope tight as you go." His face drifted out of sight, and then all I could see was the light from his headlamp. Then he had reached the level of the tunnel; he stepped off the ladder and cast away the safety rope. I pulled up the rope and used it to lower the equipment. "Be careful not to fray the rope against the rocks," Max called. When the pack reached the tunnel Max shouted, and I held it there until he hooked it and took it in. We did it again and again, and the last pack took the longest of all. That was a small bag containing the gasoline lamp, and I was careful to avoid breaking it. When at last Max had it and the rope went slack, I looked over the edge and waited for him to call me down.

"Listen, I'll let the ladder out a bit; try to give you some room for your feet. Now keep your rope tight and you can't fall, remember that. Watch where you're putting your feet."

I gripped the cable with both hands and swung my feet over the edge. I fought down the pinpoint flashes of panic that raced through me in that instant before my feet found the first step, and I started down without any hesitation. I was down about thirty feet when I stopped the first time to look around me. It was a rock cylinder, perfectly round, like the chamber in the entrance cave, and slick with water. My headlamp played off the walls; they were green and slimy. Water seeped out of small cracks in the rock, coating the walls with a moving green slime.

"What's wrong?"

I saw his headlamp far below, as far as ever, it seemed.

"Nothing; I just stopped for a minute to get my bearings."

"You don't need your goddamn bearings. There's no place to come but down."

I started down again. As I went deeper I felt that the walls were closing in on me and the water flow was heavier. I stopped for another look and found that it was true; the shaft had narrowed to about half its width and the walls were fairly dripping with greenish-brown liquid. My light revealed a large crack in the wall where muddy water poured out and blended with the dirty slime around it. Max called to me again; I could not make out the words, but his tone was clearly short. It started me moving downward. Soon I saw the light from his headlamp just under my feet; then the rock wall fell away into the huge hollow that Max had described. The tunnel opened from the center of the hollow, and Max stood in the mouth, reaching out to me. He had fastened a safety rope inside the tunnel, and that held him fast in the shattered mouth. Now I saw what he meant: the whole face of the tunnel was a mass of fractured rock, and the hollow made the step a long one.

I reached out to him and our hands touched; but just the fingertips. I lunged for his hand and the ladder turned; my grip slipped and one of my feet slipped off the rung. I wrapped my body around the cable, clutching the safety rope tightly under my arms.

"Easy, don't twist like that," Max said. "Get yourself together again and just hold still."

My struggling foot found the rung as Max reached out from the tunnel. Again our fingertips touched; he stretched and had my hand. I could hear the wire scrape against the rock above as he pulled me inward. My right foot swung in an arc and touched the floor of the tunnel, but a piece of it broke away. I jumped back, as though the rock would suck me with it to the bottom of the shaft. Our hands slipped apart and the ladder swung out into the shaft. Max pulled back and dropped to his knees with a sigh.

"You know you're going to have to come off that ladder," he said.

"I can't."

"You've got to, unless you can goddamn fly in here. It's either that or back up."

"No . . . let's try it again."

"All right." He stood and stretched out to the end of his safety line. "Now listen, get another grip on my hand and just hold still, okay? I can pull you almost to the edge. It's just a baby step after that. And remember, you've still got your safety line, so you can't fall, okay?"

His face was warm and encouraging in the glow of my headlamp. We stretched toward each other and our hands met. Max clasped me tightly around the wrist and pulled me close. "Now," he said, and I jumped out, flinging the ladder away with such force that it clattered against the opposite wall of the shaft. My foot hit solid rock and I slipped forward to my knees. I rolled over and lay on my back, breathing hard, while Max knelt beside me. I was still spread-eagled when Max got up and walked away in the gloom. "Those steps I was telling you about go down from here," he said.

I joined him at the end of the passage. It opened

into a large circular room, not unlike the others we had been through, and five or six tunnels branched away from the room in various directions. The steps dropped from the third tunnel on the left as we came into the room, a long winding column into darkness.

"Slave labor built those," Max said; "I don't think there's any question about it."

"Indians?"

"Sure."

"Have you been to the bottom yet?"

"To the bottom of these steps, yes."

The steps were long and gradual; they went in a full spiral and ended on another level perhaps a hundred fifty feet below. It was almost a copy of the upper chamber, with six twisting caves branching away from a central room. At the edge of the room the wall had been broken away, making another entry to the shaft. Max went close to the break and looked down. "At least I can see a bottom from here," he said.

I joined him at the ledge. "The rock seems to be stronger here."

"Wetter too. Watch you don't slip."

He gripped my arm and I looked out into the shaft. Grimy water dripped down my neck. Far below I saw a blurred whiteness, just outside the effective range of my light. In some distant corner of the cave I heard the sound of falling water.

"What's that white stuff?"

"Sand, surely."

"Then we're almost there."

"Depends on what you mean by almost. It might be a hundred fifty feet or another four hundred. I'd guess something between."

"Can we make it?"

"We can try it. There's another cable ladder in the big bundle. Let's look through some of these caves first; if we can find more steps, maybe we won't have to use the cable."

We decided to make separate excursions into the tunnels, to save time. Max warned me about straying, or going too far, but the first tunnel came to a dead end at a small room just thirty feet in. The walls of the room were dry, and I guessed that they had been cut into the tunnel. It looked like an old storeroom; a few ancient tools and the remains of old wood boxes were stacked in a corner. I touched one of the boxes with my boot and it collapsed. There was nothing more to see here, so I went out to the large room and paused for a moment at the second tunnel. I heard a noise, undoubtedly Max returning, so I waited there for him. The noise stopped, and still Max did not come. I listened for a long time and heard it again, a click-click-click from the mouth of the shaft. It came louder as I moved closer. At the opening I lay flat and inched my way to the edge. All I could see from there was that blurred whiteness. I turned off my lamp and lay in absolute darkness; for a long time I did not move, and the only sounds were the drippings of the slimy water around me. Then it came again, sharp metallic clicks from below. For half a second I thought I saw the reflection of a flashlight somewhere, but I blinked my eyes and it was gone. The noise stopped too and it did not come back. I fought down an impulse to call to Max, for surely it *was* Max moving around on the bottom; but I kept silent and pushed my body back from the edge. I turned on my headlamp and shrugged it off; decidedly, I was wasting time, and I moved ahead for a look at the second tunnel. This too dead-ended after a few feet. The third tunnel was deeper; it turned only once, then went straight back into the rock for about fifty yards, where I found a crude dungeon cut into the rock in an L shape. The bars were thick logs, rotted almost to mush now. They sealed off the entire room and were broken only by a heavy wooden door. The door too was mushy, but it was reinforced by steel bars and plates. It was held in place by heavy steel hinges; a steel pin held it shut. I tried to pull the pin, but rust had fused the metal around it. So I looked into the prison by peering with my headlamp between the bars.

Almost immediately I saw two corpses chained to the walls. My light caught the first one suddenly; a white skeletal face, less than two feet away, grinning hideously at me from the darkness. I jumped back, slipped, and fell, then realized that these bones had been here for a very long time. I looked again. Both were heavily shackled, with leggings and hand irons. The one nearest me had been chained by the neck as well; the iron collar held his face upright and forced him to look straight out at me through the bars. His arm had fallen off; it lay on the floor beside him, the iron still clamped tightly around the wrist. *So this was what the Spanish did to Indians who didn't behave.* I moved my light and saw other bones deeper in the L of the dungeon. There were at least five, maybe more. One still wore armor; *Spanish armor.* Then these bodies were not Indians, but Spaniards. *The Indians revolted and killed the masters;* it all fit Harry Gould's version of the Caverna del Oro legend. Behind me, sunk into the wall, I found an old torch; the wall above it was charred black. That made it easy to figure: this was a Spanish torture chamber; when the Indians rebelled they turned the torture against the torturers and left them chained here for all eternity. I tried to imagine the scene as the torch burned down and left the men hopelessly imprisoned in total darkness. I shivered. And I got out.

Max was waiting for me at the edge of the shaft. He had brought down two of the large bundles from the upper chamber and was unrolling the other cable ladder. "I take it you didn't find any more steps," I said.

"There was another staircase, yes, but it's buried under rubble. It looks like part of the roof fell in. How about you?"

"There's an old dungeon at the end of this tunnel; four or five people were chained there and left to die. Spaniards, I think."

He looked up and my light fell full on his face. I saw that he was very excited and the high pitch of his voice confirmed it. "No doubt about it, about the Spanish activity, is there?" He came close to me and took a huge nugget from his pocket. "Look at this."

"Gold?"

"Gold ore, and really rich; you can bet me on that. And I think we'll find the main mine at the bottom somewhere."

I stood nervously near the shaft the whole time he was working on the ladder. I was listening again for the noises that I thought had been Max but now knew had not. I looked over the edge, but now I heard nothing and saw nothing. Except for the sound of a faraway waterfall, the place might have been a tomb. I pondered it: The light might have been imaginary, but the noise had been real; if the noise had been real, the light had probably been real too.

"How far down did you get before you came to the cave-in?" I asked him.

"I didn't get down at all. I had just found the steps, and it was all buried from that point on. Why?"

"I thought I heard noises . . . down there."

His voice dropped to a half whisper: "You mean just now?"

"No, earlier. I had just come out of the first tunnel and I heard the sounds of metal striking rock."

He shook his head.

"Another thing—I'm not real sure of this, but for

what it's worth—I thought I saw a light down there too."

We were both quiet for a long time. We listened. Then, as I had, Max shrugged it off and went back to work on the ladder. The events of the past forty-eight hours ran through my mind like a fast-motion film.

At last he said, "How could there be anybody down there? The only rope from the top was that old one, and we know nobody came down that."

"At least you know," I said.

He tilted his head up and his light caught my eyes. "What do you say we worry about what's down there when we get down there. Here—help me over the edge."

He lay flat and squirmed out to the shaft. Water dripped from the mouth in steady streams, wetting both of us thoroughly as we struggled to get him a secure hold on the ladder. He started down; I lay in a puddle on my belly and watched him go. His light got smaller and still smaller, until he blended with the fuzzy whiteness at the bottom.

It was my turn. Max was looking up at me from the pit; the light from his headlamp filled the shaft and cast up shadows from jutting rocks. I clutched my safety rope under my arm, lowered myself carefully over the edge, and began my long climb to the sandy floor.

17

THE SANDBAR WAS ABOUT THIRTY YARDS LONG; THE sand was almost like salt, fine and white. A stream ran through, splitting the sand into two short slabs. Somewhere beyond was a larger stream; I could not see it but I heard it and felt it. The air was heavy with it; the moisture left my face and arms slick. Water poured out of the shaft at the bottom, forming a pool that fed the stream. I had to drop the last six or eight feet to the bottom because the ladder did not quite make it. But the sand was soft; I sank to my ankles and was cushioned from the drop. Max was standing nearby, looking around. I came close to him and together our lights pushed back the darkness.

We were in an immense chamber, probably the bottom of that great room we had seen from the upper cave. Behind us was a wall of rock; overhead, a sloping ceiling. But *out there*, away from the wall, was only empty darkness. We played our lights around us in a circle, but the only solid wall in sight was the one behind us.

"What a hole," Max said; "a man could walk a few

feet away from here and just never find his way back. We'll have to be damn careful."

He set up a flashing red light directly under the shaft. "The first thing to do is see if I'm right about your friend Barcotti," he said.

He was. We found Kenneth Barcotti's body at the far end of the shaft. The skeleton was badly shattered. He had fallen squarely onto a huge rock, smashing his skull and back and breaking both arms. "At least he didn't suffer," I said, kneeling over the remains. The clothing was almost completely rotted away, but I found part of a billfold that still contained a driver's license, renewable in 1957. I took the wallet and stashed it in my pack. At least now we could write an end to the disappearance of the friend of my friend.

There was still much that could not be so neatly wrapped up. To Max, the Barcotti element was done and he had no more interest in it. He moved away from the remains and crossed the sandbar to the stream. I followed about ten feet behind him. The stream ran down to the larger stream, a swiftly moving water flow about ten yards wide. We went along the edge of the water, with the flow, and soon the sand thinned and disappeared and the rock was slippery under our feet. We got up higher, where the stream plunged under the earth and the walk was easier; then the ground sloped downward and the stream burst through again and the walk became a climb. At first the slope was gradual, but it deepened quickly. I slipped and fell into Max. He gripped me around the arm and we steadied each other there.

"This is as far as we go," Max said; "come on, let's get back, quick!"

But he had slipped too, and was struggling from his hands and knees. His grip on my coat broke and I began to slide backward. I gripped a rock and looked around for another handhold higher up. I found Max's hand; he had crawled up to a higher level and was kneeling there, waiting to pull me up. At the top we both rested.

"It's one of those tricks of gravity," Max said; "it seems to be sloping gradually, but actually it's steeper than you think. Listen."

The only sound was that faraway waterfall, ahead of us now.

"Is that from this stream?"

"Damn right it is," he said. He got to his feet. "Come on, I'll show you."

We backtracked upstream for about seventy yards. There we crawled out of the sloping channel and walked in a long arc away from the stream. We came downstream again, this time keeping to the high ground fifty yards from the edge. "We were in a river-bed," Max said; "it's just a trickle now, but the river must have been fifty yards wide at one time. Maybe it still is, at certain times of the year. Later in the summer, when the snow really starts to melt high up, I bet this place is a roaring bitch."

We were walking very slowly now, and his hand reached out and gripped mine. "Easy," he said. Ahead, the ground dropped away, insidious because it first looked like a short drop in the floor. Ten feet from the edge Max motioned me down, and we inched the rest of the way on our bellies. Below us was an extension of the cave, how deep I may never know. It had to be at least as deep as the original shaft; maybe twice that. We saw nothing solid in that black void, not the slightest hint of any wall other than the wall beneath us. I turned toward the waterfall; the water flickered at me as it tumbled over the edge and out of sight. Max followed it down with his light until he lost it, and for several minutes we just listened to the sound of it. The roar was muffled, like some small earthquake that you feel but hardly hear.

"How deep do you think?" I said.

"A thousand feet; maybe more."

We pushed away from the edge and followed the stream back toward the sandbar. The return trip seemed longer; actually it took only a few minutes, probably less time because we were surer now of our footing. As we came to the sand Max stopped and looked around; I saw that the flashing light he had left under the shaft was out. "That's funny," he said; "I know that light had new batteries."

We found the light just where he had left it, but a large rock had smashed it beyond repair. Max looked up into the shaft, playing his light along the walls. "I guess a rock could have fallen from up there somewhere, but there aren't many rocks in this sandpit, even under the shaft. It does seem funny that one would fall just now and hit our light. Doesn't that seem funny to you?"

"What are you thinking?"

"Just remembering the noises you heard down here. It's possible that somebody has beaten us to the mine. Maybe they're trying to scare us off."

"Maybe they're doing a pretty goddamn good job. I don't like fooling around with people I can't see."

"Yeah, well, let's not push any alarms yet, okay? We've still got a lot of exploring to do."

He set up another flasher—his last—in the sand, some ten feet from the shaft opening. We moved out again, this time going upstream. We cut diagonally across the sandpit, joining the stream at the far end. Max did not try to cross the water; he followed the stream on high ground, above the riverbed, and I came a few steps behind him. I looked periodically at the flasher; long after we had passed the edge of the sandbar I was glancing nervously over my shoulder. Then the ground sloped upward and I heard the sound of a new waterfall, ahead of us, and I turned my attention to what was ahead. Soon I saw a great sheer wall loom up and I felt a heavy spray against my face. We moved along the rocks behind the spray and came into a wide trail cut into the rock and leading along the side of the wall.

The climb was short, ending just thirty feet above the floor. There the trail turned inward and bored into the wall. There was a slight hollowed rock platform there, where the miners had worked long ago. We did not go in; we probed into the mine with our lights. The roof had crumbled in at least three places; rotted timbers had long ago collapsed, leaving the floor littered with shattered wood and rock debris. Deeper, a bad cave-in had sealed the mine, making passage impossible.

"That's that," I said.

"Not by a longshot. I'll be amazed if this is the only mine in the cave. There's a lot we haven't seen yet."

We backtracked to the floor and followed the wall into a great concave dip. There was still an outline of trail, even at floor level, and we kept to it, coming to an end at the deepest part of the dip. *And there they were:* two great wooden doors, blocking our way like guardians of a medieval castle. They were old and strong and forbidding; burned into each were symbols that I now knew by heart: The Maltese cross.

Max was beside himself. He threw down his bag and hugged me around the shoulders; he scrambled over the few loose rocks and pulled at the doors with his fingers. That was futile, and he stepped back for another look.

The doors were reinforced with strong steel bars, badly scratched in places with the unmistakable signs of pryings. Max played his light along the floor to reveal two smooth arcs of earth where the doors had been opened backward.

"Christ, somebody's been in here." He pulled again

at the door with his fingers, but it did not move. I helped, but even the two of us could not budge it. "Crowbars—that's what we need," Max said. "Damn it to hell, I knew I'd leave something upstairs. You stay here and keep watch."

He was gone, just that quickly. I called, "Wait!" but he either did not hear or did not choose to hear; he clattered over loose rock to the floor of the cave. I moved to the edge of the trail and watched him go, a tiny bobbing light picking its way toward the dull red flasher. I wanted to go with him, wanted desperately for us to be together again, and I called louder. He did not stop. The darkness closed in around me and became a threat. I eased back against the doors. From there I could not see Max or the red flasher, *so the hell with it;* I was stuck there alone until he returned, and now the thing was not to worry about it. I filled the time with other things: speculation on the nature of the Spanish who had worked here and what we might find behind these doors. I looked at the Maltese cross and touched the oak; it was still hard and very thick. But these efforts to divert my attention waned and my jitters returned. I looked at my watch and sat against the doors to wait for Max. But he never came.

Thirty minutes later I was too nervous to wait any more. I moved away from the doors and stood on the edge of the trail, peering into the cave for some flash of light. I saw nothing; even the red flasher was out. My first reaction to that was cold fear, but I overcame that with reason: Max might have put it out, for any possible reason. I called his name loudly; only echoes came back at me. I turned off my headlamp and crawled down in the shelter of a large rock to wait and to think.

The foot noises came first: the sound of someone walking toward me on the rock floor. But he was coming without a light: *That was insane!* I stretched my body over the rock, straining my eyes for some sign of light. The footsteps stopped and I heard other noises; a shuffling, an unpacking of tools. Then there was quiet, so absolute that it strained my nerves to the breaking point. I screamed Max's name, knowing that now there could be no answer. I cringed down in the hollow of the rock to wait.

There were cave noises all around me, I know, but I never heard them. My mind was tuned to other sounds that weren't there. I concentrated on hearing them above all others; what followed was a twenty-minute stretch of absolute silence that almost shattered my nerves. I moved my leg which had become cramped and I kicked loose some rock. The sound was jarring, but even more so was the sound *out there* that answered it. I jumped up and turned on my headlamp, casting the beam in a quick circle around me. Nothing. I turned it off, and immediately there were more noises just outside my light's range: a scurrying, the uneven click-click-click of spiked shoes, then nothing. Again I waited; that terrible silence fell over me and I began to talk to myself: *Easy now, easy; he's trying to flush you out, make you do something stupid.* I could make a run for the shaft, but a run across this back floor would be more than risky; it would be suicide. *Something had to be done.* Yes, something. I moved out of my hole and peered into the black. I could wait him out; make him come to me. That was the obvious tactic; that was what he would expect of me if he knew me at all. As he must. He would know that I was holed up, waiting in mindless fear for him to come to me. If I could fool him, if somehow I could get back to the ladder before he understood what I was doing, maybe I had a chance. I crawled away from my rock and was lost at once; I groped behind me until my fingers felt the wood of the doors. And I knew that fifty feet out on the floor my sense of direction would be completely shot and I would be crawling blindly. There was an alternative: I could follow the trail back along the base of the wall to the waterfall, then feel my way along the stream until I felt sand. That would take a very long time, and I doubted that I had the nerve for it. No, I would get one fix and go directly across the floor. I moved down from the base of the rock and slipped in a pile of loose gravel. I slid down a short embankment to the floor; something hit my head and knocked my helmet off. It rolled away from me, but I could not tell where. Instant panic: *the light, my God, the light!* I scrambled around on my hands and knees, groping for it. My foot kicked it and it rolled away; I whirled around and lunged toward the sound, fell hard on the rock floor and lay there, a lump forming in my throat. *Christ!* I was up again, feeling the rock frantically, and I blundered into the helmet a few seconds later. By then my hands were raw from the jagged rocks of the floor. I fumbled with the headlamp, and it came on with a frightening flash. Something scrambled back in the darkness; I whirled and aimed the light where the noise had been, but I saw only a dark form moving away. *Come back here, goddamnit!* I jumped up, stumbled, fell again, and almost lost the helmet. I strapped it to my head, turned off the light, and waited. Noises, somewhere in the dark; my light reached out again . . . to nothing. *Maybe he's throwing rocks, maybe that's his plan, keep me going in circles. . . . Come out, you sonofabitch! I've got a gun here. I'll blow your goddamned head off!* I shouted again; the sound echoed and drowned me out. I was shouting like an idiot. *Come out!* It was a sob now and I struggled for control. I sat in something cold and wet on the cave floor and tried to gather my wits. I flopped back and lay looking up, though there was no way of telling that but from the pressure of the floor against my back. I might have been hanging from the ceiling looking down or hanging from a wall looking east or west. *Enough of that! I've got to keep my head. I can't lose control.* . . . There were enough cards stacked in his hand as it was. He knew this cave well; that much was obvious. He knew it far better than I did. He had been here many times, enough to know it in the dark. None of that made sense. If the answer to this cave of gold had really been in my subconscious and nowhere else, how could *he* know it so well now? How could *he* walk through it without a light? It didn't make sense. I sat up and listened. *Nothing. Time to move:* I had to make the shaft. I crawled until I heard another noise, then I whirled and turned on my light. *Nothing.* I cursed my stupidity. I was giving him a good report of my progress, and all he had to do for it was sit back and throw rocks. He might even be maneuvering me toward some drop-off, herding me like a goddamn steer into the slaughterhouse. I sat still for a minute and thought about it. It was more than a remote possibility; so I would fool him, I would use my light once and no more, *get my bearings, get a sighting, and strike out swiftly until I was there.* That was the only way: *Surprise him, fight him. I'll fight him. I'll kill the sonofabitch if I get my hands on him.* My hand tightened around a rock; I threw it away. There were plenty of rocks around; I could always find a rock. Right now I needed to move, before *he* had time to figure it out. I stood and turned on my light and looked around for identifying marks. There were none. I had crawled away from the wall and was isolated somewhere in the center of the big room. I had nothing to work from, but that was that, and crying about it wouldn't help. I turned off my light and got down on all fours. For a minute I stayed there, trying to guess where the shaft might be, where I had come from, and if there were any obstacles along the way. I struck out quickly, crawling over semisharp stones and pausing now and then to pick up one and cast it into the darkness. *Two can play that game.* I heard the waterfall some time before I felt it; then I heard the rushing of the stream and felt the water on the rocks and the spray in my face. *Sonofabitch!* I had turned completely around and was crawling back toward the wall. I moved straight to the stream after that. *The hell with it, the utter complete hell with it:* At least now I knew where I was and about how far I had to go. The water stung my hands; *they must, they must be two red pulps now; knees are bad too.* I was in the water to my elbows; had to, *have to keep going until I feel the sand under me.* The sounds of the stream were all around me, and the sounds were good; they helped cover my splashing. Faster . . . My hand slipped into a hole and I fell off balance and tumbled into the stream. The water swept me along, how far I did not know, until I found the bottom again and pulled myself out. I moved along carefully now, feeling the edge of the riverbed for some faint trace of sand and finding none. Where the hell was it? Could I be going the wrong way after all? Could I have gotten into another stream which even now was carrying me into a deeper part of the cave? The urge to use my light was too strong. I flipped the switch and there, not ten feet from me, was Max, propped against a rock, staring away at nothing. His head was brutally crushed; blood and brains were everywhere, and I saw red long after I doused the light and ducked again into the water. I reached my saturation point with that; the lump in my throat became a sob, then a low moan. I lost track of time and distance; I found myself crawling disjointedly through the water, still groping for sand and finding only slick stone. Suddenly the ground sloped downward and the river began to run fast. *This is it; I'm there; I've made it.* I moved with it, flowed with it, and it dipped again and ran faster.

I stopped, letting the water wash over my back, but it was very difficult to hold myself there. The rock under my hands was slimy and the water worked around them to pry me loose. I was sucked free, and I knew then that I would never reach the sand; I had gone past it and was tumbling down toward that bottomless pit. The red alert flashed through my mind; I grabbed for any projections along the bottom. A rock came loose in my hand; I found another and another and held myself there, stationary for a moment against the heavy flow of water around me. But my fingers were giving out; I was losing ground and could not last more than another few seconds. *Now, now, nothing left.* My fingers slipped over the rocks and I found my voice and screamed across the cave. *Help me, help, help me, for God's sake* ... someone was coming ... *light against the darkness:* Was it my imagination? It came as a shock, one shock added to all the others; *someone coming, hurry, whoever! hurry!* The light came slowly toward me, bobbing over the uneven steps of the one who carried it. It was a headlamp, yes, and the man limped as he came down from the sandbar to the riverbed. He came slowly, as though hoping that the cliff would do his work for him, but he carried a large crowbar and was prepared to finish it himself. He came to the edge and looked down at me; the light blinded me as I tried to look past it, and his face remained a shadow. He raised the crowbar; I lowered my head and took the blow directly on top of my helmet. I looked up; he was rearing to strike again, this time, I knew, at my arms. I released my slipping hold and the crowbar struck solid rock. My feet hit bottom, and I pushed my body toward the edge, lunging for another hold. My fingers scraped along the edge, breaking all the nails before my hand closed around a sharp piece of granite and held me there. He rose above me again, striking at my arm with the crowbar. The blow glanced off my shoulder; I grabbed for the bar with my free hand; and for a second I had it by the tip. He jerked it, lost his footing, and sprawled on his back. He swore and tried to roll over, but he had slipped too near the edge; yes, he was in trouble now, and I had the only chance I would have. I crouched so low that the water came over my chin and lunged halfway out of the stream. I gripped his pantsleg; he kicked at my face with his free leg, and I heard him scream in pain as his foot hit my shoulder at the base of the neck. I clawed my way up his body, shifting my attack from his good leg to his bad, and when I had it I twisted it, twisted with my whole body, until I could almost feel his agony. We both slipped into the stream; only then did I let him go and fight my way back to the edge. He never had a chance and his scream never ended; it just got farther away. Harry Gould never stopped screaming until he hit bottom.

18

I CLIMBED OUT OF THERE AS THOUGH MY LONG FEAR of heights had never existed. I jumped from the floor, caught the lowest rung of the ladder, and pulled myself up hand over hand. I moved quickly up the slimy shaft. Later I couldn't remember much about the climb, even that most frightening part when the ledge had crumbled away at the top. I had to shimmy past the crack in the dark, while the damaged light from my headlamp flickered sporadically. I do remember the dark and the snow; the night was full when I came out of the lower cave, and snow was falling as I ran through the ankle-deep water and out into the valley. I had a hell of a time finding the jeep where Max had hidden it, but that was nothing compared to the job of driving over that mountain pass in blowing snow at night. By the time I reached the base of the mountain above Taylor's Gulch the snow was so thick that I could hardly see ahead of me. The defroster was blowing out hot air full force, and still the window was fogging over. I felt dizzy, as though I were going into shock.

I decided that the best, quickest way out was to go to the inn. There, perhaps, I could lie down and think through what had happened; come to some conclusion about what it all meant and what I should do next. In truth, I would have made better time going back to the motel in town, but once I was on the Gold Creek road my head cleared and there was no turning around. I came to the rim and shuddered at the black outline of the old mansion. What really pulled me up short was light below me, in the inn. For a moment I hung there, uncertain and half afraid; then I decided to move in closer. I inched down the road, using only my parking lights, as I had done in this valley so many times before.

I came into the town and turned full face toward the inn. One light burned in an upper window, and there was light behind every window on the lower floor. The upper light came from Jill's window, and then I saw her red Volkswagen parked in the street ahead. There were no other cars anywhere. I moved ahead cautiously, and I left the jeep's motor running as I stepped into the snow and moved toward the door.

She met me there, coming at a run when she heard the jeep. "Jim!" There was alarm in her voice. "Where have you been? Where are the others?"

I must have looked a fright. I stared at her for several seconds, looking behind her into the room and half expecting to see someone else. Then I remembered that there was no one else. "Are you alone?"

"Sure I'm alone. Aren't the others with you? I've been here all day, ever since this morning when I got back from Pueblo. I thought you must all be out in the woods, but then it got dark and then it started to snow and I didn't know what to think. Tell me what's been happening."

I began to unwind. My breath came out in a gasp

and my knees buckled and I almost went down. She jumped down from the boardwalk and put her arm across my shoulder. "You're hurt. Here, come inside and let me see what I can do for you."

Inside, I stretched out by the fireplace in Gould's den. She ran out to shut off my motor, then came back and got a good fire going. Together we stripped off my wet clothes, all of them, and she wrapped me in blankets from one of the beds upstairs. Afterward she poured me a generous shot of bourbon from Gould's liquor cabinet. Slowly I felt the tingle in my feet as the blood circulated through my toes.

I didn't know what to say to her. She sat there watching me warm, and there were so many unanswered questions between us that I didn't know where to begin. "Gould tried to kill me," I said at last. That seemed about as good a place as any. "He did kill Max."

She was speechless. I went on, giving her only the bare facts of the day. "I think we found the cave of gold. Gould seems to have known about it for a long time. He was waiting for us at the bottom, and he got us separated and bludgeoned Max. He almost did the same to me."

"Where is he now?"

"Dead. We fought and he fell over a cliff. He couldn't have survived."

"I can't believe it."

"You can believe it. Look, I don't want to talk about it now. I'm still not sure where you fit into this."

"That's why I came back. We've got to talk."

"I don't understand why you left in the first place."

"I had to get away from here, to sort things out in my mind. And I wanted to consult with my boss. You've heard the name Leland Smith?"

"I guess I know about Leland Smith, if he's the same Leland Smith who knew Robert Holland. I hope

219

you're not going to pretend you don't know who Robert Holland was."

"No, no more of that. I'm a psychologist, and yes, I work for the same Leland Smith who was once Robert Holland's friend. Lee is a psychologist, based in New York. He runs a clinic there with another doctor named Lorenzen. I've been working with them for about two years. My assignment was to observe you in connection with an experiment that was started by Robert Holland just before he died. I have to tell you that none of us understood the full implication of that experiment until very recently. But because of the nature of my work, I couldn't let you know who I was or why I was here. Then, a couple of nights ago, when you came into my room and found the book, I knew it was all over."

"I must have been pretty clumsy."

"The balcony was wet; your footprints were still on my floor when I came in. When I looked inside my suitcase I knew you had been through my papers too. I knew you would question me about the journal, so I decided to leave at once and try to persuade Lee to come out and explain it to you himself."

"But he wouldn't come."

"He couldn't. His work schedule just didn't break for him. That's why he sent me here in the first place; he just couldn't come himself. And I botched it."

"Botched it?"

Her cheeks reddened. "I got too close to my subject."

"Is that what made you come back?"

"Partly. Lee and I talked it out on the phone; he convinced me that I should come back and level with you. I got here this morning, but the place was deserted and the door was wide open. I've been waiting for you ever since."

"I guess it makes sense," I said. "Right now I'm

not sure what makes sense and what doesn't. I'm tired and hungry and I've got at least a hundred questions."

"Let's take it slowly," she said. "I'll fix us a dinner and afterward we can talk some more."

I must have dozed while she was cooking, because the next thing I remember was a meat-and-potatoes aroma coming from the kitchen. For a while I sat in the chair with my eyes closed, savoring the fact that I didn't have any more mountains to climb. It was over at last. But it really wasn't over, not yet, not quite. In my restlessness I began to look around the den. I looked with increased insight, and my looking became a new search for answers. I found the tiny door beside the liquor cabinet, quite effectively concealed by the surrounding paneling. I couldn't open it; undoubtedly the key lay in Gould's pocket, at the bottom of that terrible drop. On the back porch I found some tools, and it was a simple job to pry it open. Beyond was a narrow corridor which led up a creaking set of stairs to a secret room in the center of the inn. This was the room that Gould called home. There was one unmade bed in the corner and a lamp on a night table beside it that cast a dim light across the place. The room was no more than twelve feet square and there were no windows of any kind. The furniture was sparse and it was crude: a handmade dresser, the bed, an old filing cabinet, and that was all there was. On the top of the dresser I found a ring of keys. The largest key on the ring was an Oldsmobile key; an engraved key with a distinctive head that had come new with the black car from the factory. Beside the dresser I found the shotgun propped against the wall. The barrel was still blood-spattered and there was a long smear of blood across the stock.

Finding it was shocking in its own way, even after all that had happened. I let the significance of the room wash over me; then I propped the shotgun back in its place and pulled on the handle of the filing cabinet. It too was locked, but now I had neither the patience nor the inclination to look around for keys. I wedged the claw hammer into the drawers and pried them open. Only the top two drawers contained papers of any kind. The first folder was a record of correspondence between Gould and a Denver goldsmith, dating back to the early 1950s. The very first letter mentioned a "find of historical significance," and subsequent letters told of transactions with Spanish coins and artifacts that had netted Gould, over the years, more than fifty thousand dollars. I recognized the goldsmith's letterhead; I had once used it as a primer for a fire.

I heard a noise on the stairs and Jill pushed her way into the room. "This is where he lived," I told her. "Look at that." I pointed to a calendar above the bed, one of the old-fashioned semisexy kind showing a girl carrying groceries and trying to keep her skirt down in a wind. The year on the calendar was 1959.

"He killed them," I said; "that's the gun he used to kill them with."

"Who?"

"Vivian. My wife. And the man she was living with."

"The people on the hill?"

"Yes."

"But why?"

"Because I had found his cave of gold, and the man living with Vivian had followed me up to the cave. I didn't tell you before, but there was a man camped on the mountain across from us the night of the snowstorm. That was the man Vivian was living with on the hill. He must have followed me up to the cave the next day and got a good location on the mine. Gould saw it all. He had to have been watching both of us from his jeep at the top of the lumber road. It must have set him off, pushed him over the edge, and he decided to kill us both. Vivian was there, so he killed her too. He probably dumped the bodies into one of those mineshafts."

"You really think that's how it happened?"

"I'm sure of it."

"Even though you never saw the bodies?"

"But I did see the man's body, only at the time I thought that Vivian had killed him. But no, Gould must have taken their Oldsmobile and dumped her body on that first trip, then come back for the man. He didn't want to risk carrying a body in plain sight on the back seat, even in that deserted country, and he could only get one of them in the trunk because the man had loaded it with climbing gear."

She looked puzzled, as though I were going too fast for her. I knew that she didn't yet have all the pieces, but neither did I, and I didn't want to lose my thought pattern explaining to her what was obvious to me. I went on: "There may have been others too. I wonder now about Kenneth Barcotti's death . . . he wasn't the kind of explorer to let a rope go bad on him." I rummaged deeper into the filing cabinet and found a folder marked "Caverna." Inside were yellow newspaper clippings telling of the legend and a wad of notes written in a scrawl that was impossible to read. Buried in the middle of the folder was a rough but detailed map of the cave, showing the entrance over the top and down the shaft. It had been drawn in pencil and was dated 1953. Drawn in much later, in very dark ink, was a floor-level mine that opened to the outside.

"He must have found the way in through the top, just like us, only twenty years ago, before his leg went bad. Later he found a mine on the floor that was almost clear; with a little digging he had it open, so he could walk in without all that climbing. It should be simple to find: all we have to do is find his jeep. He couldn't do much hiking, so if we find the jeep we'll find the mine too."

I felt her hand on my shoulder. "Forget it for a while," she said; "come on down to dinner."

But there was no forgetting it. Once I had my teeth into it I had to push ahead to the end. We talked it out over dinner; I filled in some of the gaps for her and we hashed over some of the rough places. But when all the talk about Gould and his cave of gold was done, nothing had been settled between us.

Getting into it again was awkward. Finally I said, "I wish you hadn't lied to me."

"So do I. But listen, it wasn't all that much of a lie. The part about MacDougald and Barnes wasn't real, but I am an amateur writer and photographer. Mac-Dougald and Barnes is the name of a law firm near Bridgeport. I worked there one summer, and it was a good summer, so when you asked me about it I just threw out MacDougald and Barnes. I can see now that I should have used the name of a real publisher. You checked it out?"

I nodded.

There was another long, awkward pause and I decided to move ahead to something else. "This whole thing started with a set of mountain pictures. Would you know anything about that?"

"We sent them to you."

"We?"

"Lee sent them. If you want to be precise, your friend Robert Holland sent them fifteen—seventeen years ago. He was dying when he came to see Lee that last time. He gave Lee four sealed packages; two for you and one each for your former wife and Keith Barcotti."

"Keith?"

"Kenneth Barcotti's brother. Let me try to run it

through for you. Robert Holland had just been fired from his job at the university because of some problem—"

"My little newspaper story."

She shrugged. "Whatever. Lee never mentioned that part of it to me. But I do know that Robert Holland's job was very important to him; by then hypnosis was his life. He would call Lee on the phone almost weekly to confer about one case or another. His big dream was to set up a clinic where hypnotic subjects could be studied scientifically. Lee knew all about you because Robert raved about the things you were into then. Robert said you were the best subject he had ever seen, but then he got fired and started drinking again. That was concurrent with Kenneth's discovery of the cave.

"Kenneth called Robert from Denver, extremely excited. But then the last thing Robert wanted was to hear from an old friend, and he tried to brush Kenneth off. Kenneth had been looking for this lost cave for ten years then, and Robert had enough problems of his own. But this time Kenneth had found the cave; all he had to do was get the gold out and he'd be rich. But I guess that takes some doing."

"You might say that."

"Kenneth couldn't do it himself without alerting the whole countryside; suddenly he had a lot of things to worry about. He was afraid of pirates, even the federal government, especially since the cave is on federal property. He offered a third split if Robert would come to Colorado and help him. At the same time Kenneth called his brother Keith, to get him in on the project. But Keith couldn't be reached; he rents fishing boats out of Miami and was away at sea. So Kenneth sent Keith a letter explaining it and asking him to come to Gold Creek as soon as possible. By the time

Keith did arrive, Kenneth was missing and Robert was on his way back east.

"When Kenneth first called Robert, Robert didn't have busfare. Kenneth sent Robert some gold from the mine; Robert made more than two hundred dollars selling it. Lee thinks that was when the idea first began to grow: Robert saw what he could do with the money; he could set up his clinic and never have to depend on anyone for support. So he came to Colorado, and he and Kenneth explored the cave together. Kenneth never came out. Robert told Lee his line snapped when he started down the shaft."

"No," I said. "Gould cut it."

"Perhaps."

"I know it. Kenneth wouldn't climb with a defective rope. It would have been a simple thing for Gould—just reach out from one of those side tunnels and cut it. Simple. It must have scared hell out of Robert."

"Lee has a tape he made with Robert, and some of it is explained in there. Robert tells how the line went limp and there was a long scream. The line broke and Kenneth fell. Robert never knew how or why. He got out of there fast. Went back through the caves to the jeep. He had the idea of getting help for Kenneth. Then he started to understand that there wouldn't be any help. Kenneth was finished. Back in Pueblo, Robert became ill. He was hospitalized and a fatal liver disorder was discovered. He died within the month."

"And he never went back to the cave?"

"He probably intended to. The doctors told him he might live several months with proper care, but I guess Robert wasn't the kind of man to live out his life in a bed. Yes, even then he probably intended to go back and set the wheels of his dream in motion. Only when he realized how sick he was did the plan begin to change. He came east, paid a visit to you, I believe, and then went to see Lee."

"Yes."

"By then the alternate plan was fully developed: one grand experiment, a demonstration of why he had lived. He put you into a deep trance?"

"Yes."

"And later told you the experiment had failed?"

"That's right."

"And you never saw him again."

"Right."

"Well, the experiment did not fail. If anything, it was too successful. Would you like to know what happened that night?"

I laughed uneasily. "Will it hurt?"

"I hope not. Will you try it?"

"I have to try it."

She got a small tape recorder from her room and we went into Gould's den. She told me to lie on the sofa, facing away from the fire. When I was fixed comfortably, she came around to face me and turned down the light.

"I'm going to hypnotize you, and we're going back to that night, April 5, 1956. We're going to relive that night just as it happened. For a few minutes it *will* happen, exactly as before." She took from her pocket a man's watch, a fine gold piece on a chain fob. It didn't take long; I gave myself up to it completely, and soon the room darkened and everything faded but that golden globe swinging before my eyes. I could hear Jill's voice; that never went away. I knew all through the trance that she was asking questions and I was answering them, but there came a time when that other world was more important and her voice was a dull echo. I knew I could open my eyes and be awake; I could bring myself out of it any time. I just didn't want to.

I went deeper. . . .

And Robert entered the room.

We stood looking at each other for a long moment. We were both embarrassed. He said can I come in, I said sure why not. But I was sorry about his job and he was sorry about Vivian.

He asked about her. His eyes were dull.

He told me he was dying.

He had come to ask a favor; one final Jake Walters experiment, the last thing he would ever ask of anyone. How could I refuse? He dimmed the lights, as dim as they are now, and we began. He took me deeper than ever before, but there was no attempt to call up Jake Walters. He took a manila folder from his briefcase and brought out two mountain pictures.

"You will see these pictures again, and when you do you will find this place and make a public record of this experiment. You will receive the pictures by mail and you will use them. I will show you how."

He unrolled a large road map of the United States and spread it across the table. "These are your roads—Route Fifty to Pueblo, Colorado . . ." His voice droned on, explaining the route in detail. My conscious infiltrated the trance: *That was why I was so uneasy on the interstate: on Robert Holland's 1955 map, the interstate did not exist.* He had topographical maps too, showing the Sangre de Cristo Mountains in detail, with dirt roads to Gold Creek and Taylor's Gulch. There were more photographs of the road, of both towns, of that little stone building where Robert Holland had spent all of one afternoon carving letters in a wall. He drew a precise verbal blueprint of the cave's location, then erased the trance from my conscious memory.

It was over.

Robert brought me out of the trance . . . it was exactly three-thirty A.M. as my eyes focused on the wall clock. He gathered his papers and tapes and mumbled a few words and left.

And Jill said when I snap my fingers you will be awake and you will remember everything that has taken place and you will be awake and refreshed.

She snapped her fingers. It was over.

"And now you remember," she said.

"Yes."

"All of it?"

"Yes."

"Good. Sometime I want you to listen to this tape and compare it with the tape Robert Holland made seventeen years ago. I think he'd be gratified to know that you have relived the experience in detail. Your reporting of what was said was accurate almost to the word."

I was emotionally drained. The blankets slipped down from my shoulders and she tucked me in again. When I didn't say anything she said, "Shall I finish up?"

I nodded.

"After that Robert went to see Lee. He was in Indianapolis then, trying to get a practice started. Robert told him he would be dead soon. He asked Lee to do these things: On specified dates he was to mail these packages to you and to Vivian and to Kenneth's brother."

"Why them?"

"Robert felt he owed Kenneth something. Remember, Keith was supposed to have been in on the cave trip, and would have been if circumstances had worked out differently. Robert felt that Kenneth's share of whatever was found in the cave should go to Keith. As for your wife—well, I'm not quite sure how to put this."

"Go ahead; please don't worry about my ego. That was smashed years ago, where Vivian is concerned."

"She and Robert had an affair, I believe? All I can tell you is what Lee told me: Robert didn't see her at all the way you did. Apparently he loved her. Lee thinks they might have been married if Robert had lived."

There was a long pause, then Jill said: "There was a reason for the two pictures sent to you, and for the time lag between them. It had been more than fifteen years since that last experiment, and Robert felt the stimulus had to be strong. The time lag also gave the others a chance to get into position. You were all like chess players on Robert Holland's mental chessboard. Time for Keith and Vivian to get together and drive to Colorado ahead of you—which they did."

"In fact," I said, "they got here a little *too* soon. I can just picture Vivian stirring around alone in that big house day after day. I guess when I finally didn't come, Keith decided to go to Virginia."

"He might have been planning to confront you with it. But it wasn't necessary."

"No. I was already jumping out of my skin. Keith didn't have any way of knowing that, but he might have been watching my house for days. It must have been obvious, even to a stranger, that I was about to take a trip. So he contacted Vivian and she hired Amy."

"Amy?"

"That's another part of the story. It doesn't matter now. What was in the packages Robert sent to Vivian and Keith?"

"Personal letters explaining it; some tangible proof; maybe a few coins from the mine to establish the value of it. I don't think either of them needed much convincing. Keith knew about the cave from Kenneth's letter, and Robert had told Vivian before he joined Kenneth for their trip. My guess is that Vivian contacted Keith. Undoubtedly her letter from Robert was more personal, and probably more meaningful. She probably thought that Keith had a piece of it that might add to her information and provide a whole answer. Then later they decided to work together."

"Well, what about Leland Smith? What did he get out of it?"

"Lee was just Robert Holland's messenger boy. He still can't believe that a friend would use him that way, but I can understand how disorganized Robert's mind must have been in the last few weeks before his death. We had no idea of the significance of those packages; Lee never opened any of them. That was Robert's wish, that the experiment be carried out exactly as he planned it, with no interference from anyone. Lee thought it was a simple age-regression experiment that you had all agreed to ahead of time.

"It wasn't until much later, when we got a letter Robert had left for Lee with his attorney, that we became aware of the dangerous situation you might be getting into. Lee called your home, but your daughter said you were on a trip. That frightened him; he planned to meet you here, but there were pressing matters and he couldn't get away. So he sent me to work with you and report back to him on what was happening. But by then Robert's plan was in motion and we were afraid to interfere. I didn't know *what* he might have planted in your mind or how you might react to being suddenly confronted by it."

"What was in Robert's letter?"

"It was a precise explanation of the experiment, his theories behind it, and what he wanted to prove. There were copies of letters he had sent to Keith and Vivian and quite a lot of money—expense money in case we had had trouble finding anyone. Keith was easy; he was still renting boats in Miami. Vivian was another matter. We had to hire a detective, who finally tracked her to Houston, where she was working in a nightclub. Any more questions?"

"No. I'm sure there will be more, though."

"Just don't force anything."

"No, I wasn't thinking about myself; more about the questions the cops will ask. We'll have to make some kind of official report, you know. Jesus, how I dread that."

She touched my arm, then reached over and turned up the light. I took a deep breath.

"I guess there is one more question," I said; "the one that started it. Who the hell is Jake Walters?"

"Do you want to find out?"

"I guess I'll have to now."

"When you come to New York," she said. "That's the time to find out about Jake Walters."

She was right. I raised my glass and she touched it with hers. I thought about Judy and home and Jill and now. Outside the wind picked up and the storm settled in for the night.

JOHN DUNNING

THE BOOKMAN'S WAKE
❏ 56782-9/$5.99

DEADLINE
❏ 00352-6/$5.99

THE HOLLAND SUGGESTIONS
❏ 00353-4/$6.50

Now Available from Pocket Books